Anna Kavan

Anna Kavan, née Helen Woods, was born in Cannes – probably in 1901; she was evasive about the facts of her life– and spent her childhood in Europe, the United States and Great Britain. Her life was haunted by her rich, glamorous mother, beside whom her father remains an indistinct figure. Twice married and divorced, she began writing while living with her first husband in Burma and was at first published under her married name of Helen Ferguson. Her early writing consisted of somewhat eccentric 'Home Counties' novels, but her work changed after her second marriage collapsed. In the wake of this, she suffered the first of many nervous breakdowns and was confined to a clinic in Switzerland. She emerged from her incarceration with a new name – Anna Kavan, the protagonist of her 1930 novel *Let Me Alone* – an outwardly different persona and a new literary style. She suffered periodic bouts of mental illness and long-term drug addiction – she became dependent on heroin in the 1920s and continued to use it throughout her life – and these facets of her biography feature prominently in her work. She destroyed almost all her personal correspondence and most of her diaries, therefore ensuring that she achieved her ambition to become 'one of the world's best-kept secrets'. She died in 1968 of heart failure soon after the publication of her most celebrated work, the novel *Ice*.

A SCARCITY OF LOVE

ANNA KAVAN

A SCARCITY OF LOVE

PETER OWEN
London and Chester Springs, PA, USA

PETER OWEN PUBLISHERS
73 Kenway Road, London SW5 0RE

Peter Owen books are distributed in the USA by Dufour Editions Inc.,
Chester Springs, PA 19425–0007

First published by Peter Owen 1971
© Rhys Davies and R. B. Marriott 1956, 1971, 2009
This Peter Owen Modern Classics edition 2009

ISBN 978-0-7206-1327-8

A catalogue record for this book is available
from the British Library

Printed by CPI Bookmarque, Croydon, CR0 4TD

1

THE START OF SOMETHING

TALL and turretted, alone on its hilltop, the castle seemed to have come straight out of the middle ages, intact. People seeing it from a distance seldom noticed that it was partly in ruins; which only had the effect of making it fit more perfectly into its setting, inevitable as another outcropping of the ochreous rock crowning most of the hills around. To storm and sunshine alike it presented this aspect of rocklike indestructible timelessness. Only at dusk, when the tide of night already covered the sea and the lowlands, it could seem ethereal like a vision, floating above, still in sunset radiance, insubstantial as cloud.

The young doctor, now driving towards it in his shabby car, possessed more imagination than is common in his profession, and to him it symbolized all the magic of this southern land. A northerner himself, he'd been fascinated when he first came to work here by the hills and rocks and terraces of this warmer country, by its silvery olivetrees and its vines. He was thrilled to discover here a wild beauty unknown in the industrialized over-populated north. It excited him to feel the wild hilly country of forests and boulders and dense thorny scrub pressing so close to the villages and the stony fields, making civilization seem slightly precarious. It was like going back to the time to which the castle belonged; a more adventurous, more mysterious age; beside which the present day appeared greyly mediocre.

He had liked the people very much too; at the start they had seemed to accept him. But now he was uncertain, both of their feelings and of his own. Though he still felt the charm of the south and the southerners, gradually, since the hot weather began, his attitude had become modified; he was no longer quite so whole-heartedly enthusiastic as he had been, about the one or the other.

Now it was August, and he was experiencing a revulsion against the heat, the torrid sky had become a bit wearisome to him. At times he longed for the moist cool climate of his home, feeling out of his element here, a stranger in a strange land. For this reason, most likely, he now seemed divided by some barrier from the people around him, who sometimes gave the impression of shutting him out. Probably he was excluded only in his imagination. But, anyhow, the young man—though far too busy to brood over his feeling of not belonging—was no longer quite as happy as he had been, and, slightly disappointed with reality, unconsciously fell back on the world of dreams.

In this he was encouraged by the fact that, being the junior in the medical partnership, to whom most of the visits were left, his job entailed much driving about the sparsely-populated area of scattered hill villages and lonely farms. Since there was very little traffic on the rough inland roads, he had easily fallen into the habit of dreaming as he drove along; and the castle, almost always in sight wherever he happened to be, provided a natural point of focus for his dreams.

What sort of people lived there? To what strange species did they belong? He couldn't think of them as ordinary beings; as the couple his partner described; as the Count he himself had met, and his unknown wife. It seemed to him that, living within those ancient walls, they must be different; some of the magic of the young world must have been born in them, some lost beauty or wisdom of times past.

A birth was soon due to take place there: or rather, it was supposed to take place in the regional hospital, where the senior partner had booked the best room for the Countess, before he left to attend a conference in a neighbouring country. Now, while he was still away, a message had come to his young assistant, which made it seem that the child would be born in the castle, after all.

The young doctor had never yet been inside the place. He felt an excitement that was part apprehension as his old mass-produced car boiled and spluttered its way to the top of the steep incline, and, switching off the engine, he stepped out at the foot of the soaring walls, pale, clean, sun-baked, wind-swept, like a dry sea-shell. At once he was aware of the silence, of being high up above the world, with precipices all round. Strange, to be up here, in the remote stillness under the sky, a few wisps of cloud passing, as if within reach of his hand. Already he could feel the spell of the place reaching out towards him, to draw him in.

He gave himself a sort of a mental shake as he rang the bell. He liked to think he was a very normal young man. Most of his dreaming was done unofficially, without the authorization of his conscious self, his mind functioning on

6

two different levels. So now, while consciously he attributed a slight nervousness to dislike of taking his partner's place, his deeper self was concerned for his dream, which it feared might be damaged, or even destroyed, by the reality of the castle. In his busy but rather lonely life, with hosts of acquaintances but no real friends, his familiar dream seemed a thing to be cherished—though, of course, only in secret.

But, when he was inside the castle, he couldn't help feeling the stir of excitement again. It was so incredibly, so exactly, right; the glamour and mystery of the dream transferred to the plane of reality. He was a little overwhelmed by the spectacular sweep of the wide staircase; the faded, resplendent figures, staring or weirdly gesturing from the walls; the shadowy galleries; and, above all, the indescribable atmosphere of an antique tradition—all this was magical to him; his dream castle translated into real life. He was enthralled, absolutely.

No doubt about it, the castle was perfect. What would the Countess be like—would she break the spell? He was shown into her boudoir; where at first he could hardly see his prospective patient in the dim light. Crossing the big, rather bare room, which made the world of the crowded blazing beaches outside seem vulgar and unreal, he tried to remember what his partner had told him about the young woman on the *chaise longue*. Nothing, certainly, to prepare him for what he saw; though what was so unexpected about her he couldn't say, advancing under her cool, detached gaze, as she watched him from deep-shadowed eyes.

He saw that she was tall and remote; and she should have been slender and elegant. Elegance and slenderness belonged so essentially to her that these qualities were to be felt, in spite of her swollen body—unaffected by it. She gave an odd impression of being dissociated from her condition, as if pregnancy were something unsuited to her—a trick played upon her—to which she rose superior by an act of will. A dauntless determination seemed to emanate from her, together with her remoteness. Her voice and manner were quiet, almost laconic; and, in this supremely feminine situation, even a bit masculine, thanks to the effect she produced of standing apart from herself. Her indomitable opposition to natural forces so irresistible aroused in the young man a half-amused, half-admiring sensation. And her curious air of remoteness appealed to his imagination, making her seem of the same stuff as his dream, and therefore acceptable.

But the Countess's determination soon proved an intolerable nuisance to him. She was determined absolutely to have

7

her way; it never seemed to enter her head that this might not always be feasible. First, she ordered him to recall his senior; then, when he told her the other man couldn't possibly get back in time to be useful, announced that she would at once enter the hospital.

The good-natured young doctor was gradually growing exasperated by her cool assumption that people existed only to serve her. And she had an insulting way of not seeming to see him, looking past him somewhere, as though he were too insignificant to·be noticed, while she reclined there, like a queen. She might as well have told him to his face that he was incompetent; that she wouldn't trust herself to his care.

"I'm afraid you don't understand the position," he said with chilly restraint; going on to explain that the small hospital was much over-crowded, the private rooms invariably booked months ahead. He spoke with a frigid politeness meant to demonstrate his independence, to show her he wouldn't be used as a doormat by anybody. Feeling better then, restored to his usual equanimity, he half-hoped that he'd offended her and would be allowed to drop the case altogether; he was sure she would prove a most difficult patient.

"If you'd prefer to call in another doctor—" he was beginning; when she interrupted him, saying "No, certainly not—I should hate that."

Recognizing him for the first time, she looked straight at him with eyes that seemed the colour of clear sea water, where it covers deep rocks; and suddenly a quick appealing smile went over her face, lighting it with a swift almost wistful charm. It changed her completely: extraordinary, the difference it made, the smile, and the almost shy charm; for an instant she looked like a very young girl, touching.

The doctor was astonished and moved, though the transformation lasted barely a second. Back she went then to her former aloofness; and he observed that the extreme charm of her smile was due to its contrast with her habitual severe expression. But now he knew that the assurance and arrogance and remoteness concealed the diffidence of a very young girl: and the knowledge gave him a feeling of dream-intimacy; as though they'd met and made friends in a dream.

She sent her maid when he was ready to go to show him a quick way out, the private approach to her rooms. Descending a spiral staircase, he emerged on to a terrace shaded by huge evergreen oaks; straight ahead, in blazing sun, was the main door where his familiar old car was waiting. Seeing it, he was all at once in a violent hurry, remembering the double duties he must perform that day. But, before he could start off, the Count appeared, a big tall powerful-looking man, whom he had met once or twice in the course of local affairs; he now immobilized the car by putting his foot on the running-board.

Already preoccupied with the technical details of the work ahead, the young doctor only wanted to get away. There was no need for any more talk. But, even through his impatience and preoccupation, an aura of anxiety made itself felt: an exaggeration, he supposed, of the nervousness common in men about to become fathers for the first time. His good nature made him repeat what he'd told the Countess, adding a few words about the efficiency and experience of the trained midwives with whom he often worked, and the normality of the case.

Surely that was enough. His hand moved automatically towards the starter. But, to his surprise, the Count suddenly leaned right into the car, gripping the door with both hands, begging him to find a bed for his wife somewhere . . . there *must* be a vacant room . . . if not in the hospital, perhaps in a private home, or in one of the towns further along the coast. He didn't care how much he had to pay — expense was no object . . . All this came out in a rapid undertone, at times almost inaudible, as the speaker's mouth was intermittently contorted by a nervous spasm. The doctor glanced at the convulsive grimace, then lowered his eyes in embarrassment to the hands still gripping the car as if to prevent its departure by force. He knew that he was supposed to say something, but hesitated, embarrassed; and the other, misinterpreting his silence, continued: "I do hope you haven't got the impression that there's anything . . . any personal discrimination . . . lack of confidence . . . of course it's nothing of that kind — nothing to do with yourself . . ." Now he was the one to appear embarrassed, awkwardly looking away, then blurting out, almost as if he were referring to something shameful: The fact is "that Regina — that is, my wife — is particularly anxious not to . . . that the child should not be born here . . . in the castle . . . it's a kind of fixation . . . And you must have seen for yourself that she's very self-willed . . . highly-strung."

Feeling perhaps that he'd given too much latitude to his dreaming self, the young doctor had, sometime during the last few minutes, had a reaction against the castle and its owners. He was now exclusively the normal practical busy man, the dreamer quite in abeyance. Why shouldn't the woman have her child at home like other people? It all seemed a

9

ridiculous fuss about nothing. He felt an impulse to detach the Count's clutching fingers, and drive away. But his natural kindness was shocked; after all, the man had been decent enough to explain that no personal slight was intended. His own hostility seemed irrational.

He had always considered the Count rather a fine specimen physically, a robust sporting athletic type. Now, glancing at him again, he noticed with surprise that he looked haggard, worn out. But he had no sympathy with him. The Countess was young and healthy; there was no reason to suppose the birth would be anything but perfectly normal. The fact that the man was obviously worrying over it seemed like a form of presumption; a claim to undue importance. And there was another more obscure source of hostility, of which the doctor was hardly aware, which he certainly could not have defined. The approaching birth formed an extra bond between the couple and the castle, a shared mystery, from which he was excluded. Again this feeling of being shut out . . . To a certain extent he had neutralized it by giving himself the dream freedom of the castle. So now, deep within him, he felt resentfully that these people had no right to exclude him. None of this came through, though, to the surface. Consciously, he was bewildered by the unexplained dislike with which he regarded the harrassed well-set-up fellow, as he promised to do his best, before driving down the hill as fast as he could.

It was a sultry day. All the heat which had been accumulating throughout the long summer seemed to hang like a weight of lassitude in the air. The doctor's dog, flat out in the shade of a tree, didn't get up to welcome his return, merely beating the dust with a languid tail. But the young man plunged into the work waiting for him as though he were thirsty for it, thankful to get back to his own environment after the strangeness of the castle. He seemed to have been away from himself and his own existence; it was a little while before he could take things for granted again.

At the back of his mind was the undefined notion that his dream had changed somehow, let him down. He had had enough of it; for the moment, at least. He wanted to forget all about the castle. But, though he knew it was a waste of time, he conscientiously put through several telephone calls to various nursing homes, keeping the promise he'd made to the Count. There was, of course, no vacant room. So he sent the senior midwife ahead with what was needed, knowing that he could leave all the preliminaries in her hands. He had worked with her so often that she was

10

more like an extension of his own personality than an assistant when they were on a case together. Now he could really forget the castle for the time being. It was a great relief to feel reinstated in his own life, functioning easily and naturally once more, knowing what had to be done and doing it coolly and well.

When the time came, he drove up the hill again with reluctance, but comforted by the knowledge that the nurse would be there. Not quite consciously formulated, was the thought that he now had an ally, and would not be quite alone in the strangers' camp.

The sun was still powerful, though getting low in the sky. The country-side seemed deserted. But, just as he reached the spot where the public road joined the private way to the castle, he met a little procession of men and women coming from it. There seemed to be something slightly strange about them, about their stares and gesticulations and the twittering of their excitement which penetrated to him; the young man wondered vaguely what they could be doing there in the sweltering heat, so far from any village; thinking, "Some tenants' deputation, most likely," dismissing them from his mind as he drove on.

This time, anticipating a longer visit, he parked his car in the shade of the oaks before ringing the bell. He waited a minute. Nothing happened, so he rang again. He stood in the shade of the building. But in front of him everything merged into heat and dazzle, heaven and earth fused in one incandescence; pale gravel, bleached brittle grass, the heat-heavy shimmering sky — all the same colour, no-colour, of a world sucked dry and empty of all but the glaring heat.

This southern summer . . . it seemed to have been going on far too long . . . he felt his sudden nostalgic longing for the coolness of mists and rain, glancing up at the molten sky, against which the dusty foliage hung without depth or motion, as if cut out of metal. Not a sound came from inside the castle: and outside there was nothing either; no sound of animal, bird or machine, only the ceaseless small crepitations of insects, dry and feverish, like the voice of summer itself.

What was happening? Why didn't they open the door? It was locked, of course, but he tried it again, twisting the massive ring with both hands. Suddenly remembering the private entrance, he had some difficulty now in finding this other door, half hidden by the rampant growth of a creeper, which thrust its inquisitive snake-heads into his face as if to obstruct him. It was locked too, but he heard someone moving inside, and called out: "Hello there! Let me in — it's the doctor!"

A hand began awkwardly fumbling with the old-fashioned fastenings, and, irritable in the heat, impatient of this further delay, he shouted: "Hurry up, for heaven's sake! Haven't you ever opened a door in your life?" The next moment it did open; to his amazement, it was the midwife in her white apron, who was standing there.

In his mind, she was identified with the order and normality of daily life; that she, and not one of the castle servants, should open the door, was so far from the normal order of things that instead of apologising for shouting at her, he demanded almost as rudely: "What are you doing here? Why aren't you with the patient?"

"I came down to see if you'd arrived so that I could let you in."

It was a relief to him that the woman seemed, as usual, calm and composed. Perhaps there was some quite ordinary explanation of why she'd come to the door. He had longed for coolness, and the interior of the castle was beautifully cool. At first he felt refreshed. But as soon as the heat and glare were shut out the atmosphere of the ancient building seemed to touch him too closely, flowing round him like deep cool silent water. The spell of the place was once more coming over him. This time he resisted it: on the other occasion, it had got out of hand; so now he made up his mind to remain altogether the conscious normal young man; he wouldn't let the dreamer into the picture at all. But this was not easy. He felt as if some mysterious invisible thing were encroaching upon him, alien and even dangerous to his real, as opposed to his dreaming, self. He and the nurse seemed to stand like two insignificant islands in a sea of strangeness. "Where's everybody?" he asked her. "I rang several times at the other door, but nobody came."

"There's nobody else here," she informed him. "The Countess sent all the servants away."

"Sent them away — why on earth did she do that?" He did not really want to know. The question was automatic. Here, he felt, was something strange and abnormal, an eccentric act, belonging to the sphere of the castle magic, with which he wished to have nothing to do. So his mind divided, instead of listening to the answer, he watched inwardly the funny little procession, explained now, twitch and twitter its grasshopper's cakewalk across his mental screen. He heard the word "sterilise" spoken, and, coming back to reality, saw the nurse's white figure fluttering like a gigantic moth at the dark shadowy end of the passage. Ending her complaint about having no one to help her, she finally said, just as she disappeared:

"I think, doctor, you ought to go straight up to the patient. She seems rather overwrought."

"The cheek of it," he thought, mechanically starting up the spiral staircase: since when had he allowed his subordinates to tell him what to do? But his indignation was only on the surface. The internal division which he'd created deliberately a minute ago now seemed to continue on its own account, outside his control. While his consciousness resisted the spell of the castle, his deeper self was surrendering to it, becoming more deeply enthralled as he climbed up and up, round and round. All of a sudden he was startled by the Countess's voice, so clear that for a second he thought she was speaking to him.

"Why should I trust you?"

Without realizing it, he'd got to the top of the stairs; but the people on the other side of the open door had not yet heard him. He coughed warningly before he entered the big bare room, swimming in the green gloom of its closed shutters. Remembering the nurse's remark, he suspected that he was interrupting a scene, only able to make out the two figures standing like combatants, face to face. Advancing further, he came opposite another door opening into a lighter bedroom: and the sight of the midwife's clinical-looking preparations in there, a glimpse of his everyday background, reinforced normality for the moment; magic seemed to recede.

To his surprise the Countess, as far as he could make out, still wore the clothes in which he had seen her before: why hadn't the nurse got her undressed? But he couldn't see her distinctly; she remained an imprecise pattern of lights and darks. Her pale face, framed in dark hair and oddly unrelated to the ungainliness below, seemed to glance at him from an immense distance, before turning back to her husband. "How am I to know if it's true that they've all gone?"

The young doctor looked from her to the Count, whom he could see more clearly. Since their last meeting, he seemed to have gone to pieces altogether, in spite of his quiet reply. "I promise you there's no one in the house but ourselves. I'll swear it if you like, on my word of honour." He was making an effort to appear calm. But he looked broken: his face wore the half-frightened, half-incredulous expression the younger man had seen on the faces of people just told they were suffering from some grave disease.

"*Your* promise — *Your* word of honour . . . " It was

surprising how much contempt the woman conveyed without changing her quiet sardonic manner and speech. The doctor looked at her in sudden antipathy, suddenly feeling a peculiar arrogance in the way both these people ignored his presence. What infernal impudence it was, on both their parts, to continue their private quarrel before him. The acquired receptiveness of his profession, combined with an extra touch of personal sensitivity, made him acutely aware of the hostile atmosphere the two generated. It disgusted him to see them facing each other like deadly enemies at a time calling for tenderness and affection. He resented the way their antagonism seemed to degrade the birth about to take place, which was his province, for which he felt a personal concern. And, at a deeper level, he resented their hostility as an obscure manifestation of the castle magic; of the secret he longed to share. It was as if he had been shut out of his own dream. It was too much; and though, consciously, the last thing he wanted was to become involved, he seemed compelled to break in.

"If you're talking about the servants, I know they've gone," he said rather harshly. "I passed them down on the road." At once he could feel the secret part of him, which he'd been suppressing, coming to the fore, bringing a new emotion he didn't recognise.

He had addressed his remark to the man. But, before there was time for an answer, he heard a sharply-indrawn breath, not as loud as a gasp, from the countess, and was just in time to catch her as she swayed, almost falling. For a second her strange eyes looked into his, dark as rocks under clear water, filled with a cold fear no determination could hide. Here was an involvment she could not refuse: for an instant he saw in her eyes something outraged, astonished. Then they dulled, went drowned-looking, sightlessly staring and drowned in pain. At last, at close quarters, her face came distinct, beaded suddenly, as with seed pearls, with small gleaming globules, and stamped with a pre-assumed determination, now automatic; a sort of stubborn Red Indian stoicism, determined to endure silently to the end. Her body had gone strangely limp and heavy, inert, a lifeless deadweight in his arms; as he stood looking down, searching for some trace of the girl who had smiled at him, seeing only this stubborn arrogant look of fixed endurance — the look of a Red Indian at the stake — sealed off, a thousand miles from him.

Yet, with all the force of his emotion surging up from its secret spring. he wanted to say: "Let me in . . . let me into the secret with you . . . let me share it, whatever it is . . .

14

whatever it means . . . I'll do anything, sacrifice anything . . . only don't leave me outside . . . "

He was shocked and confused, not only by the force of his uncomprehended feeling, but by the conflict between the conscious "real" self of his actual life, and the other unauthorized self, which, having gained the upper hand temporarily, was making its illicit dream world seem more important than reality. He was ready suddenly to throw his normal self overboard, in his longing for identification with the reality of the dream. But his everyday self struggled back into ascendancy when he felt the Countess beginning to stir, her body losing its limp heaviness, returning to life, detaching itself from him. Seeing awareness coming back to her face, he looked away quickly, not wanting to seem to have taken advantage of her — of her moment of anguish. He felt bewildered, neither quite in nor quite out of his dream state. But his voice sounded the same as usual, telling her that she ought to undress, to lie down — he listened to it in vague surprise.

"Not until he's gone." The Countess again turned to her husband, whose stammered protests, "You can't do this to me—you can't send me away," grew harder to understand as his nervous spasms increased in frequency. He seemed to have regressed, in his pleading, to his adolescence, dominated perhaps by some stern mother figure; speaking with the queer nervous hitch, an immature querulousness. "Let me stay . . . " This plaintive bleat sounded almost comic, coming from the big handsome man; and as if he realized it, he suddenly tried to make his voice curt and incisive. "I *will* stay . . . It's my right . . . "

But the wife made short work of this effort, reducing him to immediate silence by retorting: "I hardly think you're in a position to talk about rights . . . the rights of the case are all on my side . . . I'm keeping my side of the bargain, much as it disgusts me . . . "

They both seemed to have forgotten the doctor again, speaking as if he were not in the room. This time he didn't mind; the fact of being ignored now seemed to miss him somehow. Still under the spell of his own emotion, he listened intently, as if their words must reveal the secret he longed to share.

"I promised to give you an heir under certain conditions," the Countess was saying: "conditions you have not fulfilled—."

The man had put up his hand to cover the jumping nerve, as if to hide it, protect it, from her. Now he let his hand

15

fall, exclaiming: "You're unreasonable, Regina . . . It's not my fault that the hospital has no room . . . Come, now, be fair . . . " As if impelled by an irresistible impulse, he started towards her, with a curious effect of reluctance, as though moving against his will. But, almost immediately, her voice stopped him dead."

"Don't come near me!" She backed away from him heavily. "Don't dare to come near me — ever again!" Her arm rose, palely gleaming, from her full side, the hand bent back at right angles, blocking him with spread fingers, in a dramatic gesture which the reality of her condition somehow deprived of falseness.

The Count did not move again. But though his body remained motionless, it seemed to the on-looker that his spirit was still drawn to the woman as by a magnet; unmoving, he still seemed to approach her across the dividing space; while she, aware of his disembodied pursuit, kept retreating further and further, as from something unclean, until she was stopped at last by the wall. The doctor felt as if all this were happening in a dream. Her movements had the slow unconscious stylized precision of a sleep-walker's. Fascinated, he watched with all his eyes her somnambulistic withdrawal, and the absent formality of her final pose, back to the wall, both arms stretched wide. The slow motions seemed to have an almost hypnotic effect upon him.

Now she moved her head, sending a ripple along the length of her hanging hair: and his eyes lingered on these dark undulations in the peculiar timeless magic fashion of dreams, stretching their brevity into something enormously long, reaching all the way back to, and merging with, a forgotten memory of his childhood. So that he saw as in a vision the wavy dark glistening strands of wet seaweed he used to bring home from the beach, treasured magic barometers, when he was six years old. He felt a sudden deep thrill of excitement, a mystery deeper than that old spell. The young girl who had smiled at him suddenly seemed very close, as if they'd been children together. In some mysterious way she had come back to show him those moist sea-ribbons of the past, with their strange rain-magic, sharing the secret with him. The dream encounter was real enough to quicken his pulse and send a tremor across his nerves. "You're getting warm," a voice seemed to say, as in the children's game: while, like a great invisible flower, anticipation swelled and blossomed in sudden beauty. "Warm . . . warmer . . . " He couldn't have said which was more real, this voice, or the Count's stammering complaining tones which replaced it.

"Why you should suddenly be so hostile . . . angry . . . bitter . . . I simply cannot understand . . . "

Vaguely, the young doctor saw the Countess, who had retreated as far as possible from her husband, as if he were leprous, facing him from the end of the room. "Do you want me to tell you . . . to put it all into words . . . ? "

Reluctantly, he heard her voice, heard the hysteria rising in it, as it threaded in and out of his dream. "I hate you for what you've done to me — to my body. It's not mine any more — It was my own, private, and I took care of it always so that it should always be strong and beautiful . . . I was proud of it . . . " He didn't want to listen to her, he tried to withdraw into his dream, to take refuge there from her voice. But the dream was wearing thin now; like a needle, her words stabbed inconsecutively through the thread-bare dream-stuff. " — forced yourself into it . . . made it a common, comic, hateful, hideous thing, like a dirty story — a vulgar joke . . . made it ridiculous . . . made me hate it. So of course I hate you . . . and your child . . . and this house —this castle of yours; I'll never be able to live here again— afterwards . . . " It was almost agony to him to hear the hysterical note in her voice, as he clung to the remnant of his tender dream, letting only as few words as possible get through to him. " — this whole shameful, disgusting process . . . it's utterly vile, revolting . . . no one should know about it . . . it ought to be hidden from everyone . . . " Then, her despair at its climax, he heard her cry: "The other was bad enough — but this . . . It's obscene, I tell you, this giving birth! A loathesome obscenity — now do you understand . . . ? "

The young doctor felt almost frightened of the voice, listening to it as if from inside a tent, which all the time became more transparent, till now it dissolved completely, leaving him unprotected. In growing dismay, he watched the Countess pull a ring from her finger and throw it violently at her husband; wildly aimed, it rebounded, and came rolling over the polished floor towards him. The young man auto-matically stooped to retrieve it; and, emerging finally into reality, looking down at the wedding ring in his hand, he felt mortified, as though the bright object were a symbol of the unbroken circle into which he'd imagined himself accepted. No symbols were needed to show him that he was still well and truly shut out. He had never been warm at all, never anything but stone cold. His smiling dream girl faded out, a dim wraith, beside these real people, who were as oblivious of him as any two human beings could be of anything. Their every word, every gesture, emphasized their mysterious sharing, and his exclusion from it.

Yet, in direct contradiction of all conscious assurance, it was still possible for a lingering belief in the dream encounter to survive, even now, relegated to the deepest recesses of his inmost self. Secretly, he could still dwell on the strangeness and sweetness of the young girl; the delicate wordless relationship he had established with this ethereal being could still give him a dreamlike thrill. But to his normal self, once again in control, the notion of any sort of relationship with the Countess — even with her dream self, and in a dream — was grotesque, reprehensible even; inadmissable.

So he thrust the dream complex still deeper down, concentrating upon the concrete situation. It was high time he took it in hand, he thought, looking at the woman now leaning against the wall, exhausted by her outburst. He wondered what had become of the nurse; she should have been there to help him. After the latitude he had again allowed the dreamer, it seemed necessary to assert the authority of his official self. He did so by telling the Count briskly: "Your wife must rest now. I'll come out and have a word with you later." He looked meaningly at the door. But the silly fellow, instead of taking the hint and going, burst into another inarticulate incoherent appeal, quite incomprehensible in his agitation.

Not attempting to understand him, the Countess said: "Go away . . . out of the house . . . I won't let this child be born while you're under the same roof. Go!" A sort of ferocity sprang into her face; a look so startling that the young doctor watched blankly while she took a few laboured steps towards the door, manœuvring her unwieldy bulk with the detachment that made it seem less a part of her than some clumsy package she was carrying. All at once realizing her intention, he felt a spasm of irritation. "As your doctor, I forbid you to go downstairs," he told her, exasperated. Without giving her time to answer, he said to the Count: "Either you both promise to co-operate with me, or I give up the case." His voice sounded unnaturally loud in the quiet room, which afterwards held only profound silence.

"You're quite right, doctor." Miraculously, the big man re-assembled himself, his dignity and composure. He even managed a smile. "You're in charge here. What you say goes." To his wife he said: "That's only fair and reasonable, isn't it?" But, getting no response, his precarious integration began to founder again in stammering and confusion. Faced by her contemptuous silence, he sank to a piteous pleading

18

that sounded almost abject: then gave up altogether, not even stammering any longer, just standing helplessly, as if witless, before her. Disgusted by the sight of his self-abasement, the doctor impatiently turned his back.

But now he had to confront the woman's arrogant self-will, which, in its way, was just as repugnant to him, just as stupid —like the senseless determination of a savage never to give in. She looked almost ugly to him at this moment, leaning awkwardly on the back of a chair where she had paused to rest. Her sallow face had a pinched look, reminding him of the lascars he'd treated during the winter, put ashore from some Far Eastern trading ship, miserable with the cold, huddled in inarticulate misery like sick monkeys. When she answered never a word to his appeal for co-operation, still keeping to her clumsy pose, fixed in that unbreakable obstinacy that was beginning to seem to him slightly mad, he felt convinced she would always oppose him. What was the use of wasting any more time on her? In a new burst of exasperation, he wanted to walk out of the room. In spite of the trouble it would land him in with his partner, he suddenly determined to throw up the case. He couldn't stand the castle any longer. He wanted to get right away from it and its inhabitants — never to see any of them again. On this impulse, he began: "We can't go on like this. Where's the telephone? I'll try and get Doctor—" Before he could finish, the Countess interrupted: "I've told you that I don't want anyone else . . . " She made a queer movement, impatient and yet somehow appealing, reaching up and then forward over the chair, so that the loose sleeves slipped back almost to the shoulders, exposing her bare arms, their youthful slenderness surprising and even startling against the shapeless matronly form. She seemed to radiate unhappiness, and a sort of appeal, as she leaned so obstinately on the chairback.

The young doctor was jolted out of his irritable distaste into a different mood. All the thoughts and feelings he'd been supressing came back with a rush, he seemed to have caught another glimpse of the thin girl imprisoned in her incongruous heaviness. And he could help her; she wanted his help. He met her eyes: suddenly they were like the eyes of a changeling to him, not quite human, lost among human beings, and looking away to some impossible lost homeland — pathetic. All of a sudden, he seemed to see through her domineering aloof self-assurance to a little waif-like air of forlornness, of not-belonging. All her stubborn intransigent qualities — her wilfulness and arrogance and that sudden fierceness — seemed no more than a child's

19

subterfuges, innocent, harmless and even touching. A tremendous wave of compassion engulfed him, sweeping away all the conceptual barriers that divided them; her wealth and position and the fact of her being his patient. None of these details meant anything to their inner selves, either hers or his own. He had recognized in her his own not-belonging, and from this subtle recognition arose again that impression of dream intimacy; something too delicate to put into words. A strong excitement beat up through his pity, creating once more the emotion without a name, to which he now surrendered unconditionally.

"All right, you win," he said very quietly, as if speaking to himself, but coming to stand close to the Countess, between her and the husband, hiding him from her. A queer little smile he had never seen flickered over his face, full of the gentle protectiveness of his deeper self, more important than what he was saying. The words didn't matter, but only the way he spoke, with the simple warm-hearted friendliness that was natural to him and rather endearing, projecting towards her all his capacity for disinterested devotion.

She looked back at him doubtfully and in silence; and with a slight shock, he thought in the depths of himself: "She doesn't know how to take . . . " How little she could have been offered in life . . . The inability to accept his goodwill seemed infinitely pathetic to the kind-hearted young man; she seemed more than ever in need of his warmth and protection. She was so touching to him, with the pathos of her clumsy shapelessness and her thin girl's arms, so indomitable, that all his spontaneous chivalry was aroused. He longed to succour and protect her and to put her back somehow where she belonged, where she wouldn't be damaged by clumsy humans. All his young masculinity went out to her cherishingly, enclosing her in the private circle of his protection.

His sharp ears had caught the sound of the midwife's ascending step on the stairs, and he said quickly: "If you'll let the nurse help you to undress, I'll go down with your husband and see him out of the house." Still she only looked at him without speaking. He returned her gaze steadily, making himself wide open to her searching eyes, with all his innate gentleness, chivalrousness; waiting upon her. "See if you can't trust me," he said, with the tender secret smile of which he was quite unconscious. "You can't fight the whole world the whole time . . . This is one of the times when you've got to trust someone — So you might as well trust me — I won't let you down."

The intensity of his feeling was like a wall around them, shutting them off from the world. They seemed to stand alone together, apart, while he waited in suspense for her decision. Everything seemed to have stopped, except the steadily approaching steps: if she didn't speak before the nurse got to the door it would be too late. But he could do nothing, say nothing, more. He had placed the whole of himself at her disposal: it was up to her now. Now he could only wait, oblivious of everything but suspense, and the steps coming nearer and nearer.

At the last moment, just as the door began opening, she softly said: "Very well . . . " Like a swift beam from the bright place she came from, the rare smile lit her face with its transient charm; its startling unlikely sweetness. It seemed to confirm their unspoken inter-relationship. She had acknowledged it with her smile. A wonderful exaltation uplifted him, he smiled at her radiantly, quite out of himself for a moment, transported, abandoned utterly to her.

The abandonment of himself brought a deep stillness and peace, he only wanted to stay in this exalted state. But here was the nurse, crossing the room with a tray covered by a white cloth; on her way to the bedroom, she paused to explain her long absence, forcing him to give her his attention. He appeared to be listening; but he heard not a word she was saying, his whole being still centred upon the other woman, for whom he poured out in generous abandonment all his northern tenderness, an almost mystic devotion, protecting and adoring her from a distance. Several seconds before the midwife's experienced eyes saw any change, something more like second sight than ordinary vision sent him hurrying to support the Countess, perceiving and trying to take to himself the gathering wave of her pain. The convulsion that tore through her body shook him with passionate pity, as he bent low to catch her whispered words: "Take him away . . . quickly . . . out of the house . . . "

Her eyes were darkening, clouding over with pain and fear. He watched understanding already fading out of her eyes, as she forced the words through her lips, which set afterwards in the thin stoic redskin line, not to open again this side of the worst. "Don't be frightened . . . it won't be too bad . . . try to trust me . . . " Urgently, he forced this last message through to her, to the frightened waif who had given her trust to him. Quietly and very distinctly, he said again: "I won't let you down."

When he had relinquished her to the midwife, he stood for a second rather vaguely, as though only half present, exhausted by the strange experience of self-abandonment, a little bewildered. But he collected himself at once, passing a handkerchief over his face as if to remove the last trace of his recent emotions, which were already becoming dream-like and indistinct — irrelevant to the situation.

He went across to the Count, who had been standing all this time at the door, crushed and unmoving, as if dazed. Now he went with the young doctor, without a word, hardly seeming to grasp what was happening. The young man, quite back to normal, felt sorry for him as they went down the stairs. It couldn't have been exactly pleasant, after the things his wife had been saying, to watch someone else whispering to her. He wanted to explain or apologize: but it seemed impossible to do this without implying that he'd taken a liberty of some kind. So they reached the end of the spiral without a word having been spoken.

The Count paused here under a narrow window, standing as if deep in thought, yellow sunset light running over his shoulders, solid-looking as golden syrup. What if he refused to leave? the other was thinking, his normal self siding with the unfortunate man: it seemed hard luck that he should be turned out of his own home. Yet the promise made in the name of his dreaming self had to be kept. Anxiety forced him into awkward speech: "I think your wife must be humoured for the moment." Getting no response, he added bluntly: "You'll have to keep away till after the child is born."

Simultaneously the Count seemed to arrive at some conclusion in his own mind, in consequence of which his whole manner changed suddenly. With no trace of stammer or hesitation he said: "Yes, I must go." Suddenly he stood up straight and resolute, becoming once more the fine strong powerful imposing figure the doctor remembered, shedding the neurotic diffidence and anxiety that had seemed so incongruous, together with the suggestion of immaturity. All of a sudden he seemed to have recollected that he was an adult man in a responsible position, not only responsible for his own destiny, but for others also. He strode forward and opened the door: and unexpectedly the huge lurid sunset came flooding in upon them, overwhelming. Range beyond range, the cloud mountains filled the sky, and through their passes poured the slow glaciers of gold light, overflowing and drowning the world. To the young doctor, who had not been prepared for it, the enormous ominous spectacle in the sky seemed to throw their small human affairs out of perspective; when he recovered from the brief distraction, his companion was already outside, preparing to shut the door between them.

"Wait! you haven't told me where to find you," he said quickly, putting his hand on the door, feeling an illogical desire to detain the man, now that he was actually going. He looked at his portentous silhouette, darkly outlined against the sombre floodlight, and now pointing dramatically into its dazzling heart, and wondered what could have caused the abrupt metamorphosis, changing an ineffectual weakling into this masterful, almost forbidding shape.

"Look! You see that little pavilion? That's where I'll be. It's in sight of all the windows on this side of the castle. You can easily signal to me when the time comes."

The doctor's eyes followed the pointing hand to a sort of tumbledown summerhouse some way off, perched on the edge of the precipice, nothing beyond but the sky, and a weird pale spectral immensity, like an hallucination, tilting up to the unnaturally high horizon — suddenly he recognized it as the sea. Overlooking the ghostly faraway water, the desolate little place had a somewhat sinister aspect to him. Somehow he didn't care for the look of it. But if the Count wished to wait there it was no business of his. His restraining impulse had passed, he let his hand fall from the door, making some affirmative sound when the other said: "Just wave something. I'll be looking out." There was a short pause. A sudden gravity and tension seemed to have come on the Count. The doctor could feel that he was waiting, as if for him to say something else. But to that black featureless silhouette he had nothing to say.

The door shut, he heard the gravel crunch under receding steps, and turned back hurriedly to the staircase. He was in a hurry to get back to his patient. But for the next few moments, while he climbed the twisting stairs, the vibrations of the Count's unknown emotions seemed to pursue him; he was haunted by the thought of the derelict little pavilion, rather horrible to him, above that ghost of a sea. With what thoughts would the solitary figure waiting there, unoccupied, stand gazing out at the sunset, at the twilight, at the dark . . . ?

His own thoughts were diverted as soon as he got to the top; he was kept busy after this for some time. He didn't think of the Count again until the healthy girl child had been deposited in an improvised cradle. Then, while the midwife was attending to the mother, he went into the corridor, and, choosing an empty room where he would not be seen or heard, opened the window and looked out.

The night had become pitch dark, not a star, not a glimmer, he couldn't tell earth from sky. But he picked up a small table lamp and waved it in what he guessed was the direction of the pavilion, and then sat down on the sill. He was very tired; but, as was normal with him, he felt content and relaxed after the neatly-finished job, simple as it had been. His mood was altogether normal; and though he had not exactly forgotten his earlier dream-like experiences, tiredness, and the period of concentrated familiar activity that had supervened, made them seem as remote and irrelevant and unimportant as last night's dreams. As soon as he heard footsteps below, he called out: "Everything went off perfectly . . . a fine little daughter . . . congratulations," as though for a man to be shut out during the birth of his child were quite normal too. Disregarding the peculiar tone in which the Count echoed, "a daughter," he continued his professional patter. "I know it's disappointing when you'd set your heart on a son and heir. But just wait . . . you'll soon be an adoring papa . . . I've seen it happen again and again . . . "

As if it belonged to another person, he listened to his voice, its tiredness overlaid by a rather phoney geniality, losing itself in the huge hot darkness. He hadn't the energy to find it again. Too weary even to think, he sat in a kind of stupor, feeling darkness settle heavily round him. Vaguely, he had the impression that things he didn't want to remember were coming closer to him in the dark, becoming more real.

"Will you do me a final favour?" The voice from the terrace below startled him back to life. "Will you say good-bye to my wife for me?"

"What?" The young doctor jumped up in sudden consternation. "Are you going away, then? Without seeing the child?" He leaned far out of the window, staring, straining his eyes in a vain attempt to pierce the darkness, distinguishing only the blacker mountainous mass of a tree. Somehow, his inability to see the speaker seemed to interfere with his understanding of what he'd said, though the voice had come up firm and distinct, as when he'd heard it at sunset. Now it came again.

"The servants will be back in a few minutes. I want to slip away before they get here."

"But . . . you can't just go . . . " he said stupidly, unable to think of anything better. He felt strongly, without knowing why, that the Count's departure must be prevented. It was up to him to stop it, since there was no one else . . .

"On the contrary, it's the only thing I *can* do." This was said with such determination that it seemed futile to go on

24

protesting: he told himself without conviction that he was justified in making no further effort. Nevertheless, responsibility weighed heavily on him. Under cover of darkness a mysterious unknown danger, related somehow to the Count's departure, seemed to be creeping closer. Only he knew of it; only he could avert it by keeping the man here. And he could do that — how?

Perhaps by talking to him: suddenly it occurred to him that perhaps he ought to explain . . . that women during the puerperal period . . . that his wife . . that any abnormality would almost certainly pass when she got over the birth . . . that he had only to be tactful and patient a little longer . . . But the prospect of putting all this into words was too much for his stupefied brain, it appalled him. And it would mean reviving all the memories he was trying to lose; admitting their validity. *Were* they valid, then? Had the Countess really behaved so abnormally? His thoughts slid off into vagueness, fatigue. He was still being tugged in different directions by his conflicting impulses, when the disembodied voice said:

"Goodbye, doctor. And thank you for all you've done:"

"But I've done nothing . . . nothing at all," he thought guiltily and yet vaguely, troubled by the sad-sounding voice. He would have preferred it to speak sarcastically than with that lonely sadness, coming out of the huge indifferent dark like the voice of a lost soul . . . All of a sudden he realized that he was listening absently to the diminishing thud of footsteps; the invisible man was already walking away — It almost seemed that he'd deliberately absented himself in a dream until it was too late to detain him. Conscience-stricken, he flung himself over the sill so recklessly that for a moment he lost his balance; instead of calling the Count back, he could only gasp inarticulately and inaudibly into the thick dusty foliage of the creeper outside, while his nose was filled with the strong medicinal smell of its leaves, crushed by his blindly-clutching hands. By the time he'd jerked and squirmed himself back to safety and got his feet planted on the floor again, no steps were to be heard.

The young doctor felt rather a fool as he brushed himself down and straightened his clothes. He let his thoughts dwell on this last ludicrous contretemps, and its cause sank further and further into the background, until it was lost altogether; the notion of danger forgotten, thrown, with his guilt and responsibility, into some convenient limbo of weariness and preoccupation. Dead-tired, he yawned as he went back to take a last look at his patient, stumbling over

25

the steps up or down that were everywhere in the old building, quite impervious now, in his tiredness, to the castle's glamour.

However, he shook himself into some alertness as he went into the room, clean and tidy once more, where the Countess was lying, very pale and quiet, her eyes closed, her body very flat now under the sheet. She might have been sleeping; but the young man knew that she was aware of his entrance. While he was wondering whether to give her the husband's message, she asked, almost in a whisper and without opening her eyes: "Has he gone?" breaking the silence she had maintained since the birth began.

"Yes. He asked me to say goodbye to you for him."

Automatically checking her pulse, he stood looking down at her still face, made masklike by the closed eyes, its detachment exaggerated to absence. He felt vaguely that something was not as it should have been; but, knowing he was too tired to be of any more use, he laid her hand down again, saying: "Rest quietly and don't worry. I'm going now. The nurse will attend to everything." Tiredness like a drug in his brain, he made for the door; but almost at once her voice arrested him, jolted him out of his stupefaction.

"Before you go, please tell her not to bring the baby in here." There was a moment's pause while he turned and came back to the bed, before the quiet voice continued without the least trace of emotion: "I won't see it. I won't touch it. I refuse absolutely to have anything to do with the child. For tonight I suppose it will have to stay. But tomorrow it must be taken away — far away. Otherwise I shall go myself."

The young man gazed at her, frowning, not knowing how to answer. Her expressionless voice baffled him, he felt as if he'd come up against a brick wall. She kept her eyes shut, and the lowered lids seemed to set two blank screens between her and himself. Helplessly, he wished she would raise her eyelids. But they stayed down, sealed down by that inexhaustible obstinacy of hers, which now more than ever seemed to him slightly mad.

Fighting against the toxins of his own fatigue, he struggled for some adequate response; but his head would not come clear; everything seemed vague and confused, nothing was definite. Looking at the Countess, who, throughout the birth, had been an anonymous female figure to him, about whom no feeling was possible, he still seemed to feel nothing. He only wanted to get away, to go home. His castle dream had turned into a kind of nightmare he wished to forget. His job here was done. He had delivered the child; there his responsibility ended. It was no concern of his what happened now to these people and the life they had made. He would mind his own business—go home to forget them. But, even while he was thinking this, he knew it was an over-simplification, produced by his conscious self in collusion with his tired body. And, though he wanted to deny the existence of any other self, to renounce the dreamer and all his works, he could not disclaim the memories, despite his attempt to suppress them, with which he was being bombarded.

Yet there seemed no connection between the subtle wordless relationship he remembered and the woman before him. It had been so dreamlike, tenuous, practically non-existent; and the girl, quite non-existent, someone he had met in a dream. He was still frowning down at the woman of flesh and blood, whose face the blank absent look covered like a veil, when suddenly the memory of how he had stood as if alone with her, isolated in the circle of his own intense feeling, became far too clear and vivid to be dismissed as a convenient dream.

At last her eyes had begun to open, very slowly, as if with great difficulty, or reluctance. He waited, eagerly watching, suddenly sure that everything would become clear as soon as he looked into her eyes. For an instant something obscured the two strange pools of dark icy water, a sudden shadow, or shudder, or flaw of wind, went flying across, almost too fast for his eyes to follow, leaving them again clear and cold. She seemed to be looking straight at him with cool detachment; but the blankness he'd seen in her face was in her eyes too, giving them a curiously unfocused look, as if she didn't *quite* see him.

But the young man had received his expected revelation; that curiously acute perception of his, almost like second sight, had recognized in the flying shadow a fear so radical that the very mechanism of seeing had winced, the eye itself shrinking from what it might have to transmit to the waiting brain. Would she be able to bear the sight of the world again? Would she ever again be able to bear her life, herself, after what had happened? And, while his consciousness received this message passively, he became aware of another communication, most unwelcome, which made his heart sink. Relentlessly crystallizing in him was the knowledge that he was committed. After all, his responsibility was not ended. He could not go away and forget the castle. He couldn't just mind his own business; or rather, the woman lying on the bed *was* his business . . .

All his normal instincts set up a violent protest. In real

life, the thing was impossible, unthinkable simply. She was the Countess, one of the castle people—how *could* there be anything between them? He felt almost panic-striken; in what madness had he become involved?

She was still looking at him with that strange lack of focus, sightlessly almost; suddenly it reminded him of a child which has been terrified and will not look anyone in the face. As if it had burst through, swept aside, some enormous dam, compassion flooded his being. Fear was carried away by the strange, melting, outgoing sensation that left him powerless, weak, as though all his blood were draining towards her. In spite of his exhaustion, he felt something of his former ecstatic abandonment of self, like a pouring out of his life's blood for her. Seeing her lying so quietly, with her shadowed face and her arms tired at her sides, he knew with a certainty not unlike rapture that he was committed irrevocably. No doubt was possible now. A mystic transfusion seemed to have taken place, not of blood, but of his inmost essence, joining him to her beyond all question. Something was here that he could never repudiate.

Without his knowledge, the gentle smiling inward look came on his face, all the warmth and tenderness of his secret manhood going out to her, to wrap her in encouragement, peace. "Stop thinking and go to sleep," he said to her, smiling, indulgent, and full of kindness. "Tomorrow we'll discuss everything. It's too late to do anything now. For tonight you must rest." He was thankful, in his deadly tiredness, for this respite: though he knew it was only that—from the irrevocable there could be no escape.

His face became weary again, responsible, once he was out in the passage. Still he couldn't go home. There was still the mid-wife to whom he must give some explanation. Going to find her, aware from the whispering in the air that the servants had now returned, he was almost envious of their freedom, feeling the heavy burden of responsibility weighing upon him, for ever more. Yet he had taken up the load of his own free will; in a sense he had chosen it, and would not really have had it otherwise.

Thinking, "Poor little devil," he stood for a moment looking down at the sleeping baby, before he began to tell the nurse what seemed necessary, dead tired, leaning against the wall.

Suddenly, there was the shocking shattering crash of a shot outside, as if the whole night had exploded. An immediate commotion broke out in the room, the startled woman exclaiming, the child waking and starting to cry. With a dreamlike feeling of repetition, the young man leaned far out of the window, stretching still further to get away from the noise behind him. He was aware of the unseen walls, perpendicular, above and below him, seeing in an instantaneous flash of imagination, the nocturnal landscape outspread, radiating from the castle, its mysterious heart and centre, transformed by darkness into a dark tower, smooth, tall, magical . . .

The night itself was a little lighter. Low down in the sky, a livid discolouration, a kind of luminous bruise, showed where the moon had risen behind the clouds; and against this dim blur the broken roof of the little pavilion appeared like some rifled dishonoured tomb. He felt as though all this had happened before. He knew, and yet he refused to know, what was coming. Something dangerous, hugely exciting, was racing towards him like an express train; but for one more second, the excruciating thin cry of the newly-born filling his head, he held off the knowledge of what it was.

2

NOT WANTED

THE girl in the end bed had turned to the wall, gradually
turning further and further over in her determination to disso-
ciate herself from the rest of the ward, till she was lying
practically on her face. All she could see was a section of
the shiny yellow floorboards, at which she'd been staring so
long that the knots and grain of the wood had turned into
maps and faces and a goose on a string. Now there appeared
a pair of old shapeless slippers made of mud-coloured felt
with the vestiges of a green overcheck, moving over the maps
and faces, between polishing rags and a mop, accompanied
by a strong smell of Javel. The wardmaid was late, and in
her hurry became a little careless, pushing the end bed
slightly askew and forgetting to straighten it when she moved
on, chattering all the time to the women along the ward. The
girl at the end was glad when she'd gone and her own tensed
muscles could relax again. She felt the sort of relief that
comes when an irritating wind has died down.

Her eyes were still fixed on the same spot on the floor,
where she could now see a corner of her suitcase which—since
in the madly overcrowded hospital even the baggage room
was full up—had been left under the bed. Now it protruded
just far enough for her to see the red label bearing the printed
words NOT WANTED ON VOYAGE, and, in her handwriting,
Mona, which was her first name, followed by the name of the
man with whom she had come to this southern country some
months previously. It had been simpler to travel as his wife
because of the reservations; and, since his departure, she'd
continued to be known by his name, not having had sufficient
energy to move to another place where they had not been
together.

Although the calendar said Spring had come, it had still
seemed winter in the north, the city people still going about
like conspirators, wrapped and muffled, hoarding each one his
diminished private resources of health and spirits, every face
wizened and a bit miserly, at the end of the long winter that
was like a seige, difficult to survive: only a few hard spikes

and buds in the parks—unconvincing promises in which nobody believed, if they-so much as saw them, hurrying past in the still biting wind. Like everyone else, she'd kept on mechanically, not quite alive under her heavy clothes, in a sort of winter-trance of monotonous comings and goings between the places where she lived, ate and worked, slept and amused herself. Nothing had seemed quite real, nothing, certainly, of any importance; she had been surprised because the man took her carelessly imparted information seriously, treating the physiological detail as though it mattered. Slightly bewildered, she'd agreed that of course he was right, the thing must be got rid of without delay; and was beginning to wonder what steps would be necessary to that end, when he'd told her about the specialist in the south and the simple little letting in of air which he'd perfected. "I'm sick of waiting for Spring," he had said. "I'll take a month off and drive you down there and we'll get some sun and some decent food and liven ourselves up again." That had put an end to her hibernation. The winter numbness had gone. Suddenly the project became exciting and gay, she thought only of being alone with him in exciting new places, and the little vexation faded into the background.

"But still, he ought to have made me do it at the beginning," she thought now, transferring the blame, not quite fairly, as she well knew. Yet it was true that she'd fallen under the spell when they came through the tunnel; that she hadn't been able to think sensibly any more, drunk on the loveliness of it, the sense of a wonder-world made for love and pleasure —a sort of eternal holiday. The tunnel went under the mountains. They drove into it in winter, everything still northerly, frostbound, hard; the problems and tensions of wars old and new like a cold fog in the air. And at the other end they came out into a different world entirely: southern sunshine, the first olive trees, anemones, the spring air enchanted; wild red tulips waving their bright silk flags in the grass. She had fallen straight into a dream: impossible to waste precious moments of it on the other sordid little affair. When he said, "Why not get it over?" she always answered, "Yes, soon." She always meant to do it sometime: but not today; today was too precious—tomorrow, perhaps, or the day after. When he ceased to speak of it after a while, she had pretended to believe that he too was under the spell. Time passed, and she let it pass. The month extended itself in unreckoned bliss.

Then, suddenly, it was summer, and tourists swarmed everywhere; the lovely private places they had discovered were theirs no longer. Quite suddenly, everything changed, and she was afraid, feeling the dream slipping between her fingers, and unable to hold it back: watching him grow preoccupied, restless, before her eyes; watching him write and receive letters, his thoughts straying away from her to other interests, about which she knew nothing. Jealous of those rival interests, refusing to admit that life was not to be an eternal holiday after all, she clung to' him all the more desperately because she was not one of those to whom the sharing of emotion comes with natural ease. It had been difficult for her to fall in love. In some part of her she had felt it almost like a loss of integrity. And now it seemed that the thing which it had cost her so much to give was being thrown away lightly, no longer wanted. It made her bitter as well as frightened. But still she was unwilling to let him go. They fell into an ugly habit of bickering.

Now it was too late for the little simple air-letting, she had waited too long. "I wasn't going to force you into it against your will, but I hope you know what you're doing," he'd rather nastily said: "I hope you've thought it well over. Because, though of course I'll be responsible financially, I can't be *ultimately* responsible, as I've always told you."

Oh, yes. He'd always been perfectly honest and outspoken with her: she was to blame for keeping her dream too long —trying to keep it long after it was really over, so that he'd got bored with it, and thought she was a bore—or worse . . . She remembered those words of his which had finally put fullstop to the whole thing at last. "I suppose you're hanging on to that baby so that you'll have a hold over me for the rest of your life." As if she were a common blackmailer. After that, even she couldn't delude herself any longer: she had to acknowledge that it was over; to speak the words that would let him go. Never again would she feel the world made wonderful for her joy. The disillusionment had been harsh and brutal, hacking through the delicate membranes she had so painfully grown to connect herself with him, leaving her with the shock and the torn bleeding ends of all her out-going feelings. Never again, she'd thought: never again.

Her eyes were still fixed on the label, and, not wanting to think of the man who had gone away, or of her dream's decline from its enchanted perfection to its ugly and cruel end, she let them move on to the next word, which was her name. Mona. Could any name have been more idiotic, ugly, unsuitable? At school they'd called her The Moaner, not that she moaned more than anyone else, but because of the name. When she was sixteen and trying to teach herself to strum on the ukelele, she wanted people to call her Moana instead. But although there was only the difference of a single letter, they never remembered; somehow it never caught on. Recalling this failure, all the countless other failures fell upon her, pressing at the back of her eyes, filling them with slow tears from some apparently inexhaustible spring inside her. Mona the Moaner—prophetic it must have been. How many days had she been lying here doing nothing but cry?

Three days . . . four days . . . ? Too long, anyhow; it was time she stopped crying. Like everything else, like her life, tears became meaningless, boring, if they went on too long. There was nothing but heat and discomfort and wretchedness left in her life now: her head ached, her eyes, with their swollen lids, felt hot and prickly . . . Dwelling deliberately on these unpleasant details to strengthen her determination to get rid of her life, she turned a little way on to her back, though not so far as to reveal her face to the rest of the ward. The sun, she noticed, had just come round to the windows: for the rest of the day the ward would be like an oven, insufferably hot, the girl in the spinal jacket would soon start whimpering. She closed her eyes on this undesirable world, and concentrated on getting out of it at the earliest opportunity. There must be no more bungling. She wouldn't fail next time.

After he'd left, she had felt too shocked and lethargic to move to another town, or even another hotel. It was high summer, fearfully hot, all the hotels along the coast were packed to overflowing; where would she have been able to find a room? Later on, nearer the time, she meant to move inland to one of the larger towns, where there was a good hospital. But the birth was still nearly two months away. So she stayed where she was for the present, overcome by the heat, and by her langour and depression, postponing decisions from day to day.

Then suddenly she was ill, and they said the baby had died—that they couldn't hear any heart-beats. She was relieved to be getting it over two months earlier than she'd expected. Now there would be some money over from the sum he'd left her; enough perhaps to start her on whatever she decided to do afterwards. "You'll write?" he'd said when they parted: "you'll keep in touch? You know I'm not ratting on you—I'm perfectly willing to do my share." She had promised to let him know how things went. But she fancied he must have known that she wouldn't write; that

33

there was one certainty in her mind—to make contact with him again was the one thing she'd never do. She only wanted to forget him and the whole affair. To pretend it had never happened. So now she pretended she was going into the hospital for an ordinary operation. She'd got that point clear in her head, at least; she still believed it would have been all right if things had worked out that way, and she could have gone on pretending afterwards that she'd had some important growth removed. But the child spoilt everything by being alive.

"Why couldn't you have died, like they said?" she had whispered furiously to the hideous little red wrinkled horror, when they left her alone with it for a minute. The sight of it gave her a nasty shock—unforgettable. It was such a horror; and yet so unmistakeably alive and human. A nightmare of a little homunculus that they'd brought out of her. They told her it had a fifty-fifty chance of survival. "Die! Die!" she had willed silently, all day long: and even in her doped dreams some murderous wish had persisted. The following evening the child had died; she wasn't surprised. How could it have survived all the extinguishing will she'd directed against it? But the damage was done. It had wrecked her half-made plans, like the little demon it seemed. Impossible now to forget it or pretend it had never existed. She had seen its horrid shape with her own eyes. And, as if that wasn't enough, solemn great institutions like church and state had to concern themselves with it. Serious grown-up men with important positions stuck their fingers into the bloody mess. No one, however, took any interest in her personally, or in the fact that, by the time she'd done all they told her, paid all the fees, and bought the plot for the grave, she had no money left. But they apologized for discharging her from the hospital almost before she could stand on her feet, explaining how overcrowded they were and how badly her bed was needed. And they told her she ought to rest for a few days before travelling.

Sitting in the taxi, she had realized for the first time that she must think what to do. After the shock of the little red living horror that had come out of her so unexpectedly, her brain seemed to have stopped working. Even now she didn't really think. It was just that there was nothing else to be done in these circumstances; she felt nobody could even expect her to go on living. She got out of the taxi at the quiet end of the beach, telling the driver to take her bags to the hotel.

34

It was late afternoon, but lots of people were still on the beach. She lay down under the pines at the top of the low cliff, waiting for them to go home. It was pleasant there after the heat and smells of the ward, the pine needles were soft and comfortable, and there was a breeze off the sea. She slept, and watched the tide coming in, filling the pools and inlets among the rocks, driving the last stragglers away as it covered the sandy crescent where people bathed.

She took the flask and the sleeping pills out of her bag and swallowed as many of them as she could before the flask ran dry. Then she couldn't get any more down. But she thought she'd taken enough to do the trick, and, to make sure, she meant to slide down into one of those deep channels below where she was sitting. With luck, she'd be carried out by the tide and never seen again. If she was washed up somewhere, they'd just have to bury her along with the rest of the rubbish at the public expense, since the grave on which she'd spent her last penny wasn't big enough to hold her as well as her child. For some reason this almost amused her. She was so intent on making a good job of what she was doing that she didn't think about death at all.

But she didn't make a good job of it in the end. She delayed too long, or else the pills acted quicker than usual because of her weakness. Anyhow, she lost control, sliding down on the slippery pine needles, she couldn't see where she was going, she couldn't steer herself into deep water. The last thing she remembered was a sensation like settling into a warm hip-bath.

And then the damned hospital again. Though it might have been hell: it really was hell coming round after the sleeping pills. And everybody so furious because she was again taking up one of their precious beds—angry faces all round her. She got the impression that they cursed the officious idiot who had fished her out of the shallow pool and brought her in. She cursed him too. She was harder to kill than her child, unfortunately. She heard people arguing about her; whether she should be deported, or put into a prison or an asylum. Too miserable to care what they did with her, she lay and cried and wouldn't speak to any of them.

Even in a prison or an asylum there would be chances, provided one was determined enough. She was still trying to plan a fool-proof suicide when two orderlies came into the ward and started wheeling her and her bed out of it. "Where are you taking me? What are you going to do with me?" she

wanted to ask them, but could not, her three-day habit of
silence being too strong; in part a defence mechanism, and in
part inability to bridge the gulf still dividing her from the
living. Other voices, however, asked for her, all the other
women sat up and took notice. There were questions from
every bed. The red haired young orderly grinned and made
vulgar jokes, while the other man, older and sour faced, said
not a word. The ward was left guessing,.and full of excitement. "What a godsend I've been to them," thought the
girl. "Hours of free entertainment . . . far better than the
radio . . . I ought to pass the hat round." She kept her eyes
shut until after the bed stopped moving, and the orderlies'
retreating steps were no longer audible.

Cautiously looking then, she saw that she was in a small
room full of queer-shaped dusty machines; the walls covered
by charts and diagrams and before and after photographs of
deformed limbs. There was a dusty institutional smell, but it
was cooler than in the ward and she was alone. Without
trying to guess why she'd been brought here, she accepted
the situation as one of the unpredictable strokes of luck, good
or bad, apt to occur, apparently without rhyme or reason, in
institutional life, thankful for the coolness, and the fact of
being alone. As a large round clock on the wall loudly ticked
time away, and the sounds of the hospital came as if from
afar, punctuated by the clash of the lift doors, she thought
she must have been forgotten; she hoped it would be a long,
long time before anybody remembered her.

Suddenly, without warning, the door opened and a young
man in a white coat hurried in, and shut it quickly behind
him. She recognized him as the one who had rescued her,
when a gang of students, gathered round her bed, had been
pestering and tormenting her with their jokes and questions.
Because she was grateful to him for telling them to leave her
alone, she now made an effort to collect herself and to listen
to what he was saying.

"I had them wheel you in here because it's the only place
where we can talk without being interrupted. But we've got
only a few minutes, so I'll have to come straight to the point
and skip the preliminaries."

He spoke to her in his ordinary voice, just as he would have
spoken to anybody, not as though she were a lunatic or a
delinquent. Again she was grateful, increasing her effort to
behave rationally, so that his confidence should be justified.
"I'm listening." Her voice seemed to creak as if it hadn't
been used for a hundred years. Embarrassed, she touched

the heavy dark brown hair straggling across her cheeks and pushed it behind her ears.

"It's a confidential matter," the young man said, standing with his hands in his pockets, leaning against one of the machines. "It concerns other people besides myself—rather important people. So I must ask you to respect the confidence . . . I'm relying on your discretion . . . "

She nodded gravely, noticing that his eyes were not dark like those of most southerners, and surprised that she should have observed this detail, for she did not now look at the people who spoke to her—scarcely saw them. Why did this young man's unremarkable face seem to stand out from the rest? She remembered the students, at whom she thought she had not looked; surprised again to find she had quite a clear collective impression of dark, tanned, good-looking young men, very sure of themselves, rather conceited, each one flaunting his peacock's tail of adoring females behind him. They weren't sadists, but spoiled boys; not really cruel, or hardly at all. It had only been spiteful teasing to which they'd subjected her; probably because they sensed that she was not the adoring kind. The difference between them and this young doctor, only a few years older than they, was, of course, the fact that he really saw her — saw she couldn't stand teasing just then — while they only saw her in relation to themselves . . . Suddenly conscious of how she'd been staring, she made a quick startled move, pulling up the sheet as if to dive under it; then looking down awkwardly at her hands, folding and re-folding the dingy white stuff. When he spoke again, she was struck by something familiar in the intonation of his voice: all at once she recognized it, knowing that, like herself, he was from the north. And this reassured her; he was more to be trusted, she felt, than these sou.hern peacocks, with their conscious good looks, always waiting to be admired.

"I'm going to ask you to do me a great favour," he said his voice so natural and matter-of-fact that it seemed as if it couldn't be saying anything really strange, in spite of the words: "I'm afraid it may seem odd — unprofessional . . . I only ask because it's so important to me . . . and because of what happened the other day. Because I assume you don't much care what becomes of you. And, if one thing seems much the same as another, it's just possible that you might do it . . . "

He paused, and she asked: "What is it you want me to do?" glancing up at him and then quickly away with her

37

dilated eyes. Her face was still closed and numb-looking as it had been these last days; but she could feel the numbness wearing off; the young man had melted it with his friendly informal manner, piercing it with his penetrating clear gaze, and this was uncomfortable for her, she felt exposed before him. "How hideous I must look," she thought, for the first time. She hadn't given her appearance a thought lately, as if misery had made her invisible. She could feel him looking at her, uncertain whether to trust her, and now he said: "You do realize, don't you, that nobody must know — You won't repeat a word of what we're saying?"

A spasm of resentment caught her unawares; she felt insulted, turning from side to side helplessly, as if she wanted to jump out of bed. Then, with the too-easy tears stinging her swollen lids, she twisted her face away from him to hunt for her handkerchief under the pillow, while; in a choking disjointed voice, she exclaimed: "I never want to speak to anyone . . . about anything—only to die . . . " It sounded childish and feeble, but she couldn't help it.

"So why should you bother with my stupid secret?" This approximated closely enough to some part of her feeling to make her look at him in surprise, still holding the handkerchief to her mouth. "Of course you needn't help me out if you don't want to. I just hoped you might, if you were so indifferent to everything." With a disarming smile he went on: "As for the secrecy, that's because of the other people . . . it's not *my* secret . . . that's why I have to be so careful. Don't go getting it into your head that this baby belongs to me — my only connexion with it was bringing it into the world."

"Baby . . . ?" she repeated in a whisper, ignoring all the rest of what he had said. Her already pale face had suddenly gone dead white. He was watching her and could hardly fail to notice the change. But for some reason he chose to ignore her obvious agitation, and to go on in his matter-of-fact way:

"Yes. There's this child, you see, that must be got away from here, up to the mountains. I promised the mother I'd find someone to take it as soon as possible. But it isn't easy, as you can imagine, to find the right person . . . someone able to look after it who's also completely discreet. There are plenty of capable nurses; but how many of them can be trusted to keep their mouths shut? I've been pretty well at my wits' end, I can tell you. Then, suddenly last night it occurred to me that, as you don't seem to care what you do, you might be willing to take it on . . . I don't know what your circumstances are, so I won't talk about payment; although these people have plenty of money and are prepared to be generous. You may say that side of the affair doesn't interest you. So I can only tell you that you'd be doing something very worth while; something more than a great kindness; for which everybody concerned would be mighty grateful—including myself."

Although from his tone he might have been referring to some prosaic business transaction that took place every day, his hearer was still staring at him out of horror-dilated eyes, speechless, appalled. At the word " baby " a kind of panic had overwhelmed her, supplanting thought, reducing her mind and emotions to chaos. Unclearly, it seemed to her that he was proposing to bring the homunculus back to life . . . the homunculus for whose death, she realized, she felt responsible . . .

The young doctor was apparently oblivious of all this. Or else he was giving her time to get over the shock, only occasionally glancing at the bed, as he roamed about among the remedial apparatus, now and then pausing to test a spring, to slip his foot into a stirrup, or on to a pedal, or his hand into a clamp; maintaining meanwhile a desultory sort of mono-logue, not exactly for her benefit — it sounded more as if he were speaking his thoughts aloud. "I'm no enthusiast for in-creasing the population . . . the world's grossly over-populated as it is. I don't believe in keeping people in it against their will. If anyone wants to get out, let him go and make room for somebody else, and good luck to him—that's my attitude."

The girl on the bed didn't take in what he was saying, simply staring at him, blank with horror, not understanding a word. Gradually, however, as he unconcernedly went on talking and fiddling with the machines, the very aimlessness of his behaviour began to pacify her, assuring her of the absence of danger. His casual sounding voice, carelessly running on in the background, did its work, soothing her, dispelling panic, preparing the way for thought to return.

"Before you take any irrevocable step, it's only reasonable to make sure it's the right one — once you're dead you can't change your mind and come back to try again. You feel positive now that you've had enough of your life, and for all I know that may be a reasoned decision — you may have perfectly good and sufficient reasons for wanting to get out . . . I can't tell . . . I know almost nothing about you. But I do know that you're not in a fit state to decide at the moment. Your present judgment isn't reliable . . . You can read up all the technical reasons why it's not if you don't know them already . . . "

Caught by something implied rather than by the actual words, her attention started to come back to him from some distant place, across some dim borderline. And he, seeing this with his perceptive eyes that missed almost nothing, began to speak more directly to her. "The sensible thing would be to give yourself two or three months to get over all this . . . to get your system back to normal again. Then, if you still want to die, I shan't prevent you . . . I might even be helpful . . . and in the meantime you'll have done a valuable piece of work, and got me out of a tight corner."

The girl had come back now; re-entered her life as a thinking being. Selecting from his soliloquy those points that appealed to her, she decided that he had offered to help her out of the world on condition she did as he asked — thus making the proposition acceptable. She could tolerate the idea of the child on these terms; now, instead of resurrecting the hateful homunculus, it seemed that it might exorcise that horrid little red ghost. "Do you really mean it?" she asked, already almost consenting. He had made everything seem normal and reasonable again, talking the nightmare away with his casual voice, simultaneously restoring her commonsense by taking it for granted.

"Of course I mean it," he said, smiling with sudden attractive warmth, his ordinary young face suddenly vivid and charming. "You make yourself responsible for this baby— go to the mountains with it for three months, and, incidentally, get well yourself and get well paid at the same time. And then, when you're quite fit again, if you still think your life isn't worth living, I'll see if I can do anything to help you out of it." His white coat unbuttoned and trailing behind him absurdly like a debutante's train, he came to the bed and held out his hand. "Is it a bargain?"

"Yes, it's a bargain," she answered. She hadn't expected ever to smile again; but she felt her lips curving in response to his smile, no more able to resist its warmth than her hand could refuse the warm vitality of his clasping hand.

These were the things over which Mona was pondering, as she sat, not many days afterwards, in the train, travelling towards the mountains, the child asleep in an old Japanese basket suit-case beside her. The train was a slow one, and it meandered to and fro between the villages and small towns, sometimes running for some miles in another direction, but always turning back to the distant slopes, which never seemed

40

any nearer, as if they receded, mirage-like, before its creeping persistent advance.

The young doctor had made all arrangements for the journey. It was he who had decided that she must travel by this local train instead of the fast one, on which there might have been someone who would have noticed her with the child, and asked questions. Keeping up the atmosphere of secrecy, which struck her as rather absurd, he had himself driven her to the station, not of the town where the hospital was, but in one further along the coast. They had started very early, before anyone was about, before the heat and dust of the day and the crowds of tourists had settled like a blight over the landscape.

At this hour, some of the night's freshness still lingered with the dispersing mists, everything seemed new-washed, the empty bottles and tins and miscellaneous debris left by the holiday crowds not in evidence. At one side of the road whispered the watered-silk sea, almost colourless, almost motionless, milky, etched with fine turquoise ripples. On the other, the lovely pale vista of hills and hollows spread like a great crumpled drapery to the ethereal cloud-topped crests of the range in the background. Looking at all this, the girl was reminded poignantly of her lost dreams, and of those first days when the enchanted scene unfolded its unbelievable beauty — out of this world; magical. She caught a glimpse of the lost spell, looking towards the castle, dreamlike on its hilltop, presiding over this delicate landscape of dreams.

It was most painful to her to be so vividly reminded of what was lost. Instinctively, at this unhappy moment, she looked at the man beside her, who had brought her back to life, upon whom she had come to depend. Spending a few minutes with her each day, he had kept her going by not sparing himself, giving generously of his vitality and his confidence and support. Somehow he had carried her through the first difficult dealings with the world outside the hospital, making himself her bridge back to normal life. When he looked into her face, she always had the feeling that he understood her as nobody else ever had done, as if he saw through to her inmost thoughts and needs, so that, when he spoke, he said precisely the thing that would help her most; the thing for which she seemed to have been waiting without knowing it. So now it gave her a most unpleasant shock when he failed to respond to her silent appeal, seemed not to notice it, looking — not at her — but away to the castle, if he took his eyes off the road. For the first time he seemed unconscious of, or in-

41

different to, her need. It was the first time he had ever failed her, and it was a shock; a shocking revelation, too, of her own dependence.

* * *

At the station, the young doctor did everything possible for Mona's comfort on the tedious cross-country journey, even enlisting the sympathy of a motherly-looking passenger on her behalf, mentioning that she'd been ill and would appreciate some help in looking after the baby. But the girl couldn't forget the few moments when he had seemed oblivious of her, which made his attentions seem insincere and distasteful. He had formed her one precarious link with humanity, and now the link seemed to have given way. Watching him critically, observing the readiness with which the other woman succumbed to his modest natural charm, so different from the calculating self-conscious charm of the south, she felt that she herself had also been tricked by it; trapped into doing something she didn't want to do at all. She hadn't really considered the fantastic bargain they'd made, letting herself be swept along blindly by his spontaneous èlan, submitting to his influence. This influence had now been withdrawn prematurely, and she began to have doubts, apprehensions. All of a sudden, she felt that she couldn't go to this unknown place with somebody else's child. The whole thing seemed crazy, she was seized by a wild desire to escape from the whole situation.

But she'd waited too long. The young man had already got out of the train, which was due to leave; and, when she rushed into the corridor, the door was shut between them and would not open. She could only stand gazing desperately at him and making frantic signs through the window, as in some grotesque nightmare film. Their eyes met; for an instant she had the familiar reassuring sense of contact, as though he knew all her thoughts and feelings even better than she did. She waited in agonizing suspense for him to do something to save her — to open the door, or call the guard — get her out somehow, while there was still time. Why didn't he hurry? She stared down despairingly into his face. Surely he couldn't have misunderstood what she was trying to convey?

"Don't worry . . . Everything will be all right . . . I'll be writing to you . . . " His voice came to her strangely muted through the thick glass. His foreshortened face, the eyes screwed up in the sun, looked preoccupied, absent, as if he had half-forgotten her already. With horror and incredulity it was dawning on her that he didn't mean to help her out. She'd let herself in for this thing, and would have to go through with it to the end.

The train lurched forward along sharply-curving tracks, and was almost at once out of sight of the station. She stayed where she was in the corridor, overcome by sensations of hopelessness and defeat. It had all happened again, was her confused thought; and again no one had cared; no one had moved to save her — why had she expected it? People never did care. She felt that the young doctor had used her for his own ends, betrayed her, as her lover had done — she'd been sold; sold again. Idiot that she was, would she never learn that no one could be trusted? She should never have tried to make contacts; emotional relations were not for her. Even at its height, the love affair, on which she'd embarked with difficulty and trepidation, had seemed, partly at least, a treachery to herself. Now her true self suddenly asserted its independence, demanding to be avenged.

Suddenly she forgot her fears; her face lost the desolate helpless look that made it pathetic, becoming heavily introspective, secretive: she clenched her hands on the bar across the window, experiencing a sudden revulsion against the whole race of men. She had never been one for gregariousness; even at school she hadn't had many friends. She should never have deviated from her solitary pattern. From now on she would live in her isolation — for herself alone. Suddenly, the memory of her love affair had become hateful to her — it had all been a sickening mistake, disgusting: the thought of being entangled in the sticky meshes of romance made her shudder.

So strong was her will to keep herself to herself, that she shrank even from the strangers in her compartment and from their curious eyes. It affected her with instantaneous disgust when she saw them preparing to be friendly and sympathetic, staring at her, intrigued, sensing a drama of some kind. She would not look at them or even think about them — much less speak to them. Never again would she allow anybody to know what she was feeling. She took off her hat and sat gazing out of the open window, unrelaxed, turned away from them all, the warm wind lifting her heavy hair, alone in their midst. Her fellow passengers found this unsociable attitude rather offensive. They were puzzled by her expression and bearing, neither of which seemed suited to her age or sex. Put off by her chilly aloofness, her 'No Trespassing' sign, they shrugged their shoulders, exchanged a few muttered remarks, and then ceased to take any further interest in her. Which was what she wanted. She was determined to live alone in future, even if she had to live among human beings.

The baby, of course, was a slight complication. She was not very skilful in handling it at the best of times; and today, in the jolting train, she was clumsier than usual, holding the child awkwardly so that it felt insecure, refusing to take the bottle for which it had been whimpering. The cries grew louder and turned to screams; it got red in the face, limbs and body went rigid. She didn't know what to do. Her new-found detachment wasn't equal to this; impossible to be detached from the tense bundle of rage she was holding. Some of the horror of the little homunculus returned to her as she looked helplessly at the thing in her arms. Such a passionate fury of life, such a tough single-minded will to exist, there was in that egoistic morsel, exclusively absorbed in its own needs, and clamouring relentlessly for their satisfaction, though the heavens · fall. Because she'd failed to provide something it wanted, it seemed set against her in such a frenzy of opposition that she was taken aback.

The motherly woman, offended by her stand-offishness, had been looking on with a certain satisfaction at her discomfiture. Now she took pity on her, or, more probably, on her charge, and offered assistance. The child was transferred to her arms, where, with exasperating promptness, it began sucking away in perfect content. Despite her wish to be left alone, the girl was only too thankful to let someone else cope with the situation. She really admired the businesslike efficiency with which the other made the infant clean and tidy after its meal, and put it down again in the basket to sleep. Nevertheless, it was a relief to her when, at one of the larger stopping places, there was a general exodus from the train, and the woman got out, as did the other occupants of the carriage, in which she and the sleeping baby were left alone. At last she could relax now, leaning back in her corner.

But her detachment had been shaken and was not quickly recovered. Against her will, she kept remembering those screams . . . that clenched convulsed little body with its stick-like arms . . . and that red face, so like the other ugly red midget face she so longed to forget. Revived by the demonic brat now peacefully sleeping, the whole hot hellish nightmare came back to her, the hours when she'd lain, willing her own child's death. It had died in the early evening; and in the evening of the same day *this* one had been born . . . Half aware of some superstitious notion lurking, atavistic, behind these thoughts, she pushed them all out of her head.

She'd almost forgotten what it was like to feel cold: sud-

denly noticing that she was shivering in her thin dress, looking
down in surprise at the gooseflesh of her bare arms, she got
up to pull a sweater out of her bag. Absorbed in her thoughts,
she hadn't looked out of the window for some time. Now
she did so, and, to her astonishment, the mountains, which had
always seemed the same distance away, on the horizon, were
suddenly quite close. They seemed to have advanced to meet
her with giant strides while she wasn't looking, and were right
upon her. She looked with amazement at the great dark
wooded slopes, slanting up overhead, and felt a stir of excitement.

The train dived into a tunnel, emerging in deep cold
shadow, green like the ocean-bed, no sky visible, nothing but
rocks and trees crowded together, crowding up close to the
line. After the brilliant sunshine and the vivid landscape
behind, the forest was sombre, cold, rather ghostly. Leaning
over and peering up, the girl's excitement quickened at the
sight of a gigantic precipice of bare rock, immense and forbidding and slashed with snow, far up in the pale, pure blue
sky. Suddenly she was glad she had come to the mountains;
it seemed right and inevitable, she felt she was drawing near
the fulfilment of a secret wish.

Her home-country being almost all at sea level, she hadn't
seen snow mountains till she came to the south. At first they
were no more than a part of her wonderful dream. But, later,
when things began to go wrong, she found herself gazing at
them for minutes together, watching them in a particular
way. It got so that she never forgot the mountains for long.
Not that she had any definite thoughts about them. They just
seemed to come into her head suddenly, and then she would
have to look. It comforted her, in the confused unhappy
welter of her emotions, to see the mountains always tranquil,
remote, in their lonely splendour; untouchable, serenely in-
violate. It was an obscure comfort to her to know that man's
hectic world wasn't the only one — that there were others,
where agitation and passion and bewilderment had no place.
When her love turned into a chaotic fever-dream, in which she
was tossing, hallucinated, frightened and miserable, she had
longed to escape to the cold, austere, changeless beauty and
peace of the snow.

And now that it was all over, now that she felt she had
finished with the human race, that she loathed and detested
them all, defiling and despoiling the globe with their litter
and hateful noisy machines, her thoughts turned gratefully to
the lonely regions men couldn't contaminate; to the deserts
and polar ice caps and, above all, to the mountains. The

mountains they could never debase; the mountains remained proud and glorious and untouched as they had been created. It suddenly seemed that the real reason she'd agreed to the young doctor's crazy bargain was because the mountains had fascinated her and drawn her to them. She had felt a vague longing for identification with them; and now they had called her — hence her excitement.

So far she knew nothing of the mountains, having only looked at their exterior from far away: now suddenly she wanted to know them, to see into their inmost heart. She became impatient with the ghostly cold forest, that seemed to go on and on, interminably, on those lower slopes; sunless, lifeless, only the spectral grey rocks flitting past in the sub-aqueous gloom. The engine puffed stolidly upward, letting out a screech now and then. Otherwise, silence; no call of bird or animal in the forest; no voice in the train.

The girl wandered restlessly into the empty corridor, and peeped, rather shamefaced, into the next compartments — which were all empty. She seemed to be the sole remaining passenger. She felt that the human world had been left behind, as if the station where so many people got out had been its frontier. But she didn't yet seem to be in the world of the mountains. It was more as if she'd been held up half-way, in the chilly dimness that seemed neither day nor night.

The trees thinned at last, she began to see gleams of light and late sunshine ahead. At last the train was coming out of the forest, hurrying, as if escaping to the grassy uplands beyond. The dense foliage had disguised the steepness of the climb; she was astounded by this high plateau, above the tree-line, right under the mountain tops. Climbing still, the track ran on between lumpish mounds and ridges of rock and grass slopes yellow with western sun, infrequent little streams brightly threading down. A towering dead grey bluff reared an impassable-looking barrier straight ahead, at which the train was charging like a mad bull. Shrieking triumphantly, it shot through a short tunnel, out into the shallow green cup at the other end; a lost little valley, so unexpected, and so remote and strange, that it seemed to have fallen from some other planet into the lap of the topmost peaks.

This was the place for which the train had been making all day. Now it slowed down, while the passenger gazed out at the hulking great summits, squatting round ponderously in a circle, their hunched shoulders of naked rock tattooed by patches and streaks of snow in weird cubist designs. The sun, on the point of vanishing behind one of these vast agglomerations, still poured golden light into the shallow bowl, at which

46

the girl gazed through a dazzle of gold. A cold thrill pierced her, passing beyond excitement to some more sinister feeling, like dread, which she did not examine. Now, indeed, she was looking into the heart of the mountains. But, heavens, what desolation! After the endless forest, the little high valley of grass and stones was like the end of the world in its remoteness; the very last place in the world, it seemed to her, right under those fearsome pinnacles in the sky. The great heavy rock-masses seemed too near, crowding oppressively close to the shallow, fragile-seeming bowl, squatting round ominously, as if at any moment they might move in and crush it out of existence. She saw that the valley had its own eerie charm, an unearthly virgin stillness and delicacy, under the great brutal masses of rock; then the sun disappeared. The hollow filled instantly with pure blue twilight, the heights becoming more aggressively present, towering like elementals, their huge heads still bright in sunshine, while their terrible ponderous stony weight pressed down on to the earth, crushing it down into the lower gloom.

The train stopped. With difficulty Mona dragged her eyes away from the shining titanic shapes in the sky to look for the village among the boulders, lying haphazard where they had fallen, and the multitudes, oceans, of smaller stones. A few peasant houses sprawled untidily in this stony dèbris, barely distinguishable, with heavy stones weighting the roofs.

A man walking along the platform opened the door at which she was standing, and, without speaking, passed on, leaving her gasping in the high cold air, that seemed to sting like an electric shock. For a moment she didn't move, afraid to leave the train, which suddenly seemed an old friend. The train would go back to the world she knew, to the country from which, eventually, she could reach the life with which she was familiar. She had the idea that if she once let the train go without her she would be doomed to this awful cold desolation for ever more, she would never get back to her life.

Well, she had done with the world hadn't she — or the world with her? There was nothing left for her to live for — far better to die, and have done with it: the mountain world seemed like a form of death. Her eyes returned to the stupendous peaks, standing aloof in monstrous, godlike indifference. Again the thrill went through her: and this time a wish came with it, clear-cut and definite as a call, to leave the failure, the mess, the pointlessness, of her life among human beings — it was exactly as though the mountains had called her to them. Her eyes began to shine with a rather feverish brightness, the cold stung bright spots on her cheeks. Excitement burned in her like a fever, as, balancing the baby's basket awkwardly under one arm, she climbed down from the high train, and arrived, tottering, on the platform.

So here she was. But it still didn't seem quite credible that she should have come to this ghastly lost village at the end of the earth. The child had slept through everything quite serenely. Once more she was momentarily amazed by its tough infantile egoism, seeing it lying there snug in shawls and blankets, supremely indifferent to all happenings, provided its own comfort was not disturbed. She put the basket down on a bench, and stood beside it, shivering, waiting for someone to come, half stupefied by the cold, which, away from the stored warmth of the train, seemed to touch and shrivel her like a witch's curse. She felt slightly sick at the high altitude, looking about rather vaguely. The little station was desolate in the gathering dusk, a bell clanging somewhere with muted resonance, a sound of primeval dreariness in the icy electric air. Away at the end of the train a few indistinct figures moved, occasionally uttering harsh cawing cries, taking no notice of her.

The mountain tops were gradually fading, ghostly grey shapes overhead, breathing down bitter cold. It was too much of an effort to go on looking up; at this height, her body felt heavy as lead. So she gazed, out of her stupefaction, at the plants growing in a tough bristly mat at the edge of the platform, each one woody and branched like a miniature tree. And that was just what they were, she perceived, tiny oak-trees, dwarfed by the altitude to the size of thistles; a whole forest of midget oaks, two or three feet high. She stared and stared at the odd phenomenon, a perfect example, it seemed to her, of the peculiar eeriness of the place. What arboreal kink could have brought them, with the whole wide fertile earth at their disposal, to these barren slopes, where they could survive only through such a freakish distortion? It made the place seem stranger to her than ever; weird beyond words.

Behind her back, the train was starting to glide past the platform, back the way it had come, this being the end of the single line. As if of its own volition, her body swung round. But she forced herself to stand still, watching the train slide away. She'd finished with the world; let it go. But as soon as the train was out of sight she felt frightened, as if she really had cut herself off from humanity now, for good and all. Rather desperately, she tilted her heavy head to gaze at the mountains, in search of some recognition there, since she had ceased to belong to the world of men . . . In some muddled way she was afraid that the mountains, too, would reject her, vanish, like the train, leaving her stranded between two worlds.

Suddenly something seemed to catch at the heart in her breast, as, startlingly, in the darkening sky, the heights burst into flame. One after the other, the summits caught the last fire of the setting sun, burning in final splendour around the sky, the snow rose-red, the rock many violet shades touched with gold and deep lustrous blue-black shadows; a magic circle, blazing, austere and splendid, over the night-bound world. She was amazed by this unexpected and awesome beauty, transfiguring the great gruesome masses of rock and ice, making them glow with unearthly glamour — it seemed to her like a sign of acceptance. Her cheeks burned, her unnaturally bright eyes shone still brighter, reflecting the strange effulgence, which seemed to show that the mountains had taken her to themselves. Then, as suddenly as it had come, the jewel-colouring vanished, the heavy indifferent crests at once began to grow ghostly and indistinct, withdrawing from her.

For a moment she felt disappointed. But then, remembering their blank stony indifference and apartness that had appealed to her in the first place, their absolute indifference to human life, she was glad that the glamour had gone. She wanted no more to do with glamour or any such feeling.

The air already seemed colder and darker. And now the girl saw a distant figure coming along the platform, carrying one of her bags in each hand. Wearing a curious high-crowned hat that brought him straight out of a medieval folk-tale, the man seemed to advance at the pace of the advancing night, drawing the dark along with him, or himself borne on its tide. She was shaking with cold. But as soon as she saw him she seemed to stiffen; to go very still and remote, matching herself with and against the elements of this icy region. She had broken off contact with the human world; this was where she belonged.

She looked up at the now disembodied summits, terrible great ghost-shapes of luminous pallor floating on the dark sky, almost phosphorescent, with black gaps of shadow where darkness came pouring through; dim, huge, breathing down iciness. Deliberately she identified herself with their in-humanity and utter loneliness—with the fearful cold otherness of the non-human world. She would not feel the terror of it; she would not feel anything any more. She drew the horror and awe and loneliness of the mountains into herself; willing it to freeze her into some substance so rocklike that it could

49

never melt, never be broken, harder than stone and colder than ice; so that no one should ever again have the power to hurt her, or even come near her. She had a sudden sense of solitude, peace, then; of detachment, as though she had been perfected, and made invulnerable like the mountains. She was standing on the platform waiting for the man to come up to her with her bags; and also she was watching him from somewhere a long way off, from some inaccessible height where she stood isolated, aloof, inviolable, as the awful inhuman mountains.

A little wraithlike cloud had materialized mysteriously in the crystalline frozen air, almost transparent, one or two stars looking through coldly. Like a gentle reminder, a few big summer snow-flakes fell from it, turning as they fell: at which the child, waking now, seemed to stare; seeming to watch the white flakes come drifting down, without haste, without hesitation.

3

SOMETHING MISSING

THE parents belonged to the old southern nobility, said to have royal blood, of which they were among the few specimens still extant, and they gave their daughter the name Regina, giving her little besides, far too dignified and remote to display any affection they may have felt for their child; their kind seem to be dying out of the world through sheer aloofness. Nature, more generous, gave the girl a suitable regal appearance, height being desirable in a queen. Except that she grew up too tall for conventional tastes, she was a beauty; her figure perfect, her flawless ivory skin lovely with its velvet bloom against the contrast of her luminous bronze hair.

She was, even as a child, very aware of her beautiful body, which she made a separate entity in imagination, the object of all her devotion and the centre of all her fantasy-life. Driven in by the stern and repressive circumstances of her girlhood, all the feelings that should have been drawn outwards to normal love-objects centred upon her own physical self, finding in her wonderful body something besides a most precious possession, more like a valuable favourite slave, to be tended meticulously and jealously guarded. And this substitute for the more usual lonely child's fantasy-playmate developed, as she grew older, into something perhaps not entirely normal; an obsession, almost, with her secret loved one.

When she married, straight out of the schoolroom, the titled rich man her parents had chosen, she was bound to resent his interference with the lovely body that was her private treasure and joy. The whole physical relationship revolted her, each repetition of the sexual act seemed a rape, and, when pregnancy thickened the fine lines of her figure, she began to hate the man for debasing her beautiful darling. Outwardly, however, she gave no sign, trained in the stoic tradition of silent endurance.

The husband was really in love; but, used to being adored by his womenfolk, he felt that, having given his affections to his young bride, he'd done all that was necessary. He never

51

thought of trying to understand her, and was genuinely amazed, when the birth came as the climax of horror beneath which her silence broke down, by the revelation of a hatred he'd never even suspected. By forcing him, in her passionate sincerity, to believe she would really rather die than let him touch her again, she pierced the otherwise invulnerable armour of his sex-superiority, and inflicted the one truly moral wound, the one unforgiveable insult. He could hardly have survived her rejection of him in his male function: to give birth to a girl seemed an additional insult, an unnecessary and cynical gesture on her part, and it finished him off.

His suicide came as a relief to her, pure and simple. When she heard the shot and understood what it meant, a weight seemed lifted from her emotions, comparable to the burden just removed from her body. The man who had blown out his brains on her account was the cause of her recent sufferings, and, in view of the tortures she had endured, the agonizing humiliation of her shamed body, his death seemed no more than an act of atonement that was her due.

Regina emerged from it all extraordinarily untouched, child-like, innocent-seeming, as though she were, like such sexless beings as sprites and mermaids, exempt from human emotions. But she couldn't endure the sight of the child; it must be sent far away from her. Which was not easily done without the danger of malicious gossip, the father having been a man of importance, at least locally; to find anyone who could be trusted to keep the secret while caring efficiently for the child, seemed an almost impossible task. But, by an incredible stroke of luck, the young doctor who had attended the birth and was already under Regina's spell came upon just the right person in the hospital where he worked. A young woman, a foreigner, solitary by nature, and apparently alone in the world, agreed to take the baby to a remote mountain village, while she spread the rumour that it had been sent for treatment at a spa specializing in children's ailments.

Regina was thus left free to devote herself to restoring her own perfection. Every day, in front of long mirrors, she scrutinized her naked body minutely, dispassionately, systematically eliminating each defect. She was still not quite twenty; her resilient young body, quickly recovering its supple slenderness and virginal grace, was soon virtually indistinguishable from what it had been.

But, even now, something seemed to be wrong, or lacking; she felt restless, dissatisfied, divided against herself. Her lovely body had emerged from its trials unblemished. But, though it was so nearly perfect again, she could not love it as before, or it would not let her love it — they were estranged. The unspoken words "There's something missing," began to haunt her at odd unexpected moments. Night and morning she heard them, when she brushed her hair, giving it regularly a hundred strokes, sending it flying out like a soft wing, that whispered: "Something missing . . . mis.s.s.s.s.ing . . . " fifty times into one ear, fifty times into the other.

The young doctor was now so deeply in love that he had overcome his original scruples concerning the differences between them, and, more than anything in the world, wanted to marry her — to devote himself to her happiness. He saw that she was restless and discontented; occasionally his watchful eye caught a distraught movement, and she had a queer oblique way of looking past him, into some unreal reality of her own. At times there was an air of neurotic frustration about her, when she seemed to blame him; although he was always rushing to her the moment his work was done, eager to give her everything, absolutely all that he had — spending himself upon her. He tried vainly to find out what was wrong. But she would not discuss such intimate matters, fixed in adherence to the creed of silence, restraint, self-control.

His love, as a matter of fact, no longer satisfied her, as it had done while she'd felt weak and ill. She needed something else now, and though she had no idea what this might be, she rather resented his inability to supply it. As a doctor, he assumed superior knowledge of the workings of her body and mind; so she felt that he ought to have known what would reconcile her to herself.

He, on his side, was beginning to be a little discouraged: the strain of conflicting loyalties was telling on him. Always straining to get through his exacting work, always hurrying to her, and finding her always dissatisfied, he was starting to wonder whether it was in his power, after all, to make her happy. Yet there was in her a challenging quality of innocent-seeming simplicity and wistful sweetness which enchanted him; by which he was absolutely bewitched. It had only to make one of its rare appearances for him to be moved to expend himself even more — for the thought of losing her to become intolerable.

So he tried to project her vague discontent on to something concrete, within his control. The two of them had this, at least, in common; she being equally anxious to fix her nebulous feeling to an object in the external world.

Because she reacted so violently to any reference to her marriage, he didn't like to mention the child. But some months had passed since the young foreigner took the baby away, and the arrangement had only been temporary. A change would have to be made very soon. Tentatively, he asked Regina whether she would feel happier if the child were settled permanently somewhere; and was relieved by her emphatic response — yes, yes; she was certain of it.

Her mind had seized upon the idea that anxiety over the baby's future was the cause of her unrest. In half a second, she'd convinced herself that here was a way to put everything right; and, in gratitude for the suggestion, rewarded the doctor with one of those irresistible smiles that enthralled him, charmed him, and made him long to cherish her for ever more.

It was autumn, the chilly, erratic wind going about the walls suddenly interrupted her thoughts with a whispered: "Mi.s.s.s.ing . . . " ruffling the drying leaves of the creeper outside the window. Quickly glancing at her reflection — she had a habit, whatever room she was in, of sitting where she could see herself in the glass — the mirrored eyes told her it too had heard. This ghostly whispering . . . it was starting to get on her nerves . . . She felt sure it would stop if the child were disposed of for good. In sudden eagerness, with a sudden yearning, she promised the man she'd do anything — marry him — whatever he wanted — if only he could arrange this disposal. She braced herself and did not shrink when he kissed her cheek lightly, as a brother might have done. It was the first time anyone had touched her beloved body since the husband's death. She apologized silently to her darling, explaining that this man was different, kind and gentle; he'd never become brutal and overbearing like the other — this one she could control. He was presentable and devoted; trustworthy; and, for all sorts of reasons, she needed a man; which meant, with her background and circumstances, that she must have a husband. She thought she could tolerate the doctor in this capacity, in return for his services. First he would find a home for the child; then help her to get away from this place of unhappy associations, and to start a new life somewhere else.

And she was grateful to him for treating her as though she were a Venetian-glass-girl, extremely frangible, delicate. She felt she could almost become fond of him. Basically, however, he was a means to an end. He appeared to her, not as a lover, a husband, but in terms of usefulness, of what he could do for her, as though he were her property rather than a human being in his own right. Those were the only terms on which she could bring herself to accept him.

As for him, he'd have taken her on any terms. He had to have her, she was absolutely necessary to him, to his life.

It was an absolute craving he had for her. For that exquisite young girl's smile, apparently so sweetly natural, fresh and ingenuous, he'd have gone to the ends of the earth.

As soon as he could get away for a day, he drove his old car up into the mountains. It seemed too much to hope that the young woman in charge of the child would be willing to take over permanently. He could only try to persuade her. His longing for Regina was so strong that it seemed as if difficulties must melt away before it: like the heavy snowfalls which had blocked the road, until a recent mild spell had left it open for him — he was able to drive the whole way without chains. This seemed a favourable omen: and, as he drove, he never stopped musing, dreaming, about his love. Not until he was almost at his destination did he tear his thoughts away and begin to think of the stranger, whose life had been so drastically changed by his intereference.

She seemed more than ever a stranger now that health had had restored her looks. He scarcely recognized the handsome, composed young woman, who had a slightly disconcerting way of looking at him, as if she didn't see him, personally, at all. Her young face wore the fixed expression of someone much older, who, having suffered at the hands of the world, has retired from it, and will have no more contact with its inhabitants. She was consistently polite, abstract, and cold; and her eyes always kept their look of distance, looking from some remote mountain top, refusing to become involved.

It made the friendly young man a little uneasy. He wasn't really in the least exuberant in his behaviour. Yet, sitting with her in the big room she shared with the child, her cool aloofness, superiority, or whatever it was, made him feel like a big boisterous dog, that comes bouncing up clumsily, wagging its tail, for a game.

By contrast with her remoteness, his natural warm feelings seemed superfluous, gushing. He felt he'd come on a fool's errand. Already, as he put the question to her, he was thinking of the free day and the petrol he'd wasted — it might be weeks before he could take a day off again. It was very annoying: but his annoyance was less than it would otherwise have been, because he wanted to get away from this girl, who made him uncomfortable. If she turned down the idea, he could go at once.

He thought she was uninterested, barely listening. Then, to his amazement, she said that, in anticipation of his proposal, she'd already considered the matter; and calmly proceeded to name the terms on which she was prepared to take entire responsibility for the child's upbringing — reasonable terms, to which he could make no objections. He gazed at her in wonder, and with conflicting feelings. He'd never dared to hope he would achieve his object so easily. But he was not jubilant so much as incredulous; unable to believe she meant it seriously; somehow it seemed preposterous when he looked at her, at those cold, far off eyes.

It appeared that she was perfectly serious. The young man was almost frightened by the efficiency and forethought she displayed, producing a form of contract in duplicate, and calling in two members of the household to witness their signatures. Looking up from her name, Mona Anderson, written in firm black letters, as the witnesses left the room, he felt like calling them back, scared of being left alone with this formidable young person.

He supposed he must stay a few minutes, for the sake of politeness; but could think of nothing better to say to her than: "You're very businesslike." Which she received in dead silence. His open, spontaneous nature distrusted calculation in any form; some distrust must have been audible in his voice — the remark hadn't sounded as complimentary as he'd intended. Hurriedly he tried to create a more friendly atmosphere by talking about her life in the mountain village. But it was very heavy going. There was no getting past that resolute cold detachment of hers. Finally he became silent; while she gathered up an armful of sewing and sat down with it near the window, as if unaware of his presence. She seemed not to know he was watching her as she sat there, rhythmically drawing her needle through the white stuff, pure white snow light pouring over her shoulders and filling all the folds of the fabric before it spilled its frigid radiance in a pool at her feet.

The snow outside had drifted right up to the glass, immensely deep and eternal looking, filling the room with its peculiar lively reflections, moving like icy water — almost like something alive — fascinating the child, which reached up from its cot, trying to catch the bright waves rippling over the wall. The young man was feeling very uneasy at the thought of having consigned a helpless and impressionable being to the care of this cold-seeming inhuman girl: who appeared to his imagination, stimulated by the dancing mirage-light from countless ice crystals, like a figure from a winter legend. For a second, he saw her as a sort of snow queen, robed in the irridescent diamond-shimmer of frost; forever frozen, white, hard, inaccessible, under shifting resplendency of the northern lights. And, though these arctic fancies came and went in a flash, they left him with an impression of cold, which seemed to emanate from an icy core within her — a kind of secret ice-spine that would never melt. It made her attractive young body seem rather dreadful to him, with his warm love for humanity.

"Why are you doing this?" he asked abruptly; the question which had been all along at the back of his mind forcing its way out.

She looked up at him, her needle suspended in mid-air, recalled from her fixed absence. "Well . . . " she seemed to be ruminating. "I suppose for the usual reasons." She twisted round to stare at the child in its cot, frowning, as though absorbed in the problem. She seemed to take it very seriously.

Yet, in spite of the fixed stare, he was convinced that in some extraordinary way she didn't see the child at all — just the problem. The infant concerned her only in the abstract: of the individual living child, the normal rather pretty baby called Gerda, with the father's colouring and a fluff of whitish-gold hair, she was all the time weirdly unconscious. He couldn't understand it. And then, in one of those sudden bursts of almost psychic illumination, which distinguished him from less imaginative practitioners, he recognized the frustration of her robust, courageous strong-minded person; seeing how she could have made a wonderful mate for some hero-adventurer of the new age, founding with him a new race of supermen, a new universal order, explorers of outer space. Because the hero-husband hadn't materialized, she had turned, in the bitterness of her disappointment, against herself, against the life-force within her, freezing it at its source, turning herself to ice.

He didn't want to believe it. Remembering that she was the mother of a dead child, he very much wanted to believe she'd transferred some maternal love to this other baby, thus providing an adequate and acceptable explanation of her behaviour. "What do you mean by the usual reasons?" he was impelled to ask: if only she would say she had done it out of affection!

But naturally she said nothing of the kind, looking up at her questioner with that pondering portentous frown she had turned on the child, as though deliberating a problem of deep importance. Yet only a fraction of her notice seemed to be keeping track of him warily, of his actual bodily self sitting before her. She had reduced him too to an abstraction; a problem inside her head.

"Money . . . independence . . . " she replied, looking straight at him. But even as she looked directly into his eyes, there was the curious distance; she was seeing only the problem he represented.

"But you could easily get a better job — something more ambitious — with better prospects." His voice sounded slightly strained, he really didn't know what he wanted from her.

"I've had no training," was all he got, coldly, like a frozen rock thrown down from her mountain top.

Impatient suddenly to get back to Regina, he glanced at his watch, deciding that he might now take his departure. But, as he stood up to go, the child started to whimper, and he changed his mind, feeling guilty. The sound was so much like an inarticulate protest. Resolutely putting his love affair out of his head, he settled down to watch Mona with her charge. It still wasn't too late to tear up the contract, and this he determined to do, if he saw any reason for such action.

But, seeing her give the baby its feed and prepare it for the night, he could not doubt that she was completely efficient and trustworthy. It was only that her attitude to the child, as to himself, was always impersonal — the actual baby girl she seemed to pass over, somehow. He told himself that at this stage it didn't matter: the child was too young to feel the lack of affection; its physical welfare was all-important. But he felt ashamed, and very uneasy — it was almost the first time in his life that he had ever deliberately silenced his conscience, and it troubled him deeply.

As she carried the infant to the cot, it was already falling asleep in her arms, lying there abandoned and vulnerable, in the utterly confiding way of very young children, trusting implicity to that cold support. He looked at her distant eyes, that seemed inhuman to him; and he wanted to snatch away the helpless creature he'd given into her power. At this moment the baby's eyelids fluttered and rose; fringed with long, sable-soft lashes, the violet-tinted eyes seemed to look straight into his, as if in unbounded trust. He felt like a criminal. He was really horrified by what he had done; he knew he ought to take the child away—revoke the contract.

But there was Regina. He had to think of his love and his own future. Suddenly he found that he was desperately tired, almost too tired to carry on, certainly far too tired to contend with new difficulties, new problems. In a sudden panic, he jumped up, feeling like Judas, saying he had to get back at once. He hurriedly wished Mona goodbye; while she watched him from afar, from that cold place where she'd isolated herself; which no one was allowed to approach; where no one was even allowed to become real; where people existed only as abstractions, and, as living beings, scarcely crossed the perimeter of her notice.

But, plunging out in the freezing chill of the mountain evening, that seemed warm compared to her glacial atmosphere, elation got the better of his sense of guilt. He couldn't do anything but rejoice when he thought that now Regina would come to him and be happy. But from time to time he remembered with horror the two he had left behind him. He had done this horrible thing to a helpless child. Only for Regina could he have done it; and for her he could have done anything. He forced the whole business out of his consciousness. He would think only about his love, and the new life before them. But every now and then, as he drove, he felt a sinking sensation because of the act he refused to remember.

Without stopping even to eat, he went straight to the castle, to bring his news. He was told that Regina was upstairs, in a little sitting room she used when she was alone, and hurried up, unannounced, as he did these days, impatient to reach her.

The small room seemed empty when he first entered. After the cold dismal night through which he'd been driving, it felt very warm from the wood fire, crackling as it burned with a sharp aromatic smell, giving more light than the old-fashioned lamps here and there. The walls were hung with dim tapestries, and old faded portraits of children, pathetic in strange stiff clothes, and an enormous mirror in an elaborate tarnished frame. There stood Regina; it was her stillness that had made her invisible to him. Suddenly now he saw her, in front of the mirror, staring fixedly at ·her reflection, utterly absorbed and unconscious of him — she had not even heard him come into the room.

She was wearing only a thin negligeè of some sort, almost transparent. Under the thin stuff he felt immediately the fascination of her slender white nakedness, which he had never looked upon as a man, but only through the blindfold of his profession. Now he saw her beauty, and his heart began to beat furiously, as if it would burst out of his chest. How lovely she was, his darling. Yet something about her bewildered him; she seemed different, somehow. And he couldn't understand how she could be so totally unaware of him. He himself, however deeply absorbed, could never have been *quite* unconscious of a human presence; such complete obliviousness seemed to insult the identity of the other.

He was about to speak to her, when, moving her arms, she dropped the single garment she wore, and, with the charming shy eagerness of a girl with her lover, leaned towards the glass.

Her tall reflected shape came swimming to meet her, pale and slender as a long stem; her face, like the bud of some big white flower, furled and secret in its calyx of dark hair, floating on the glassy surface. The young man's eyes strained in their sockets. Her beauty excited in him an intense desire for her: but something in her face alarmed and confused him; it really looked strange at this moment. The situation seemed altogether extraordinary — not normal. The big. lonely, semi-ruinous dwelling that had survived the centuries, exposed on its hilltop, now nightbound and still more solitary in the dark, a relic of the days of were-wolves and witches; and in it, this lonely, dim-lit room, where the naked girl stood alone with her mirrored self, unconscious of everything else, like a witch at her spells.

Her face, under the shadow of heavily hanging hair, seemed to be changing before his eyes; growing smaller, whiter, more mysterious, with an indefinable sensual look, half smiling, like the faintest possible hint of something corrupt. Strange, and utterly gone from him, she stood there, oblivious, with the voluptuous inward look of a self-love no longer innocent as a child's make-believe. He was at the same time both fascinated and repelled by her expression; it, and his own strong desire for her, thrilled him and filled him with alarm.

All at once she appeared entirely different, as though a witch-girl looked out of the eyes of his innocent gentle love. It was as if he knew nothing about her, and had been wrong, completely mistaken. Already her obliviousness had dealt his warm heart a cruel blow. And now came this second shock of her strangeness. The poor young man was completely baffled, confused, as he gazed at her standing there, rapt and unconscious of him.

He felt a sudden panicky desire to escape — he couldn't face her just now. He was too tired — too bewildered. At the back of his thoughts there was always the pathos of the infant's trusting eyes. To have sacrificed it to this witch-girl, who had changed places with his beloved, made his crime a thousand times worse. Terribly shaken, he tiptoed out of the room, and fled from the house. The servant who let him out stared in astonishment at his white, stricken face.

He was too agitated and confused to know what to think. But, after a fearful night, he'd almost worked himself up to the point of deciding that the child must be taken away from that awful inhuman Mona; which would probably mean the end of his love affair. The thought lacerated him. But, agonizing as it would be, he almost wanted to tear himself free from the witch-girl Regina seemed now, not quite human either. Every time he remembered her standing naked and oblivious in front of the glass, his skin crept slightly. Uncanny, the picture seemed. Was she really, perhaps, just a little mad?

However, when he went the next day to the castle, there was his innocent young beloved, smiling at him in the way that went straight to his heart. She was so charming, so natural, so virginal, so much the sweet young girl, that the other picture became incredible, simply. Now he was the one who seemed to be going out of his mind. How could his imagination have played such a trick? It must have been some delusion, conjured out of his tiredness and the dim light; he must have confused her, somehow, with his vision of Mona, up in the mountains. Convinced as easily as that of his mistake, he now looked apologetically, adoringly, at the girl, feeling he'd wronged her secretly in his thoughts. All his longing for her revived, stronger than ever. Once more he pushed the victimized baby out of his consciousness.

"You will marry me, won't you — quite soon?" he pleaded, a little, almost imbecilic smile on his face, that was white with tension. If Regina put him off now, he really felt he would die.

She looked at him out of wide wondering eyes, like a little girl. She was wondering if she'd be able to manage him. It was a bit of a risk she was taking, and she knew it, saying, yes, she would marry him as soon as could be arranged. But to stay in the gloomy castle of whispers had become awful to her — she was dying to get away.

Forgetting restraint in his ecstatic belief, the young man flung his arms round her and kissed her rapturously. He was so transported that it was several seconds before, recalling her outburst at the time of the birth only a few months earlier, he realized that he should have controlled himself. She had not tried to resist him. She stood submissively, with bowed head, trembling so violently in his arms that he thought she was weeping. As he quickly released her, he saw that her face was tearless, but very pale, with an agonized look.

"What is it? Are you ill?" he asked, terribly anxious.

But she said it was nothing . . . she didn't want to upset him . . . she was a silly girl . . . he must take no notice . . . And she moved away, and stood looking out of the window, her back towards him, her hands clenched so that the knuckles showed white: while the young doctor reacted precisely as she'd hoped and intended, cursing himself for a thoughtless, bungling brute. Of course, it was far too soon to make love to her. He would have to go slowly, win her trust by slow degrees, prove to her that all men weren't beasts.

When she thought the suggestion had done its work, she turned round with a tremulous smile, sitting on the wide window seat, her long graceful legs stretched out in front of her like a schoolgirl's, looking about fifteen. The young man seemed to see her with new eyes, seeing her truly, he believed, at last, as a very young girl who had never been loved deeply or disinterestedly and so had never learned how to love — who needed all his loving protection. He felt such tenderness for her that tears came into his eyes.

He went across, and, quite naturally and unselfconsciously, knelt down beside her and kissed her hands, asking her to forgive him. This new vision of her as an unloved girl, who had never been loved for herself alone, obliterated the witch-girl entirely. And Regina was lovely, so sweet and gentle with him. He put his head in her lap, and she stroked his hair, murmuring: "Be patient with me, won't you?"

"I'll wait as long as you like," he promised her, on his knees. "I won't ever touch you in that way until you wish it." He felt a Galahad, making his solemn promise to her, for which she thanked him sweetly, stroking his hair.

Afterwards, he sat by her side on the window seat for a long time, holding her hands, and feeling uplifted; he would have done anything in the world for her sake. Inwardly, he vowed to devote himself to her life-long happiness, in a sort of knightly dedication, all deadly serious. It never occurred to him that he was making a ghastly fool of himself. He loved her so much; more than he'd believed possible. But without any sex at all. It was as if his sex had suddenly fallen asleep, and he wouldn't let it wake until they were married, and he'd been able to win her love. He was content to dream of the time when she'd have learned to love and trust him, and to forget her first marriage. She was still so young, he was confident that, once he had her to himself, he could soon make her forget. Then, and only then, would he be her lover, her husband. He wouldn't hurry her or force her for anything on earth.

His own love was so strong and deep it seemed inexhaustible and everlasting; he could afford to wait. Nor did it strike him as strange how all desire had gone out of it, so that, even after they had been married, he wasn't tempted to make love to her. It would be so much more wonderful when she came to him freely and unafraid, of her own free will. He never doubted that, ultimately, she would come. At the deepest emotional level he felt that, having become his wife, she must be accessible to him, finally. Meanwhile, he surrounded her with his protective, warm tenderness; a subtle sustained gentleness, unobtrusive, unfailing, deferring to all her wishes.

Regina had money of her own; not a great fortune, but enough to enable them to travel about in comfort. The young doctor would have preferred to carry on with his professional work. But he agreed to an indefinite holiday, since she wished it, and he hoped it might help her to forget the past. The forgetting process was taking longer than he'd expected. But he was in no hurry. The effort of suppressing his sex had left him curiously quiescent, he seemed to exist in a suspended state, waiting till she should be ready to come to him as his bride. Then he would have his life again as a man, full and complete, rounded and made whole as it had never been, to compensate for the time of waiting. The weeks were slipping past. Very soon now she must come to him.

Regina of course had no such intention, her loyalty and devotion to herself being absolute. She was quite determined never to yield her body again to any man, but to keep her precious darling pure and intact. It was another instance of her unbelievable luck to have found a husband so amenable, so willing to suppress his natural desires.

Everything she'd wanted had now come to pass. She'd got rid of the child; she was living far from past associations, with a man who worshipped her from a distance, and gave no trouble. Yet she still wasn't happy, though she danced and sunbathed and went riding and altogether had what is called a good time, enjoying the admiration of men wherever she went. She took it for granted that men should be attracted to her, but paid little attention to her admirers; their admiration was a tribute to the beloved body, which must be adored, respectfully, from afar. In spite of all this, she continued to feel dissatisfied and divided against herself. She was, as a matter of fact, without knowing it, slightly bored.

As the months passed, the whispering gradually started again. She'd be lying, perhaps, on the beach, drowsing in the hot sun; and suddenly she would start up, alert, as though listening, hearing only the long-drawn "M.i.s.s.s.s.ing," of the waves.

It began to get on her nerves all over again. She felt she was being bullied into doing something she didn't want to do, refusing at first even to know what it was. The sense of internal strife grew stronger as time went on and her unconscious boredom increased; in its insidious, whispering way, the voice was always driving her on towards something new. She was being impelled to explore, to experiment, to investigate further, to find out what was missing. Relentlessly, she felt herself being driven towards new experiences — towards a new man. She began to look more attentively at her admirers, not because they interested or attracted her, but because of this inward drive.

When its object dawned upon her, she was frightened. When it came to the point, she didn't really want to leave her accommodating husband, who was kind and good, asking nothing but to cherish her endlessly. She might not be so lucky next time. His presence shielded her from contact with the vulgar, brutal world. She dreaded being exposed to the rude coarseness of life. Especially, she had an absolute horror of being manhandled and mauled. But always there was the whispering, driving her on, until she felt torn in two.

She wanted her husband to protect her: from what, she hardly knew, and certainly couldn't tell him. She could only gaze at him imploringly, helpless and inarticulate as a hurt child that can't explain where the pain is, when he came to say goodnight to her, in her room. Surely he must understand her real need. He'd always been so eager to help her and shield her, with a delicate, intimate intuition that was almost feminine in its grasp of her states of mind, her requirements, emotional and physical.

But now that she was in such need of his help and protection, he seemed different, withdrawn. She'd been too absorbed in herself to notice the curious slowing-down of his whole personality, as the deep sleep he'd imposed on his manhood spread through his entire being. Deprived, too, of the stimulus of his profession, he was now no longer capable of the empathy, the sympathetic, sensitive warmth, that in former days had made him so quick to feel his way into her situation. It was as though he were not fully awake in any part of him. He'd been waiting so long for her to come to him and for their wonderful new life to begin; not till then would he wake again to his full self, refreshed and renewed.

Seeing her uneasy and troubled, he jumped at the only explanation possible to his obsessed mind. He thought she must be on the point of surrendering to him, but reluctant to take the final step. He saw that it would be a difficult step for her; but this difficulty he couldn't take very seriously; it seemed so trifling compared to the coming joy. And his own feelings were so absorbing. At last, at last, she was coming to him! He was thrilled with the ecstasy of his love, which seemed almost holy, as though he would be taking a sacrament as well as a wife, purified by the long waiting he'd endured for her, like a test of endurance — like the knights of old. He thought he had almost won through. But he must still keep his promise, right to the last. He would do nothing to hurry her, even now.

Gently pressing her hands to his breast, he looked down at her tenderly out of eyes that, though bright, had a peculiar glaucous sheen, as if he were not quite awake. "Don't worry, my darling," he said, his gentle voice slightly muted. "Don't be afraid."

She gazed at him, disappointed, not understanding what he meant, puzzled. Before, he had always been so very conscious of everything about her. Now, though he looked at her tenderly, that unique awareness of her immediate situation had gone. His tenderness seemed without meaning, taken in conjunction with those almost blind-looking eyes, which did not really see her, or her predicament.

It was true that he did not see how she felt torn apart. But, realizing that something more was required of him, he said, as she thought, rather strangely: "Everything will be all right once you've made up your mind." Then he kissed her with reverence and departed, quite unconscious of the look which followed him to the door.

What on earth did he mean — made up her mind about what? It seemed such a queer thing for him to have said. It almost sounded as if he knew towards what she was being driven, and, instead of holding her back, left her free to decide on her own line of action. Which struck her as rather insulting; as though he didn't much mind if she left him. His words had the opposite of a restraining effect; there was a strong superstitious streak in her, to which they seemed like a go-ahead signal. Everything would come right when she'd made up her mind. Very well, then, she would make it up — it was, of course, made up already. She would silence the whispering voices by doing what they wished her to do. Then she'd be happy at last and at peace with herself — in a new life; with a new man.

She shuddered, dreading the ordeal of it; the exposure to the world; as well as the struggle bound to come with this unknown quantity, this new man. But, at the same time, she was elated, glancing at her reflection with a smile of complicity that turned her into a witch-girl again. Her marriage had surrounded her with a screen of protective love, shielding her from the world: she was afraid of losing the screen; but she also saw her shielded life as tame, unadventurous, boring. The risk of danger, that wasn't too serious, stimulated her — there was always the money to come between her and any real risk; her income would always keep a way of escape open for her, in the last resort.

65

As for her husband, he had served his purpose, helping her to break out of the frame of family, girlhood, tradition, and launching her into life. He had reached the limit of usefulness, she had no further need of him. So she told herself superstitiously that he said the word — he himself had said it. He had only himself to blame.

* * *

When, shortly after this, Regina left him, with the almost middle-aged, but still attractive, wealthy American she'd picked out as the most manageable of her admirers, the young doctor — as soon as he could think sanely about it at all — was inclined to share her opinion. The shock of her departure woke him from his suspended state as brutally as if, while he was asleep, somebody had come and hacked off some part of him with an axe. He felt rather like that, drained and shattered, as though bleeding invisibly from a frightful wound.

He'd risked everything for his love — the child, his profession, everything — then, just when he'd believed he was winning, this fearful blow. Yet, in the midst of all the torture and humiliation and bloodiness of it, he wasn't bitter: he thought Regina was probably less to blame than he, with his Galahad nonsense, his ridiculous pledges and chastity vows. Now that he'd come back to normal, the mere thought of how he'd behaved made him squirm. Oh, God, how was it possible to be such a stupendous fool — such a great solemn ass?

Thankful to be awake again as a normal man, he didn't know whether he still loved her. He simply wanted never even to think about her. And he had little time to think about her or anything else. Being quite without resources, he had to concentrate immediately on earning a living. It wasn't easy; no one wanted to employ a man with his reputation. Not that he himself had done anything particularly scandalous. But the story had got into the papers somehow, embellished by sundry lurid details of the journalist's invention. A certain atmosphere of unsavoury sensationalism surrounded the whole affair: the first husband's suicide; the spiriting away of the child; the hasty and almost furtive remarriage; and now Regina's new flight. Whenever the unfortunate doctor applied for a post, the gossip would start again. For some months he led a hand-to-mouth existence, too occupied with bare survival to brood over his wrecked marriage, or over the moral issue involving the child, which troubled him even more.

It was a difficult and disagreeable time. An older man, or one less well balanced, might have gone under. But the doctor had strength, industry and perseverance; he had regained his sense of proportion and his sense of humour; and he was absolutely determined to make good in his profession. To his vast relief, the marriage, which had never been consummated, was dissolved without attracting any further publicity. The gossip was dying out gradually. When he was offered a minor post in the small hospital of a provincial town, he accepted gladly, cheerfully starting again at the foot of the ladder off which he had slipped when he married Regina. Submerging himself in work, he set about forgetting that unlucky episode.

But he never allowed himself to forget the child, resolved to make some reparation to this innocent victim, sacrificed so unavailingly to his lost love. He had no clear idea of how it was to be done. But he was always careful to keep Mona Anderson's address. And when, after working some time at the hospital, he was entitled to twenty-four hours leave, he at once set out for the seaside town to which she had taken the baby girl. A vague notion hovered at the back of his mind, much too nebulous to be called a plan. He preferred to leave it that way, and to trust to inspiration when the time came. He was a great believer in acting on the spur of the moment.

He had not written to Mona all this time, and he didn't write now. It might have been better if he had, he admitted, when he heard, on arrival, that she'd left some months earlier. There was nothing for it but to take another train to the town about fifty miles inland, to which she had moved. By the time he got there, it was evening; he was tired, hungry, and somewhat discouraged after his day of travel. For the last hour or two, he'd been steadily losing faith in the "spur of the moment" approach. He had to be back on duty by ten o'clock the next morning; whatever happened, he must not outstay his leave, he could not risk any sort of trouble, just as he was becoming accepted again as a respectable member of the community. On making inquiries, he found he would only be able to stay for just over an hour; and, seeing that the town was unexpectedly large, began to feel he had come on a real wild goose chase, and probably wouldn't even succeed in locating the girl.

However, it appeared that she was living not far away. Somebody directed him to the street, he had no difficulty in finding the entrance to the big building, standing back with its lighted windows, beyond a gravel sweep and clumps of black foliage. He went in, barely noticing where he waited for Mona's arrival, overcome by sudden acute hunger — he'd eaten nothing but a sandwich all day, and certainly wouldn't get anything during the night journey back. He was wondering whether it was too late to suggest going out to a restaurant in the town, when he heard the familiar voice speak his name.

There stood Mona, looking as handsome, as remote and coldly composed, as when he last saw her. What in the world was he doing here? she wanted to know; immediately making him feel that he'd acted with childish and irresponsible impulsiveness by coming unannounced. She herself gave the impression of an orderly and efficiently-run existence, which would never include arriving, famished, late in the evening, in an unknown town, with another train to catch in an hour. He had to remind himself of the circumstances in which he'd first met her, which proved her to be less capable than she seemed. But he still felt she looked upon him as a hopeless scatterbrain, as he said: "I wanted to see you — to have a talk."

"Well, we can't talk here," she replied, laconic, and distant as ever, looking him over with cool, far-away eyes. "I suppose you'd better come to my room." She was turning to lead the way, when he detained her by catching her sleeve.

"Look, I suppose you've had dinner already. But I'm absolutely starving — can't we get some food somewhere? Only it must be somewhere near because I've got to catch a train back quite soon."

She looked from his face to his clutching hand as if he were off his head; and he hastily let her go, his stomach letting out a dismal rumble at the same time. Perhaps she heard it. At all events, she suddenly seemed more human, the faint suggestion of a rather grim smile appeared on her mouth, as though his incompetence and general absurdity had brought her a little way down from her mountain top.

"We'll just have time to get into the canteen before it closes" — she glanced at her watch — "but only if we rush — "

At a pace that made conversation impossible, they hurried through various corridors, into the open air, where a covered way led to a separate building. Vaguely he was aware of passing numerous young people; but, in a sort of bewildered daze of hunger and tiredness, he took no real notice of anything until he was sitting opposite Mona at a table without a cloth, drinking coffee, and eating a foot-long roll filled with sausage. He couldn't quite place the big, bare room, with posters on the walls, a noisy party of girls in one corner, and an atmosphere of rough and ready simplicity, oddly combined with some exclusiveness that made him feel an outsider.

68

though nobody was in the least unfriendly. Noticing how the members of the corner gathering were inclined to stare at him and giggle among themselves, and also that he and his companion seemed to be a few years older than anyone else he had seen, he asked her a question.

"I told you; it's the canteen." Since he still looked blank, Mona added: "Of course there's a proper dining-hall too, but you can't expect it to be open at this time of night. We were lucky to get in here. This is the only college where the canteen stays open so late."

"College?" he echoed, astonished.

"Surely you know this is the College of Intermediate Studies?"

The young man sat gazing at her with a bewildered expression, the half-eaten roll in his hand, feeling as though he were dreaming — playing some dream-game of cross-purposes in which he was hopelessly lost. "What are you doing here, then?" he finally asked.

"Oh, I'm not a student," she said, with her grim little smile, evidently at cross-purposes too, misinterpreting his question, or the motive behind it. "This is where I work — as secretary to one of the professors."

"But what about the child?" More mystified than ever by her explanation, he gazed at her with an absolutely befogged look of extreme perplexity, which called forth a fresh outburst of giggles in the corner. But neither he nor Mona noticed the amusement caused by his really rather laughable expression; the girl, now almost as astonished as he, exclaiming:

"Didn't you know about Gerda? Do you mean to say you hadn't heard that her mother came and took her away from me? Months ago — to the States, I believe."

Gerda? Vaguely he remembered that this was the baby's name. But he still couldn't take in what he'd just heard. "Regina took her to America?" His voice sounded stupid with incredulity. The idea of making amends had been with him so long that it had become part of the structure of his existence: he could only slowly adjust himself to the fact that it wasn't going to be possible; that he was to be frustrated in his desire for atonement. He need not have come here at all. All his travelling and searching had been for nothing —gradually it was coming home to him.

The young woman was watching him with wonder. Seeing him so disconcerted, with that baffled, frustrated look, her own face softened. His impulsive behaviour didn't make sense to her; but it seemed so extraordinary that it broke

69

through her aloofness, temporarily. "You came all this way —traced me here — because you wanted to see the child?" Coldness and distance had gone from her voice and manner, replaced by a wondering curiosity, interest; uncomprehending, but friendly; which he, immersed in his own thoughts, didn't notice. Nodding gloomily, he answered:

"Yes. I wanted to do something for the poor kid — to give it a chance of some happiness."

"And how were you going to do that?" Now Mona couldn't help speaking ironically, reverting to her usual attitude. It was preposterous, to her way of thinking, to talk as though happiness were a commodity to be bought in a shop and handed out to anybody you chose, like a box of chocolates or a banana.

"I wanted her to come and live with me — and you too, of course," he replied simply, rather surprised that the inchoate scheme he'd been harbouring at the back of his mind should find such precise formulation. "I thought it would give her a better chance — a more normal, natural sort of background; so that she wouldn't grow up feeling unsupported, or different from other children with fathers and families."

"But surely —" Mona began: breaking off, speechless, overcome by conflicting emotions. She was, first and foremost, amazed by this disregard of the caution and forethought that had killed her own love affair stone dead, and which she'd come to regard as qualities inherent in the masculine nature, recalling the longed-for gesture not made, because those prudent qualities shunned a love too enveloping, too deep. But then, the way this man had included her with the child, as a mere appendage, was really a bit too much. And his extraordinary naive simplicity, as though he'd no conception of the realities of life — but not a clue, simply . . . "Wouldn't that have been rather difficult?" she asked curiously. "Because of your profession, I mean, and the conventions — wouldn't people have thought we were living together? Wouldn't you have been struck off the register, or something?" She watched him with a cool, straight stare as she was speaking, intrigued by this very queer fish that had come swimming up to her out of the darkness.

"Oh, you'd have had to marry me, naturally," he said, as if this were self-evident, taking a huge bite out of his roll, not looking at her: while she watched him, astounded.

"To *marry* you?" This fantastic proposition she had *not* expected, even from him, unworldly simpleton as he seemed to be. Made in that off-hand way, too, as if it were perfectly natural: after the circumstances in which he'd first found

70

her; and when he himself had barely emerged from one disastrous marriage. Really . . . She was left speechless again. Just as well that a buzzer went off at this moment, and a loud voice shouted: "All out, please!"

As he got up, the young man gulped down what remained in his cup, and then, munching, clutching the end of the roll, followed her across the room to the open door. A clock was striking high overhead; and, as they came out into the clammy night, a dim haze of drizzle, revealed by the bulb hung between the buildings, consolidated into the slanting downstrokes of heavy rain.

Mona shivered and crossed her arms, suddenly cold and depressed. It was for her one of those moments which seem to generate a sense of life's futility and sadness. She never allowed herself to brood over her lost lover: it was purely by accident that she had just now remembered his wary avoidance of the responsibility inseparable from deep feeling; and so the gesture not made, the words never spoken, that would have meant her happiness. All that old sorrow seemed now to be mixed up with this present parting from this so-different man, who had casually strolled out of the night, and was about to vanish into it again. How extraordinarily mysterious people were, only knowable (or rather *un*knowable) through their incomprehensible actions: so that, of this one she'd never know anything but the fact that he'd been, in-credibly, ready to marry her; and was now just as ready to walk out of her life for ever.

The last stroke of the hour punctuated her thoughts with its blank full stop. She saw the young doctor wiping his fingers on his handkerchief after putting the last bit of roll into his mouth, and knew he was on the point of offering his hand and saying goodbye. At this moment a light went on just behind them. They both looked round automatically at the bright window, where rows of hooks supporting all sorts of garments and student paraphernalia were to be seen — as though at the sight of this cloakroom, the iron repression she'd imposed on herself was suddenly blown off, like a lid screwed down too tightly. She was seized by an irresistible impulse to hang on to her companion till the last possible moment— not to let him go, as the other had gone.

"Just wait here a second, will you?" she said to him, darting away; returning immediately with a coat, evidently not her own, into which she was struggling. Breathless, but as if there had been no break, she added: "I'll show you the quickest way." She didn't permit herself to think about what she was doing.

71

"But . . . in all this rain . . . there's no need," he protested, not understanding the abrupt, unaccountable change that had come over her. Whereupon she, almost equally mystified, rejoined irritably: "Oh, I know there's no *need*. But I take it you don't actively object to my coming?"

In silence, in a state of silent tension, they walked to the entrance gates, where he paused again, assuming that she would turn back. "Many thanks." His voice and manner had both become stiff. "I can't go wrong now — it's a perfectly straight road."

Once more she saw him preparing to shake hands, and once more prevented him, saying hurriedly: "All the same, I'd like to come to the station with you, if you don't mind." She was grateful to the rainy dark for concealing her flushed face — at least. she hoped fervently that he couldn't see how she was blushing, as she stubbornly and unflinchingly returned his curious gaze.

"Oh, if you *like* getting soaked, *I* don't mind." He was tired and rather cross, bewildered by her persistence. Giving up trying to understand, he plunged into the wet, windswept street, where there wasn't a soul to be seen; the town seemed silent and dead as the tomb, as they plodded along side by side, not speaking, the steely cold rain driving into their faces.

When the clustered lights of the station appeared, he wondered if she'd go back. But. beginning to realize the extent of her obstinacy, made no comment when she followed him on to the platform. He was getting really curious to know why she was so determined to stick to him. The buffet was closed, even the waiting-rooms were locked up at this hour. They could only walk up and down the deserted platform, beside the gleaming wet tracks, for the few minutes before the train was due. Stark white lights glaring down, emphasized the desolation of darkness and wind and rain, not a sign of life, unless the baleful red and green signal eyes were to be considered alive. It hardly seemed credible that any train would ever stop at this ghastly spot. But at least they had a roof now between them and the rain.

Glancing at his tenacious companion, the young man saw that she was one of the very few women who retained their looks, even when drenched to the skin. She reminded him of a ship's figurehead, leaning into the wind, which outlined her prominent bosom; her severe chiselled profile, glistening with raindrops, might just have risen from the trough of the waves. Giving her for the first time his whole close attention he saw that, despite a certain indomitable air, she no longer seemed altogether the icy snow queen of his earlier vision.

72

He suddenly got the feeling that, though she was still isolated, cold and remote, on her mountaintop, she half wished to come down. The wave of bitterness that had swept her up there had subsided and left her stranded, not sure that she wanted to stay, not knowing how to get down — would she ever be able to make the descent?

He stopped under one of the glaring arc-lights to look at her, not noticing in his new intentness that she returned his gaze with an interest equal to his own. The harsh light gave her face a statue's impersonal frigid look, with the raindrops upon it; but also revealed indications of strain, which, at her age, should not have been there, as though the rarefied atmosphere of the heights was affecting her nerves. In dead silence, standing on the empty platform, they stared into each other's faces: he absorbed in trying to decide whether she really had grown more human (could the ice-core he'd believed indestructible have started to melt?); she closely concentrated in the more precise effort of memorizing his expression and features. With the help of the crude light, showing her every detail, she was constructing a mental image so exact that for the rest of her life she'd be able to call up the likeness of this strange man, who, but for a whim of Regina's, might have saved her from the isolation to which she was now condemned to the end of her days. Her memory received the imprint of his face, not on its surface, but somewhere in its depths, beyond all possibility of forgetting. And now she could no longer stand there silently looking at him: becoming aware of herself, she had to break the silence that had lasted so long.

"You must be very fond of children," she said, "to take all this trouble . . . Why don't you have some of your own?"

It was a strange question to come from that cold statue's face he was watching. But its personal nature, which some people might have resented, merely made him smile with the warm natural friendliness that was his charm. "Well, that implies a wife. And I've been rather put off marriage."

"But weren't you going to marry me, if I'd still had the child with me?"

"Yes: but that was a special case. I've always had a strong feeling of responsibility towards that particular child — perhaps because I brought it into the world. Ever since Regina left me I've felt under an obligation to do something about it. And it seemed to me I could only help by having it with me. Before I could do that, I had to make some money, make a home — get myself accepted again by respectable people. It was hard work, too, after all the publicity and gossip. I came as soon as I possibly could . . . And now it's too late . . .

all that effort has been for nothing . . . it's a great disappointment . . . " He was talking to himself finally, speaking his thoughts aloud. He'd forgotten about Mona; about the station, about the train he had to catch; about everything, in fact, but the hope of atonement, which had now been denied him. When her clear, cool voice interrupted his thoughts with the words: "It's a terrible disappointment for me, too;" he vaguely said, "What . . . ?" not having understood her.

Coolly and clearly, her heart beating wildly, she repeated: "It's a terrible disappointment for me, too," still with her level gaze fixed upon him.

Now that he had understood her remark, its implication seemed beyond belief. Incredulously, he asked what she meant.

"Just what you think I mean." The grim little smile appeared on her mouth. But now, the sound of the approaching train, for which she'd been straining her ears, seemed to force her to go on speaking, always faster and less coherently, as though in a desperate race with the growing volume of noise. "I suppose I should be grateful for small mercies — for this meeting — because I never expected to see you again. It was the most incredible luck for me, meeting you in the first place. I was absolutely done for when you found me in that hospital. I thought my life was quite finished. But you made me want to go on living. Of course I know now there was no personal feeling about it, you just wanted someone to take the child. But I was so wretched then . . . you were the only person who was at all kind to me . . . I suppose I was a bit mixed up in my head with all the dope and so on . . . I thought you might be a little bit interested in me . . . Oh, I'm not blaming you in the least — it was just wishful thinking on my part. But it was a horrid blow afterwards, when I realized . . . almost worse than the other time . . . But you'd made me feel different . . . more of a person . . . I wasn't going to let anyone wreck my life . . . I'd just live it alone . . . for my own self, I wouldn't have any personal relations with people, ever again . . . I hated everybody, and wanted to be alone. That's why I wanted so much to have the job of looking after Gerda — because it meant I could live by myself, without getting involved with anyone . . . But of course it was too good to last . . . " She moved a step nearer to him, away from the edge of the platform and from the great locomotive, now bearing down upon them, surrounded by clouds of steam, which, instead of dispersing, hung low in the damp air, so that they stood festooned, as by mountain mist, in weird whitish wreaths. "I've tried so hard to forget about you . . . but I

74

can't — it's no good . . . And to think that I might have married you . . . so near and yet so far . . . " Her slight unnatural laugh was lost in the clanking shudder which went through the length of the train, as it came to a standstill.

The platform that had been all this time deserted and windswept, abandoned to night and rain, was suddenly full of activity, noise, people. Doors flew open, passengers pushed their way in and out, trolleys loaded with pillows trundled past, baggage was hurled about, above all the commotion a mechanized voice brayed incomprehensibly. The young doctor hardly noticed the change. All this pandemonium might have been going on in some other country, outside his consciousness, where he was concerned only with the revelation of Mona's feelings, of which, until now, he'd been quite unaware. Such unawareness of a fellow being's reactions was something he would have disliked very much in another person; he was disturbed to find that he could be guilty of it himself. Remembering all the derogatory notions he had, at various times, had about the girl, quite unjustly, it now appeared, he felt ashamed and guilty. The one bright spot was that this guilt could be expiated; in some obscure way, it seemed that it might take the place of the other; he might be able to make amends after all. But before he had time to think how, Mona reminded him that he ought to be finding a seat in the train, telling him he must hurry, and giving him a slight push towards a door that was swinging open. Still pre-occupied with his thoughts, hardly noticing what he was doing, he obediently climbed into the train: and the door was immediately shut and locked by a passing official.

Finding himself separated from the girl, the young man seemed suddenly to wake up; he threw open the window, vainly searching for her in the turmoil on the platform, bewildered by the senseless confusion, in which she seemed to have vanished. Then: "Here I am," her clear voice came up from just below him. Seeing her calm face lifted to his without any expression, the things she'd been saying again seemed unbelievable: he felt he must have imagined them all; or else she'd been teasing—making a fool of him; he'd become rather suspicious of ridicule since Regina's departure.

"Of course you didn't mean any of that, did you?" he asked, feeling at a disadvantage, as he always did, before her composure. As if to substantiate his suspicion, the engine began to give vent to a prolonged monstrous hiss, as, of a huge audience expressing its contempt for him and all his works, drowning his voice, so that she could only shake her head helplessly. "Did you mean what you said?" he bellowed, with all the force of his lungs, determined to get an answer, and quite indifferent to the startled faces the passers-by raised towards him. The question had suddenly become extremely important; he had to find out.

She couldn't fail to hear this time, and nodded her head, adding loudly: "But don't let it worry you."

Again he saw her grim little smile; and something, perhaps admiration, attracted him to her; something was missing from his life which she could supply — which was incomprehensibly bound up with his will to atone. He felt a sudden excitement, as though about to compete in a dangerous race, where he might win great fame and prestige, or break every bone in his body — the odds were even. "Why don't we get married, then?" he shouted down to her in his excitement. But he saw at once that this was a mistake, watching her face go hard and remote.

"No, thanks. Pity is one thing I've no use for." The engine's hiss was subsiding, he could hear her without difficulty. "Don't insult me with pity, please," she said, cold and final, looking straight and hard at him.

"Pity? What on earth made you think of pity? I'd as soon pity *that* — " As he waved his hand at the enormous engine, gliding past with a kind of ponderous monolithic stealth on the other line, he was thinking that some part of her really did remind him of a ruthless great handsome machine, powerful, streamlined, terrifying. Through all the station's hullaballoo, he could feel this grim aspect of her, and it really scared him. But was ready to take her obsessional hard side, her fearful efficiency, partly because he wanted to help her down from the mountain, and partly because he needed her to receive his love, which lately had found no outlet. He would pour out for her all the warmth he had stored for the child; and so make reparation. Knowing now that she still had a heart alive somewhere in her, not quite turned to ice, his task would be to bring back its full living warmth. He felt the challenge of this like a difficult case, stimulating and exciting; the start of a new adventure.

"But why should you suddenly want to marry me? I can't see the point." Mona had not been able to doubt his emphatic repudiation of the idea of pity: the unflattering engine-comparison had convinced her far more surely than the most elaborate denial. So now she could look at him without that formidable hard coldness. But her expression was still sceptical; she was finding it all rather too much to swallow.

With his quick spontaneity, he replied: "I need you, that's

the point — though I've only just found it out." People would think him mad, he was well aware, barely having escaped from the claws of one woman, already throwing himself at this other's head. But he had to do it. The very craziness of his conduct was an added inducement, an additional thrill. "I'm not in love in the romantic sense — I've had enough of that. But I want you. And we're two fairly reasonable human beings. I don't see why we shouldn't make it work." He gazed at her with the glow of excitement upon his face, suddenly eager to embark on this new adventure, his eyes wide open and shining in the hard light.

She was filled with wonder as she met his eyes, so unlike the narrow, cold, guarded windows in most of the faces she met. It seemed almost a miracle to her that, in spite of all he'd experienced in his marriage, they were neither bitter nor disillusioned — quite without malice or resentment. She saw in them only an inviting, excited warmth, at the same time modest and bold; some masculine recklessness that was likeable and attractive.

"I'll do my best to make a success of it, if you'll have me," he said, slightly anxious now, because every second his need for her grew more compulsive — "will you?"

The engine gave a vindictive shriek, a violent jolt dislodged him momentarily from his place at the window, so that he couldn't be certain of what she said—it sounded like, "You're a hero," reminding him transiently of what he'd thought that day in the mountains. He'd be a poor substitute for the hero-adventurer of his imaginings; that was, if she'd have him. "Will you marry me?" he asked again, urgently. He wouldn't have believed it, if someone had told him half-an-hour ago, that the marriage which had been just a detail necessitated by convention could change so soon to a matter of vital importance to him personally. Why didn't she answer? There was so little time: the train was already moving, though slowly, while she kept pace with it, walking alongside with her head bent, as if pondering, so that he couldn't even see her expression.

"You must say yes or no — you can't send me away without an answer . . . " Unable to keep up any longer, she stopped still, and immediately started to be left behind. "You must answer!" he called desperately, seeing how, all in one instant, she seemed alarmingly far away; while he was being swept on, helpless, leaning far out in his determination not to lose sight of her solitary figure, standing alone on the once more almost deserted platform.

Battered by the wet wind, straining his eyes in an effort

D 77

to see her face, its features already indistinguishable, he shouted back: "Are you going to marry me?" The words were whipped off his lips and whirled away in the rainy dark. There was still no answer. Had she heard him? He couldn't be certain. Because of the motion, the rain, and the widening distance between them, he couldn't be sure; but he got the impression then that she nodded, as if in consent. And with this he had to be satisfied; for now, screeching derisively, the train dived underground; and when it re-emerged into the rain-filled night, the station had been left far behind.

4

MOONSHINE

FIRST thing in the morning Gerda had been told by her
mother that she must complain to the manager about the floor-
waiter's slackness. But she was feeling so ill, she dreaded the
interview so much, that it was evening, nearly dinner time,
before she could bring herself to face it. Even now that it was
over and she was safely outside the door of his office, she
couldn't stop herself trembling. Yet the man hadn't really
been unpleasant to her, as he was telling himself at this
moment; the family was far too valuable to him for that, they
spent a great deal of money in his hotel. But he wished the
woman would complain directly to him; or at least send
someone who could talk sense, instead of this kid, who seemed
more like five than fifteen, and only stammered incomprehensibly and stared at him with her big scared eyes that always
seemed to be on the look out for trouble.

And of course she found it, he thought, slightly uncomfortable because, in his impatience, he'd spoken a bit sharply. He
rather prided himself on his knowledge of psychology,
not learnt from books, but from the crude raw human
material. Watching his clients' reactions to one another,
noting how that mild, apprehensive, propitiatory expression
brought out the suppressed sadism in people, he saw Gerda,
gentle and over-sensitive, as a predestined victim in a world
of the unscrupulous and tough.

His vision of her as a kind of doomed halfwit would have
been confirmed had he known how innocently and in all good
faith she accepted, as part of her education, these dreaded
tasks, thrust upon her whenever she came back for the holidays to the expensive hotels where her family lived most of
the time. It had never occurred to her that she was made
to do such things because her mother hated doing them herself; hated being brought into contact with the vulgar
mechanics of living; hated to appear to anyone except as an
object of admiration.

If only she hadn't had to see the manager just now, Gerda
was thinking, while she felt so ill, and needed all her energy

to hide the fact — illness being the one thing above all others that her mother despised, loathed and absolutely refused to tolerate. She knew she'd been more inarticulate, behaved more foolishly, than usual; she was grateful to the man for dismissing her so soon with an apologetic message. But still she continued to tremble.

The empty, brightly-lit, mirror-walled passage was beginning to expand and contract like a concertina, while the lights shot at her with long glittering beams that darted with malignant playfulness under her eyelids. Why was the floor tilting in this extraordinary way, as if it were the deck of a ship? Unfamiliar with the symptoms of faintness, she watched its odd behaviour with a detached surprise: then, clutching, only just in time, at some piece of furniture, she subsided on slippery satin, and bent her head down towards her toes, as she'd been taught at First Aid classes.

What bliss it would be to pass out altogether, thought one part of her mind. But another part persistently reminded her of what the consequences would be: her mother's anger, her bitter sarcasm and contempt; her power of creating an atmosphere of heart-breaking exclusion and disapproval that lasted for days and days. It wasn't worth it. With this decision, came a vague impression of two huge ponderous noisy shapes, representing her stepfather and his son, Jeff; who, though so much older than she that he seemed grown up, would sometimes tease and torment her like a spiteful schoolboy, with an adult skill in finding sensitive spots.

With a long shuddering sigh, the girl presently straightened up, looking round nervously, like a person waking in a strange room. The corridor was steady again. She must go to the private sitting room, where her family would be waiting for her report. As she told herself this, she knew she wouldn't be able to move, already feeling the crushing weight of lassitude, like an invisible eiderdown, enormous, soft as feathers, heavy as lead, which fell upon her these days whenever she relaxed for a moment — a hateful oppressive mass, possessed of a stubborn determination to paralyse her. She struggled vainly to throw it off. Her body refused to move. Exhausted, she soon abandoned the futile effort, and sat drooping there, her head bent, as if weighed down by the long straight almost white hair, hanging in thick hanks at the sides of her face.

And all the time the lights were aiming their dangerous icy darts at her eyes, dazzling her, changing the aspect of things . . . which began to merge with her dream fantasies, so that she looked at vast empty spaces, strung with diamond chains. Alluring and delicately exotic, the sparkling clusters hung down, crystal fruit of some magic ice-vine, each glistening globe with its palpitating prismatic heart. They fascinated her, she could have loved them . . . if their shooting beams hadn't been so meteoric, so fierce. Again and again they stabbed her eyes with arrows of burning ice, penetrating the brain behind, till all her sick thoughts swam in their arctic glare. Slow, stately, splendid, aurora borealis opened and shut its gigantic fan, blazing on snow-slopes with rocks out-cropping, on summits of rock or cloud, massed citadels, sublime in that glacial brilliance . . . The shapes were sliding . . . changing again . . . becoming a fabric of falling white. Soft as snowbirds, the white flakes were falling, turning as they fell . . . before her eyes, which had never seen falling snow . . . (an odd antique figure in a queer pointed hat slipped along the dream's dissolving edge) . . . falling always more thickly . . . till the air darkened . . . and she was somewhere else . . . a question was being asked: where did they come from, these winter fancies, when she knew nothing of winter?

Unanswered, the question faded into the muffled thump of a far-off orchestra, several months away. It was Christmas, she'd been given the gold sandals, more beautiful than any-thing she had ever possessed . . . their beauty was magical and would transform her: while she wore them she'd lose her shyness and become gay and popular . . . she knew she would, she longed to go to the dance, the ballroom bloomed into mysterious splendour, everyone would like her because of the wonderful shoes. Then she wasn't allowed to go, although all the other young people in the place would be there . . . Alone in her room, she could hear the dance music quite clearly . . . the music of a world out of reach, which she would never be able to enter . . . a gay brilliant world of happiness, from which she was for ever shut out . . .

The curious muted thudding pulse of the rhythm strengthened, broke out of the dream. As if at the end of a long and difficult journey, Gerda opened her eyes on the pas-sage again. The shock of finding herself there; of realizing that, sitting there where anyone might have seen her, she'd fallen into a sort of sick dream, at last enabled her to break the spell of her lassitude, and stand up. But her body still felt numb and heavy; her feet no longer seemed joined to it. Looking down, she saw them moving like boats on the river of coloured mosaic flowing interminably, far down below her, as she walked laboriously along the corridor, stretching away to infinity before her — would she ever get to the end?

A dim half-recollection brought the gold shoes back into her mind. To give them to her must have been her step father's idea, since her mother never bought her anything pretty. There was no resentment in this thought. With the patience and ignorance of the young, she had for fifteen years lived a wretched life, and been hardly aware of it: deprived of all the things other children enjoyed — home, affection, companions; dragged from place to place and from school to school without being consulted, as if she'd been a dog. Her mild, trustful nature accepted this state of affairs, partly because she had never known anything better, and partly because she believed there was some fault in herself. Once, when she was very angry, Regina had said: "You should never have been here at all": words which terrified her, and which her childish imagination had interpreted as meaning she'd committed at some time a mysterious forgotten crime; the punishment for which was to be rendered once and for all subservient and inferior, a kind of family scapegoat, dedicated to the performance of all the tasks the others disliked and shunned.

Suddenly, with a sense of surprise, she found herself at the door towards which she'd been making her way; and, opening it, entered a room filled with the peculiar aroma in which she lived; the composite smell of Egyptian cigarettes, sweet-scented flowers, and the spicier, less sweet perfume her mother used. This was the way her life smelled; a ghost of this compound odour even clung to her clothes. Usually she was unconscious of it; but now it revived her faintness, for a moment the group before her appeared indistinct, two square blackish shapes, with a tall slenderness between . . . resolving itself into the typical tableau; the royal group as she saw it: the two massive masculine forms in dark dinner clothes emphasizing by contrast the tall slender elegance of the central figure, which thus attained the importance of a queen between two courtiers.

Coming into the room where the accustomed tableau had already been formed, Gerda felt an underlining of her separateness, at once made aware of being outside the group, which for this if for no other reason, seemed united against her, as if her elders resented her apartness as a criticism, regardless of the fact that it was most painful to her — anything but deliberate. The three people surveyed her silently for a moment, without a smile or any welcoming word — which, indeed, would have embarrassed and startled, rather than pleased her; the ordinary usages of politeness being suspended, where she was concerned. She knew that they were waiting for her to give an account of the interview to which they had driven her so much against her will. And it was typical of her place among them that, neither to her nor to any one of the trio, did it occur that she might have been given some advice on how to conduct it; or that there was any unfairness in holding her responsible for the outcome of it.

Yet her stepfather was considered a kind-hearted man, with the easy-going tolerance of his great size and strength, which was the source of his splendid appearance, rather than an obstacle to it, as in the case of a magnificent great carthorse. With his ponderousness and his wavy thick dapple-grey hair, he really had something of the sumptuous glossy heaviness of a prize Percheron, wearing his red carnation like the red rosette awarded to the best heavy-draught horse in the show. It was he who, in the first place, had persuaded Regina to accept her child, then in a stranger's care, and recall her from banishment. If asked now, he would have said that he was disappointed in Gerda, who had turned out sulky and difficult; meaning that she was quiet and shy, unresponsive to the loud-voiced jocularity he considered suitable for young people.

"Well, did you screw up enough courage at last?" Jeff was the first to speak, in a loud blustering tone imitated from his father, only distinguishable from bullying by its veneer of the crude flippancy passing as humour between them.

A fine-looking young fellow, broad and muscular, handsome in a red-faced, rather obvious way, he already showed signs of the elder man's heaviness, but without his attribute of majestic confident ease. Confidence in him seemed to have dwindled down to conceit, suggesting that the stallion strain had begun to regress to an earlier, commoner breed. So, where the father, though woundingly insensitive, was well-meaning, the son showed a hint of something degenerate, of the ears-laid-back viciousness of a bad tempered animal, in his persecution of the defenceless girl. Nevertheless, there was a strong resemblance between the two men; not only the physical likeness, but a common personality trait, some essential weakness, inadequacy or immaturity, which kept them both in carthorse-like subjection. It was the woman who dominated and led, mistress of all situations in life, as well as of the lives of these two, who submitted, not just gladly, but with a complacent air of congratulating themselves on her astute mastery of their ponderous might, which could otherwise have fallen into the wrong hands and been misdirected.

In Gerda's eyes, the three made a compact unit, a solid contented block, from which she stood apart, helpless and alone. Sick and dizzy, unable to speak, she felt like a victim before her judges, nodding in reply to the young man's question, feeling his eyes callously searching out the weak points in her total weakness.

"Just look at her — still green about the gills with funk! What were you afraid he'd do — bite you? might have got hydrophobia if he had . . . " Jeff's loud laughter exploded vacuously into silence, without encouragement from his elders, who, from tolerance and fastidiousness respectively, withheld their entire approval.

Gerda was so used to his crude open jeering that, in the ordinary way, she was hardly affected by it. It was only now that his conduct seemed the last straw, her protective outer layer of unconcern, acquired through the years, suddenly crumbling, tears came into her eyes, which she hastily turned away from the handsome, taunting, empty young face of her tormentor. But, wherever she looked, she could see nothing comforting or reassuring in the impersonal stereotyped luxury of the hotel room. The deep unconscious anxiety permeating her whole being suddenly directed itself against the arbiters of her fate. She had never realized their unkindness in denying her a child's elementary right to security and affection. Nor had she any idea of how much she'd already been damaged by them; her natural modesty distorted into an ineradicable sense of inferiority, and her timidity into a nervous fear of people, from which grew the conviction that she was unworthy to give or receive love. She only knew that she was afraid, not so much of the three before her, as of the distance dividing her from them, which suddenly seemed unbridgeable and immense. Nobody in the world seemed to want her; there was no one she could speak to about herself; no place where she mattered, belonged. For the first time, and even now without full recognition, she felt the hurtful blind indifference of her family; the men too coarse-fibred and preoccupied, the woman too neurotic an egoist, to notice the gentle, unreasoning, trustful affection flowering spontaneously from her youth and sweet nature. At this moment of sick sadness, the scarcity of love from which she had suffered ever since, and even before, her birth, made itself felt in the form of a childish longing for the petting and comforting she had never known.

Quite unconsciously, she turned with an inexpressibly imploring look to her mother; who, at the same instant, asked casually: "What did the manager say?" looking, not at her daughter, but at the outspread fingers of her own left hand, on one of which blazed a magnificent square emerald. Equally uninterested in what had transpired in the office and what was happening now, she seemed, by staring fixedly at the jewel, to identify herself with its cold perfection rather than with her companions, with their fatally human flaws. She still kept her eyes focussed on the ring, which flashed cold mineral fire as she waved her hand, cutting short Gerda's confused attempt to repeat the manager's message.

"Did you remember to tell him we wouldn't stay unless the service improved?"

Regina's tone seemed to the girl to have that blend of long-suffering and impatience that would have been used to a stupid servant who never did anything right. It was so acutely painful to her, it made her longing for comfort seem so futile, that, without knowing why, she was ashamed, and her eyes again filled with tears. To her blurred vision, everything in the room began to seem dim and remote. The three people before whom she was standing seemed to recede and to grow unreal. She seemed to be looking at them from a tremendous distance as unreality, like a gigantic octopus, laid soft impalpable feelers upon each sense, dividing her from all that went on.

Her head began to revolve slowly. She wondered vaguely how long she'd be able to keep any contact at all with the room. When someone lighted a cigarette the smell came to her in a wave of sickness. Smoke seemed to fill the room like a fog. She could hardly see, hardly breathe. Even her mother was becoming shadowy, unreal.

And, as if sensing this, Regina looked at her sharply, fanning away the smoke with her hand, struck by some alteration in the young girl's face, which she did not trouble to identify, beyond seeing in it an obstruction of her own influence, which could not be allowed. Her daughter must not stand there as if in a dream, her face empty, as if she were absent somewhere.

"Gerda!"

Startled, the dreamer rushed back to this situation she did not recognize. What was happening here? Through a smoky haze of confusion, she saw the room as a place of shadows and unreality, where, with a shock, she encountered the cold eyes, the narrow mouth thin with menace, in the strange small white witch's face. Already she had watched the magic green flash burn its way through the smoke. Now fascinated, she again saw the slender white snake-arm unfurl its pale coil, dart into life, striking through the sick heaviness of the smoke, like a bolt of emerald fire. She seemed to have witnessed an act of pure witchcraft.

Suddenly then, she saw that it was her mother, and was horrified by her thought. It seemed incredible that she could

85

have imagined her mother a witch — she pushed the frightful thought far out of her mind. But subconsciously she would always remember the flashing snake-arm striking enchanted fire, the thin mouth venomous with intention to hurt. Deep within her, she knew she had seen the truth.

"What's the matter with you?"

Hearing the sharpness in Regina's voice, the girl tried with all her might to become her normal self, to see with normal eyes, think with her normal intelligence. She managed to articulate the word, "Nothing." No more would come. However hard she tried, she couldn't free herself from the persistent clutch of the unseen tentacles, sticky-soft and tenacious as spiders' webs, which, as soon as she liberated one sense, stealthily wound another in their clinging mesh . . . the world was reduced to shadows, unrelated to her.

"Oh, leave her alone — let her sulk if she wants to." Jeff's voice was merely an unpleasant noise in the distance, about which she need do nothing. But then her stepfather's mildly reproachful voice, nasal and unexpected, "You'd better hurry up and get changed," jerked at her attention again. Vainly peering through the smoke in search of his face, she heard him say something about going down to dinner. But she could only focus his mighty haunches under taut black cloth, wrinkled like a black skin . . . and a great arm planted across at right angles . . . power symbols that had no more to do with her weakness than had that other symbol of abstract authority . . . hard, cold, impersonal and precise, a slender graceful upright shape, now moving between two massive escorts . . . getting out of the way, only just in time, of the passing rustle of perfumed silk, Gerda clung sickly to the door post.

At first, after the three had left her, she could neither think nor move. Clutching the door, she closed her eyes for a moment, hoping to clear her head. Immediately, she was whirled away on a fabulous journey, as if to the moon; from which she struggled back in confusion, her thoughts still all the time straining away from her, trying to escape once more to that mad lunar race-track, beyond her control.

She must not let them go. She must change for dinner. It was a fearful effort to keep holding on to them. She had to remind herself constantly that she was on the way to her room, as she went slowly along the corridors, hesitating at corners, reading with difficulty the numbers on the doors. She kept repeating the number of her own room, afraid that she might forget it; and this effort of concentration alone seemed to anchor her to her surroundings, which, in spite of it, drifted intermittently over the borderline of the unreal.

It was a time of the evening when everybody was downstairs, the upper floors deserted, a maze of identical passages, warm, brightly lit, red carpeted, lined with the closed and numbered doors, each exactly the same as all the rest. Here, the continuity of her existence lapsing, she wandered a while, sick and vacant, lost and lonely as a child-Jonah in the red intestinal passages, hot from the living monster's feverish heat — instead of shivering, she was now burning hot. "Where am I?" she asked suddenly, recalled by something familiar about the shapes of numbers, curly-tailed nines and sevens — yes, it was her own door; she had got there at last. With a tightened grip on her thoughts she forced herself to perform deliberately and with her will actions normally automatic; turning the handle, stepping across the threshold, shutting the door again.

Shutting herself into the room, seeing her few belongings scattered about, she came back a little way into the normal world. The window was open, as, long ago, in some previous incarnation, she must have left it; after the heat of the corridors, the air from outside was refreshing. But almost at once she began to feel cold, and to shiver again, so violently that she had to catch hold of the bed: at which she looked longingly, thinking of the bliss of lying there as of some unattainable paradise; repeating that what she had to do was to change and go down to dinner. At the thought of food she turned sick. Yet she knew she would have to do it, no thought of rebellion crossed the frontiers of her mind. Nothing could save her from this awful effort she had to make, of taking off and putting on clothes, and going down to sit among strangers, under the indifferent or jeering or disapproving eyes of her family, and forcing herself to eat. She was so young and friendless and sick, she felt so dazed by the misery of it all, that a few tears fell from her eyes unnoticed, and splashed on the eiderdown, where they left dark marks that gradually disappeared.

By the time the tear marks had faded out, her shaking fingers had unfastened her dress. It was beyond her to make the effort of tugging it over her head, so she dragged it down awkwardly, till it dropped round her ankles. Suddenly, catching sight of herself in a long looking-glass, her eyes dilated, a start of fear went through her, her hands flew up to her breast; while she stared incredulously, unable at first to believe in the scarlet staining her skin between the shoulder-straps. Wildly, then, she pulled down the top of her slip. On her familiar thin chest, with its delicate traced necklace of fine blue veins, the ugly red looked so alien, shocking, that she was frightened, as if she had seen an internal organ exposed. The mad fantasy world, towards which in her head she was all the time sliding, seemed now to have invaded her solid flesh. Hardly knowing what she was doing, she tried to rub out the red with a towel; then, when the rash refused to be obliterated, pulled her slip over it, covered it with her hands—nobody must see it, nobody must know.

But people would have to know. With a sensation of panic, she thought that her mother would have to be told; her mother who despised and abominated any form of illness; how furious she would be. The girl's heart beat frantically, as though her mother's anger became a pulse, beating crazily all through her. And now, looking down at her chest, she seemed to see something shameful, all the guilt she had accumulated in her life seemed to have settled there, in that fiery brand, which was also a stony invisible weight on her breathing.

All the same, she was gradually getting used to it. The first shock, the almost metaphysical horror of the thing, was wearing off. It was only a rash, after all: she wouldn't be branded shamefully for ever. Perhaps by the morning, even, it would have vanished. Though she didn't really believe this, it cheered her slightly. She need not tell her mother until the morning, and then there might be nothing to tell. In the meantime, she had this respite in which to relax. At last she could lie down and give up the struggle. Nobody could deny now that she was ill, nobody could expect anything more of her — she could rest at last. Miraculously, she'd been spared the awful effort, from which, a minute ago, it had seemed nothing could save her.

Already, at the prospect of relaxing, her thoughts were straining away, like hounds at their leads, impatiently straining to escape to that fever-place where they could race in crazy circles without restraint. But she had inherited and had instilled into her a great respect for order, for doing things in a controlled, composed manner, in the correct way. Slovenliness and laxity were base characteristics of mongrels, not to be tolerated. So now, before she could relax, she must undress and get into bed.

She kept forgetting what she was trying to do, astonished by the perversity of fastenings and the clumsiness of her hands. The sickness and the heaviness and the pain in her head were all the time working to distract her. But they were separate from her determination to get undressed. She and her body had become two separate things. Her thoughts were separate again, always threatening to slip their leashes and escape control. To cope with all these separate things was like juggling with several balls at once; if she lost control of one, everything would collapse — she knew this, as, struggling awkwardly into her nightdress, she tripped over its long folds, lost her balance, and fell on the bed. Yet she was determined to persevere, not to close her eyes until she had put on the nightgown properly and got under the blankets. But, the moment she found herself lying down, lassitude overwhelmed her, and her consciousness raced away, free at last. The bed vibrated with her shuddering. She was freezing, lying there uncovered under the open window. But she didn't notice, too preoccupied with chasing after her thoughts, tearing in wild incoherence, all ways at once.

At some time or other, her eyes opened again, and she met the hard bright eye of the light fixed upon her, shining down steadily on the muddle in which she was lying, half in and half out of her night-dress, on top of the bed. There was something so weirdly improbable about this — the light burning in the still depths of the night, the confusion, her own cold sickness and trembling, her mind gone from her in fever —, that she made another attempt to come back to herself. But while she was still struggling towards normality, her thoughts again went careering off, and she had to tear after them, in mad pursuit.

Her family taking no interest in her non-appearance, the first person to discover Gerda's illness was the maid, who, towards the middle of the next morning, went in to do her room.

The girl herself knew almost nothing about what was happening in the outside world, fully occupied with the febrile activity in her head. Ghostly shadows appeared or vanished inconsequently: and once, convulsing her with terror, there was her mother's cloud-white face of anger and icy voice. The hasty exit from the hotel, made, in the hope of avoiding notice, when everyone was at lunch; the stretcher smuggled out furtively by back ways, by luggage lift and staff quarters, to the ambulance waiting, hidden among the trees; seemed neither more or less real than the delirious antics with which her brain had been busy the whole night long.

A doctor, employed by the hotel to deal with such emergencies, arranged for her unobtrusive admission to the fever hospital in the nearest big town, co-operating with the manager, who was anxious that his influential clients should be put to as little inconvenience as possible. The position was simplified by the fact that Regina was thinking of renting for the summer a house in the neighbourhood. She had only to sign the contract and move in at once.

As it happened, no one else was infected. But the chance of catching a temporarily disfiguring disease from her daughter would have made the mother's alienation final and complete, had it not already been so.

It was inevitable that Regina, with her narcissistic devotion to her own body, should regard her child as an enemy, whose mere existence automatically damaged her more and more, underlining the passing years that brought nearer the catastrophe of old age. In a deeper way, too, of which she was aware only through her resentment, the girl seemed to injure her by perpetuating something of the nightmare atmosphere of the birth, and of the whole disaster of her first marriage. In sending her to the hospital, instead of one of the more comfortable private homes, the mother was only following the pattern of her aversion, one of the chief manifestations of which was an extreme reluctance to spend even a fraction of her income upon her daughter. Thus, while she herself was always dressed by famous designers, her child was never allowed the pretty clothes worn by other girls; was sent to inferior schools; treated in general as an expensive nuisance, as though it were an act of generosity to clothe and educate her at all, instead of letting her grow up a naked savage.

Because of the delay in treating her illness, Gerda's condition was serious for some days. As long as she was on the danger list, Regina kept up appearances by telephone enquiries or by sending one of the men to the hospital. She even paid one visit herself: but by this time the patient was already recovering; so there seemed no necessity for further displays of concern. Without openly hoping that she would die, her mother had, of course, considered this desirable possibility; and she now felt disappointed, defrauded. Her feeling was that Gerda had no right to create such a disturbance, and then get well in the end. It was as though she had been showing off, making herself the centre of interest under false pretences. After all the fuss there had been, Regina wanted to hear no more of her for a very long time.

When, in due course, she was told that the girl could come home, she was horrified and indignant. Already? Must she have her back on her hands so soon? Pretending anxiety, she asked if Gerda could not stay in hospital a little longer, until her health was more fully established.

But the doctor she now had to deal with was far less obliging than the first one; he was not in the least impressed by her wealth, and had no need to cultivate her good will. Dryly, he replied that a fever hospital was meant only for fever patients. He could arrange for Gerda's admission to a convalescent home; but saw no need for this, since she'd obviously be more comfortable in the house occupied by her family, which was known as one of the most luxurious in the district. He went on to say that she would need comfort and special care, for some time, to repair the damage to her system, which was anything but robust, and appeared to have been consistently overstrained.

His tone of scarcely-veiled disapproval enraged Regina by implying that she'd failed to look after the girl properly in the past, and was likely to neglect her again in the future. She was furious with the doctor for daring to criticize; and still more furious with Gerda, who must, as she assured her husband, have complained — though whether she really believed this was doubtful, her daughter being so obviously incapable of making such a complaint, or even thinking she had cause to do so. But it suited her to accuse the girl of disloyalty, thus justifying her own negative attitude, when the stepfather, in his easy way, said: "Oh, let her come — the house is big enough, and she hardly takes up as much room as a shrimp, anyhow."

It was as hateful to Regina to pay for Gerda to go to a home as to have her back in the family group. As for treating her with special consideration — that was an insufferable idea. She herself, and she alone, had always to be the centre of all attention. Another point was that Jeff now performed, a thousand times more efficiently, all the tasks that had been such an ordeal to his stepsister. But the doctor was insisting that she must be removed from the hospital. And now the matron wrote too, saying that it really wasn't fair to leave her there any longer; what she needed now was a little spoiling, and taking out of herself.

Spoiling! The word acted as a fresh stimulus to her mother's indignant anger. She'd always felt that Gerda had no right to the pleasures she herself had been denied by her strictly repressive upbringing: and she particularly resented the suggestion that she should enjoy herself now just when, in her own private opinion, she deserved punishment. However, as she could no longer postpone the issue, she acted in a typically selfish, somewhat infantile way, arranging to fetch the girl on a certain day: then, when the day came, putting off her arrival for a few more days; a manœuvre which she repeated several times, on the assumption that the hospital authorities were unlikely to turn an ex-patient into the street.

91

Her supreme egoism enabled her to disregard altogether the inconvenience these tactics must have caused. Gerda was the one who apologized humbly and tried to find excuses, her large eyes clouding over with the quick tears of weakness, and darkening with a wounded look that disarmed criticism; the harrowing look of an acute deficiency she knew nothing about.

She had suffered before in a somewhat similar way at the various schools she'd attended, spending the last days of term, when everyone else was rejoicing, in a state of anxiety, waiting to hear whether she was to join Regina or be left where she was for the holidays. But her own attitude had now altered. She'd never wanted to stay at any of the schools: on account of her nervousness and the way she was constantly being moved from one establishment to another, she'd never made any real friends there. Though, in the circumstances, this wasn't surprising, it was a factor in her growing sense of being an outcast, beyond the pale of affection.

Yet, contradictorily, there still existed in her a child's naive belief in some relation between personal conduct and the course of events. From all the fairy tales in which for years she'd immersed herself, she'd built up a picture of life that was quite unreal; of a world where obedience, modesty, and all the virtues extolled to children, were in a kind of mystic alliance with what is called fate or chance, which would ultimately bring happiness to their possessor.

In actual fact, fate seemed to have placed her, as if maliciously, in a position where it was virtually impossible for her to attain even the very humble form of happiness that was all she asked. But now, incredibly, her childish faith was justified. By transporting her to the unpromising milieu of the fever hospital, fate made accessible the affection for which she had always, and vainly, longed. She had searched for it, out of her mind, with the sick urgency of delirium, always hurrying after this unnamed want, the restless deficiency burning in her all the time, while fever decomposed the thoughts in her brain. Sometimes a blank would come, when she knew nothing. Then the feverish race continued, pierced by intermittent glimpses of reality, as if a door opened and shut. Sometimes, to her horror, a white witch-face would regard her malignly, with a colder-than-human gaze. And always there was the agonizing pursuit of she knew not what, fragments of reality coming through with a sinister twisted meaning she vainly tried to de-code — everything distorted by fever, dissolving in hallucination. Until at last she became aware of approaching something that had been vastly remote.

For centuries she'd been travelling towards it, crossing mountains, deserts, tempestuous seas; lost at times in a grey maze of city streets; or in dense forests where unseen menacing drums tapped their untranslatable threat; under skies sometimes black, sometimes fiery with wheeling suns, split sometimes from horizon to zenith by a terrible emerald flash. Now she seemed all at once to be racing towards that formerly remote destination, suddenly close at hand. At last she was coming awake as herself, and in her right mind — her eyes were opening on the real world.

The air above her had started to mutter and boom. And, as her eyes opened, they were transfixed by pain. She saw a tremendous flare of light, blinding, as if the world were on fire; only a few frail black bars holding back that fearful incandescence. The blinding brightness was melting her eyes, she felt them run down her cheeks like tears. Where were her hands? She couldn't find them, she had no hands. But an old, old reflex, older than memory, made her struggle to turn away from the dazzling glare. Then a woman in a blue dress, with white on her head, put out her hand, and a blessed dusk fell. The light was extinguished. And Gerda went unconscious again.

After this, reality flickered continually through her delirium. The real world stood around her for minutes together: in too-bright daylight; or in the silent cavernous gloom of night, when beds loomed, a dim herd of browsing and silent monsters, only a feeble worm of light glimmering. But she was too tired to bother with it. Persistently her weariness resisted the concrete world, which, though just as persistent, could not quite succeed in becoming real. She might have gone on resisting it indefinitely, if it hadn't been for the woman in blue, always there, to do what was needed, to pull down the blind, or to help her to drink, knowing better than she herself knew what she wanted.

The name of this nurse was Jean. Though she was quite young — when she took off her cap and shook out her thick hair, always full of electricity like a cat's, she looked very little older than Gerda — she took her work seriously, as a vocation. always ready to give of her abounding vitality to her patients. She'd been attracted by Gerda all along, sorry for her. She looked such a pathetic little lost waif lying there, conscious, but very still, only her big eyes open and moving, as though searching for something. The nurse came to the bedside to take her pulse, lifting the limp hand and placing it on her breast, so that at the same time she could check her breathing. It was more regular, the pulse slower and fuller.

According to all the rules, she should have been getting better. But something seemed to be preventing her recovery, her temperature still shot up in the evening, as though, having stayed too long in the delusory fever world, she could not find the way back.

As a nurse, she was puzzled; and as a kind hearted human being she wanted to help, to bring her out of her ghostly half-world, back to the fullness and happiness of real life. Noticing that her eyes had ceased their restless moving since she'd been holding her wrist, Jean continued to hold it lightly between her fingers, as she said: "You must hurry up and get better, so that you can go outside." A heat wave had begun, it was very hot in the wards, and those patients who were well enough, had their beds pushed out on to the verandahs overlooking the patchy grass quadrangle round which the hospital had been built.

Gerda's large eyes turned up to the speaker, strange-coloured eyes, the colour of violets that are just starting to fade. They seemed only just alive, empty of something that should have been there. Now an answer gradually accumulated in their violet-tinged emptiness: a look of refusal gathered as from far away, replying that she only wanted to be left alone — not to be brought back to consciousness of the world.

The nurse was shocked and astonished. She herself was so full of the enjoyment of life that she could hardly believe it possible this pretty little rich girl didn't want to live. But it was so. She had seen the answer with her own eyes, unmistakeable. Suddenly the pathos of that wordless reply filled her with compassion. Leaning over the bed, smiling into the too-wide open eyes, she lightly smoothed the pale hair away from the face in a quick caress. "Try and get well soon," she said, coaxing, as if to a child, her smiling look full upon Gerda's face. "To please me — will you?" She didn't consider the words or why she said them, speaking what came on the spur of the moment.

Still looking up at her, Gerda's eyes became wider still with wonder, doubting the reality of what she saw. Was it possible that she'd found what she had been looking for all this time? It seemed too good to be true. But the unreasonable fairy-tale reasoning still operating in her hurried to confirm her belief: she gave way, and let her heart yield to what she saw in the nurse's face — the disinterested interest, and the never-before-seen hope of a personal tenderness. Her lips shaped, "Yes," almost without a sound, then curved into a smile of singular sweetness, while at the same time her big eyes grew lustrous as with tears, a new melting softness filling her breast.

So, slowly, she began to recover, because of Jean. Jean, with her simple, wide gaze, blue and straight, was the first person who had ever come to her for her own sake, for no reason except that she liked her and wanted to help her and felt her need. The effect was remarkable: as Gerda got better, she slowly broke through the wall which, because she had for so long been unwanted, unloved, had begun to close her off from all human warmth. The fairy-tale belief that fate would become the agent of her happiness had worn very thin by the time Jean appeared to confirm it. Now, because Jean was her friend, she slowly conquered her shyness and began to talk a little to the patients and nurses, to smile at them timidly but with growing confidence, like a timid little animal, delicate and large-eyed, slowly becoming tame. She was a model patient, docile and grateful, always eager to help in the wards as soon as she could get up. But it was only with Jean that she laughed and chattered like any other girl of her age.

She had a slight set-back when her mother came to see her: an event causing considerable stir in the hospital, which was in a poor part of the town, where well dressed strangers were as conspicuous and as rare as swans. Gerda's bed had been wheeled close to the window. As soon as she saw the slender figure in the quadrangle below, she tried to lean out, so that Jean, standing by in case of need, for she was not yet allowed out of bed and was still very shaky, had to grab hold of her.

Because of the heat, her mother had put on a wide-brimmed hat, in the shadow of which her face had the lovely luminousness of a pearl, touched with faint rose, mysterious, beautiful. In her rose-patterned dress, she had the cool, untouched, untouchable look of a Christmas rose, in the midst of the hot, sordid ugliness of the place, and the dusty stale urban atmosphere. She raised her hand in its pale glove and waved to her daughter. But there was nothing personal in the charming gesture, she had no message for her, the words Gerda had been about to call out remained unspoken. With painful sureness she knew that none of this effective loveliness was for her benefit, it had nothing to do with her. Even the smile was meant less for her than for the audience—the whispering, staring on-lookers on the crowded verandah.

After standing there for a moment, looking at everything with a touch of disgust, Regina hurried away, in a hurry to escape from the depressing hideousness and the danger of infection. The ghastly brick buildings gave her a feeling of horror; and she was terrified of the sick, poverty-stricken people all round her, of their contagion and ugliness. It would have killed her, she felt, to be shut up in such a place —how could Gerda endure it? She felt an illogical contempt for her daughter on this account.

For the rest of the hot day, the girl lay without reading or talking. She said nothing to anybody about the visit, lying for hours, her wide open dim-violet eyes fixed on nothing. This glimpse of her mother's indifference and inaccessibility brought home to her the dreary emptiness of her former life, realized as never before, now that she'd had some experience of companionship and affection. Since her present happiness was only temporary, and would make the return to that emptiness still more bitter, Jean's friendly face seemed to smile at her from a world still hopelessly out of reach; a place which, in the last resort, she could never enter.

The effect of the visit gradually wore off. With her consciousness she forgot it. But it left an indelible scar deep within her: a fixed sense of exclusion and loss finally replaced the childlike credulity with which she'd believed life to be somehow on the side of her happiness. Outwardly, however, she continued to recover slowly, and to enjoy the friendliness of the people around her, and of Jean in particular; though she never spoke of her family, even to her.

The bored occupants of the place were most inquisitive about these rich people, so different from themselves, and at first constantly questioned Gerda: until, finding her always silent and distressed by their curiosity, they gave up and ceased to discuss them in her presence.

Regina's one dramatic visit had made a tremendous impression, really almost as if a queen had come to the hospital, greatly stimulating the interest felt from the start in the peculiar beings who sent their daughter there, instead of to one of the grand private homes. Shut up in their strict isolation, patients and staff alike were thrilled by this glimpse of a way of life that seemed magically unreal. The whole business was a sort of theatrical performance for them, giving them the illusion of being in personal touch with the enchanted regions they usually saw only on the films. There was endless gossip about the family; about the mother, particularly, and the way she neglected her daughter; endless speculation as to the cause of her unnatural behaviour. Though Gerda herself never complained, there was a good deal of resentment on her behalf. And when the time came for her to go home, and her mother still left her at the hospital, making excuses from day to day for not fetching her, quite a strong feeling grew up in the segregated community.

The topic provided a pleasant and novel excitement, enjoyed by everyone but the innocent victim, who obviously suffered from her predicament. Seeing how over-sensitive she was about being in the way, trying to efface herself altogether in her anxiety, even the matron became sympathetic, giving her the run of the place, and even stretching its inelastic routine, so that Jean could spend some time with her each day.

It might have surprised those who sympathized with the girl to know that, once she felt herself accepted, she was happier than she'd ever been in her life. The hideous institutional buildings, grouped round the quadrangle of worn-out grass, were more like home than any other place she had known. The daily-renewed dread of being removed was the only flaw in her happiness, and she tried to forget it in playing the long, serious, silent games of make-believe she had never outgrown, pretending her family had forgotten her, that she'd be left here for the rest of her life, adopted by the hospital, or that Jean would somehow save her from being taken away.

The two had become good friends, despite the differences between them. Gerda appealed to the other girl's maternal instinct, and, on her side, was absolutely devoted, so grateful and happy that she seemed a different person when they were together, enjoying her youth for the first time with a kind of wonder, laughing and chattering about everything in the world that did not concern her own family. It was so unusual to find her silent and downcast one evening, that Jean immediately asked what was wrong.

The two girls were leaning on the balustrade of a verandah, deserted now, when all the beds had been wheeled back into the wards at the end of a sultry oppressive day. Black clouds had brought on a premature twilight, and lightning flickered across the sky, as Gerda's despondent voice answered: "They're coming to fetch me in the morning."

"They won't — they'll put it off again, like they always do."

"Not this time. This time they really mean it. I know."

There was such conviction in her voice, and such a note of despair, that Jean turned to look at her, surprised, but unable to see her face.

"Well, so much the better for you if they do," she said, with deliberate cheerfulness, trying to dispel the gloom she did not understand, not realizing for an instant how miserably the other was watching the dissolution of her brief interlude of happiness. Her own thoughts, following totally different lines, broke out indignantly: "I think it's absolutely disgusting, the

way they've left you in this wretched hole all through the hot
weather, when they've got that marvellous house by the sea.
That's where you ought to have been weeks ago — lying out
in the garden, or on the beach. I believe you'd have been
quite strong again by now — "

"Oh, stop, Jean! you don't understand."

"Why, what ever's the matter?" For a moment the nurse
was completely taken aback by this distraught interruption.
Then, in a rather odd voice, sharpened by curiosity, she
asked: "Don't you want to go, then?"

"No! Oh, no!"

She saw Gerda cover her face with her hands; and immediately put her arm round her, as though to protect her helpless fragility with her own sturdiness and independence. "What
is it? Aren't they kind to you? Tell me . . . " There was
real affection and sympathy in her voice and gesture. But,
like everyone else, she was madly curious about the family
and their strange attitude; the one thing her friend would
never discuss. So many fantastic rumours had been going
about that she half-expected some sensational revelation from
the weeping girl, whose next words, "They won't let me see
you again," came as a complete anti-climax.

"Why not? Of course you'll see me again if you want to—
but you'll probably forget all about me as soon as you get
away." This time Jean spoke with slight impatience: but,
feeling how Gerda was trembling like a poor little scared
animal, she tightened her arm consolingly, trying to soothe
her, repeating random words of encouragement: "Don't cry
. . . don't worry . . . everything will be all right . . . I'll ride
over on my bike — I've often done it . . . It's not far. Nobody
will be able to stop us meeting — why should they want to?"
until, under the comforting influence of her voice and touch,
the sobs gradually quietened to the almost inaudible crying
of a worn-out child, and then ceased entirely.

In the meantime, however, a strange thing had happened.
As if the close contact of their two bodies made a channel for
it, a new understanding had come through to Jean; who was
beginning to realize that Gerda's distress was due to the lack
of something she herself had always taken for granted as an
unquestionable right, available to the least privileged of man-
kind. Though she could not know the circumstances that had
deprived her companion of this simple right to a loving home,
it was obvious that she was not to blame, but the innocent
victim of something that, almost like a curse, seemed to
darken the air around her, far more sinister than anything
Jean had imagined. In her frank simplicity, the nurse recoiled

instinctively from this thing she couldn't even name, because it was felt, not thought, and when she tried to pin it down in her mind, it eluded her, slipped away. Yet she could all the time feel its dark influence in the air; now it seemed to threaten her too, as if an evil hand had come groping towards her, from which her impulse was to turn and run. She had grown genuinely fond of Gerda; she really did want to help and protect her: but this other thing, against which all her instincts were warning her, was too strong.

Jean had always been determined to enjoy her life, and, though it contained little except hard work, she had so far managed to do so, fighting against adverse circumstances with the weapons at her command: courage, optimism, and a kind of inspired blindness at certain times. She knew there were things in the unpromising future and the drab present at which, if she were to go on being happy, she couldn't afford to look.

Intuition had always warned her when to shut her eyes, as it was warning her now. She couldn't afford to see Gerda's despair, for, if she did, she'd be forced to see life as ugly, cruel, unjust; and human beings as cruel too, irresponsible and unprincipled in their conduct, even towards their own defenceless children. In the hospital she'd already seen proof of their cruelty in blows and bodily harm. But this was something new to her; a far worse kind of cruelty, inflicting irreparable damage but leaving no outward scars; a callous, sustained withholding of all nutriment essential to the emotional life, which was thus starved and stunted at its very source.

Jean, of course, did not see it so clearly, or think in such concrete terms. She was not especially intelligent, and her mind was clouded now by her confused emotions. Allowing instinct to take control, she was only aware of an imperative urge to avoid the contamination of Gerda's unhappiness, which she had already felt spreading towards her. As, stronger than either affection or pity, the impulse of self-preservation urged her to escape, for a brief instant she had the impression that, in obedience to it, she deliberately broke some connection between them. But this feeling, which never quite came to the front of her awareness, was immediately driven deep down, far below the surface, even while in the spirit she seemed to be moving away from the girl, beside whom her body was still standing, whose thin shoulders her arm still encircled. She was terribly sorry for Gerda; but, in a submerged way, even more relieved at the growing distance between herself and the threat to her happiness.

In the same submerged fashion, she could feel the gap

widening while she spoke to her friend, rather fast and breathlessly, as if her speaking self were running away from what she'd just done at a deeper-than-conscious level; repudiating the break she'd just made — which, nevertheless, seemed the right thing, the only possible thing, for her to have done. "I'll come over on Friday — my half-day. We'd better arrange now where to meet, in case they do come for you tomorrow before I see you. I know the house and the garden, so I can find my way about. It's a sort of show place, you know, and they used to show people round — " In a flicker of lightning she saw the small face paper-white, big black eye-holes with a glitter of tears, raised to her imploringly, as in a last forlorn hope; and, with an unexamined sense of guilt, hurried on: "I know — there's an old wishing well — nobody can object if I meet you there because of the public path from the road. I'll come as near there as I can."

"Will you really come? Is that a promise?"

Touched by the wistful, forlorn little voice, the young nurse wondered why her own hasty promise sounded so unconvincing; why she could find no adequate words; why there seemed nothing that she could do. Her conscious self was unaware of the paralyzing inner conflict between the never-fully-realized act of severance, of which she now retained no recollection, and her desire to console and encourage her friend. Between the two opposing impulses, she could only smile as she would have smiled at a badly hurt child, troubled by her own inadequacy, as she said: "If you can't get there, or if things go wrong, leave a note for me under the stones."

Again lightning slashed the black sky. Gerda saw it as a bad omen, an ominous white snake-arm striking up there. Livid in lightning, she seemed to see the white witch-face of her delirium, the thin mouth pursed with venom, the dead cold jewel-eyes brilliant beyond all pleading. Her last hope expiring as the thunder rolled, she knew that Jean couldn't help her — no one could. Unless she saved herself, she was done for. She had a wild, childish notion of running away. But where to? How would she live? She was so useless, there was nothing she could do. Her continually-interrupted education, haphazard and sketchy, had not prepared her in any way for earning her living. Though she was fifteen years' old and developed physically, emotional starvation made her seem somehow unfinished. Timid, delicate, humble, she was so totally lacking in self-confidence that she almost felt she had no self at all at this moment . . . incapable of making any move . . . helplessly watching the last trailing fringe of her happiness glide away . . .

Her wide, strained, doubtful eyes had again filled with tears. But a sudden fierce spatter of raindrops concealed them, flying angrily into the faces of the two girls, spitting at them out of the darkness.

"We'd better go in," Jean said, letting her arm fall from Gerda's shoulders, distressed because now, when she most wished to speak her affection, it remained dumb. She wanted so much to say something reassuring; but her throat obstinately remained shut, no words would come. Still, for a few more seconds, the two stood there together, as if waiting for something they had forgotten; as if each hoped the other might find the words, which, unless they were spoken now, never would be. And when they finally parted it was with sadness, as though secretly they both knew they were not really saying goodnight, but goodbye.

*　*　*

Gerda had no chance to see Jean the next morning before Jeff came in the car to fetch her. Her step-brother's overbearing physical presence seemed to transform her into a little wraith, almost transparent by contrast, so thin and pale that, once he'd driven her away from the hospital, nothing whatever of her was left behind there. His big, handsome physique seemed to obliterate even her memory, so that she wasn't mentioned, no one spoke her name any more, though, for a day or two, there was some talk about the magnificent car and its driver, before a new topic caught the general interest.

Jean had nothing at all of her friend either: not a snapshot, nothing by which to remember her. After a day or two, she seemed to forget even what she looked like, this girl with whom she'd been closely associated for three months or more. A quarter of a year! Transferring to her forgetfulness the guilt belonging to the break she had made but no longer remembered, she felt obscurely troubled by Gerda's disappearance out of her life.

It really was strange how abruptly all the hospital gossip had ceased: her inoffensive little ghost exorcised so completely that she might never have haunted the place; she hardly seemed to have been a real person, included now in the curious aura of unreality that had always surrounded the rest of the family. Jean felt rather as though for a time she'd been friends with a girl from the moon; who, when she vanished, left behind a less definite memory than would have been left by a human being; something so nebulous, shadowy —just moonshine — that she could never be sure she had existed at all.

To keep an appointment with a moon-girl seemed quite absurd. But, when Friday came, having promised, off she went on her bicycle, in the cool windy weather that had followed the storm. Some sort of mental block prevented her from thinking of Gerda specifically; she told herself that the exercise would do her good, and the blow of sea air, as she rode along the coast road, against the wind, looking forward to the return trip, when it would carry her like a bird.

Arriving, soon after three, at the point where a footpath led from the road to the wishing well, she dismounted, leaned her bicycle against the fence, and climbed over the stile.

In front of her was a belt of woodland, a narrow path running down through the trees to a circular clearing with the well in the middle, and a few big stones — once perhaps part of a cairn — lying in the grass, bracken growing up tall between. Already, without going any further, she could see that no one was there: which was what she expected — if she expected anything. Blocked by the unreality in her mind, her thoughts still failed to reach Gerda's name. As she followed the downward path, she kept glancing about as if looking for someone, but not for anyone in particular. Between the trees, glimpses of the grey stone manor could be seen from the clearing, its chimneys and mullioned windows, the lower part of the house, and the garden in which it stood, being hidden by undergrowth. She gazed at it for a while, and it seemed deserted: no smoke from the chimneys; no movement outside or in; no sound of lawn-mower, or car, or dog barking, or pigeon's coo: which added to her general feeling of unreality. She'd already noticed that the fence surrounding the clearing and path was a token, rather than a real, barrier, marking the old right of way to the well through this private estate. Again avoiding the thought of Gerda herself, she merely observed that no one would have any difficulty in getting past the two strands of rusty wire sagging between the uprights.

Even when the sight of the stones reminded her of her own suggestion, it was just a memory floating about in the void. She didn't think who might have left a note there, or why, as, feeling rather ridiculous, with a faintly amused, faintly self-conscious look, she began to heave up the great heavy stones one by one; finding nothing underneath, though in places the bracken was flattened as if someone had stood there.

After this effort, she sat down on the old crumbling well-head. The under-sides of the stones, damp from recent rain, had dirtied her hands, and she set about cleaning them with leisurely, careful thoroughness, first with grass, and then with her handkerchief. She knew she was deliberately spinning out

this operation, making it last as long as possible. And somewhere at the back of her mind was the thought that someone
must be given plenty of time to appear, in case there had been
some delay. But the two ideas did not come together. For
perhaps half an hour Jean idled there, without hearing or
seeing a sign of life; then she brushed the blades of grass off
her skirt, and stood up.

Suddenly, just as she was about to go, she did at last
remember the girl she had come to meet; remembered her so
distinctly that Gerda might have been standing there, with
her waiflike look of pathos and helplessness, her big eyes timid
in her pale little face, under the almost white hair. The
memory had the vividness of a vision; yet it made the girl
herself seem no more real, recalling only those qualities that
were vague and negative — her paleness and frailness and
self-effacement — as though nothing were real about her but
her unrealness, and she had never lived in real life.

In real life there were Jean's own friends and family, and
the hospital people. Matron was real to her, and so were
the patients. But this other was simply a moon-girl, who
came from a different world. In self-defence, Jean had already
broken the link of their friendship. And now, in her mind,
she went further, dissolving Gerda herself, and with her of
course the threat to her own happiness, into the memory-
substance of the unreal, from which no sinister hand could
ever come groping in her direction.

As a real person, Gerda had ceased to exist. As for Jean,
she had kept her promise. She need no longer worry about
her, or reproach herself, or feel troubled. Gerda hadn't come,
and she hadn't written, and so she must be alright. Safely
back where she belonged, she must have forgotten about the
hospital. Strolling up the path, pausing at the stile for a last
look back, Jean felt for both their sakes deeply relieved. She
was so glad the poor little thing was back home in her own
place, wherever that was, and that pity could have an end.

· Without great determination, the young nurse could not
have contrived to extract happiness from the uncompromising
material of her life. In addition, she'd had to develop a certain toughness, and was quite resolved to protect herself, even
if this entailed Gerda's elimination. So, even if she could have
read the note, which Jeff had removed from its hiding place
under the stone, it probably wouldn't have changed her conviction that no such person as Gerda had ever been. Irrevocably she had dissolved her friend into moonshine; and their
relationship into something like the memory of an old film,

not at all true to life, which had once evoked a vicarious passing sadness.

So that was the end of that. She got on her bicycle and rode off, back to real life, and the remains of her half-day's freedom. Glancing at her watch, she was glad to see that there would be quite a lot of it left, if she hurried. She had the wind at her back now, to help her. Like a weightless gigantic hand on her back, it sent her spinning along effortlessly in the brisk briny smell of the sea. It made her feel gay to be leaving all that unreality further behind her each second. Suddenly she felt such a surge of spontaneous happiness that she began to sing, for no reason, except that she was alive, young and healthy, and flying easily through the air, carefree as a bird.

5

SOMETHING MORE

THOUGH Gerda was no less intelligent than the average girl
of her age, the circumstances of her life combined with her
nervousness and her erratic education to make her seem so.
A scarcity of love, and the consequent insecurity and inferiority-feeling, operated like a machine, specially designed to
neutralize and break down her innate qualities. At each new
school she attended, she awaited with dread the moment when
she would be relegated to the class of a lower age-group than
her own; where her companions would make her feel an outsider because she did not belong to their exact category in the
rigid hierarchy of the teens. She was too gentle to be un-
popular; but she remained apart; the difficult adjustment to
a new environment usually absorbing all her forces until, just
about the time she began to settle down and was free to make
friends, she was once again whisked away. The continuous
strain of keeping up with the others, in class, at games, in
their communal life, left her no energy to enjoy her school-
days. More than anything, she felt relieved when, as soon as
she was seventeen, her mother decided to discontinue what
she described as the useless expense of her education.

It meant that the dull, empty, lonely life she was
accustomed to lead during the holidays, dragged round by her
family as a sort of unwanted appendage, would now be her
whole existence. But at least she would be spared the constant abortive attempt to make herself like other girls, and the
painful comparison of their families, clothes, and general circumstances with her own. She knew that her mother would
never agree to pay for her to train for any profession; and her
poor opinion of herself made her doubt her capacity to earn
her own living. With a queer little unexpected stoicism, she
resorted to a habit of passive acceptance, living from day to
day without complaint, and, as far as possible, without
thought. This was her life, from which there was no escape.
What was the use of thinking about it? She would simply
endure, meanwhile making herself a different world in her
head, where no one could reach her; where friends who could

not be estranged from her would supply the affection lacking in her real life.

Her fate in real life was to be always alone, left out of everything. The one friend she had made she had not been able to keep, and she would not try to make another, to risk the pain of a second loss. She wouldn't even allow herself to dwell on the memory of that one friendship, which, because it was such a unique event in her life, seemed unreal. Distrusting the ephemeral and precarious nature of happiness, she was afraid to make any claim on even a happy memory: prefering to retire into her private fantasy world; trying neither to think of her real situation, nor to make contact with human beings.

She was glad that her family left her alone most of the time. If, as occasionally happened, someone staying in the hotel made friendly overtures to her, she would not respond; not only because she knew that to do so would arouse her mother's pathological jealousy, but also really believing herself to be beyond the pale of human relations. Though she had never found out in detail what had happened to end her friendship with the girl from the hospital, she suspected her family of being somehow responsible for the break two years before. And perhaps this was why, since then, her attitude towards them had slowly changed; her childhood's ingenuous trusting affection gradually giving place to a deep resentment; of which, however, she was hardly aware; and which only showed itself in her withdrawal into the private world, now so much more real than her life with them.

A small, slight, almost childish figure, with long pale hair hanging straight to her shoulders, she followed her elders from car to 'plane, hotel to liner, sea-coast to city, according to their whim; silent, docile, retiring; moving always in her own little circle of dissociation, as if these travels didn't really concern her — as if her real self were elsewhere.

Of the trio who ruled her life, her mother alone retained a sinister sort of significance for her. The men were no more than ponderous shadow-shapes on the edge of vision. As soon as she had learned to escape to a world of her own, her stepbrother had become unimportant, no longer able to torment her. And his father had never meant anything to her; so, though he sometimes looked at her now with a new almost appealling expression, she remained unconscious of him.

All her life she had suffered from the indifference of these people, who, throughout her childhood, had consistently rejected all she had to offer. And, now that she was growing up, she involuntarily withdrew, made herself inaccessible to them, so that she did not see her step-father's pathetic position.

Older than his wife, he seemed to be ageing almost daily. His big head with its abundant grey wavy hair, sinking now into his massive shoulders, gave him rather the look of a buffalo; — when he glanced round suspiciously, of an ageing buffalo, scenting the herd's contempt for age and waning powers. He had lost much of his genial assurance, and would sometimes look from one person to another with a sort of bewildered helplessness, as if he'd caught sight of some distant threat, against which all his money and buffalo-might, and even Regina's power, would be of no avail.

Being quite without inward resources, when he could no longer take part in any active sport, he was left face to face with that central inadequacy which had kept him contentedly under his wife's dominion. He seemed to depend on her more and more; while at the same time he grew increasingly disinclined for her strenuous round of pleasure, in which Jeff frequently took his place.

In the past, the old man had been accustomed to deplore his son's lack of ambition, unable to understand how a young fellow could be content to fritter away this time, doing nothing at all. But now, though he felt a wistful regret that he saw so little of the boy these days, he often thought how lucky it was, after all, that he hadn't entered any profession, and so was always available to act as Regina's escort — to dance, or gamble, or lie on the beach, or go shopping, or drive her about in her big American car.

He never guessed that, not luck, but his wife's forethought and deliberate planning, were responsible for this state of affairs. Years before, she'd started systematically discouraging his son's interests, focussing all the boy's attention upon herself; while inculcating the doctrine that sex was unmentionable, vulgar, and entirely superfluous; in preparation for the time when she would need, in place of her ageing husband, a companion-chauffeur, with whom she could associate without the danger of gossip or tiresome emotional complications. Jeff's indolent, luxury-loving nature had made her task easy; especially as he'd come under her influence during his most impressionable years. He was almost slavishly devoted to her, still calling her by the name, Gloriana, he'd given her ten years earlier, when he was fifteen. And he was the perfect general factotum — handsome, self-possessed, efficient in practical ways, a safe driver, and excellent dancer— into which she'd unobtrusively turned him, without either he or his father being aware of what she was doing. His essential stupidity, crudity, didn't matter, since he supplied her with the uncritical, undemanding devotion that was her profoundest need.

Her object had been to fix him emotionally at the sexless boy-lover stage of regarding her as a sort of fairy queen, radiating beauty and light, in which he'd be content to bask forever. And, to a surprising extent, she had succeeded. But, though to Jeff, as to his father, her capacity for dominance had a magic charm which had held him fascinated all these years, his youth was more assertive; there were some curious side-effects, notably one taking the form — sex being too deeply repressed for any thought of it to cross the frontiers of awareness — of an endless craving for her company. In some impossible way, he wanted to have more and more of her: wanted her all to himself; all the time; absolutely. Because of their way of life, he *was* alone with his step-mother far more than would have been possible in a more conventional settled existence. But he still felt this insatiable hunger for her, which made him irritable and dissatisfied, jealous of anyone who approached her.

There was a real bond of affection between him and his father. Yet so strong was the other feeling that, when the old man died suddenly of a heart attack, the son's first reaction was a sense of relief — now he would have Regina to himself. Then grief overwhelmed him: guiltily he remembered those recent glances of wordless appeal. Critical for the first time, almost, he disapproved of his step-mother's attitude, resenting her refusal to come to the funeral, although she had her excuse ready, a slight cold having kept her indoors for a day or two. She could say it would be risky for her to come out, since the weather, as if in collaboration with her, had changed suddenly. One of those infrequent dull spells had set in, not really cold, but dismal, blustery and overcast, which, in places where the sun nearly always shines, seem bleaker than the bitterest winter frost in a harsher climate.

The afternoon was already declining when the coffin was lowered into the open grave. The flowers seemed to burn, their colours lurid and unnatural in the grey, deadened light; a light peculiarly appropriate to this small neglected burial ground of a foreign creed, hidden behind funereal cypresses, on the untidy outskirts of the town, surrounded by the mess and muddle of incomplete building projects. The grey sky and black trees; the weedy, untended graves; the roofless houses, like ruins standing about; the silence, intermittently interrupted by the dry clatter of palm leaves in the gusty wind; all contributed their dreariness to the interment. In spite of the flowers and the costly headstone, there was a suggestion of something furtive and almost shoddy in this hasty consignment to oblivion in foreign earth of an unknown stranger; without mourners, without honour or dignity, without grief.

As he stood at the graveside, the son experienced a moment of unaccustomed insight, realizing, as nobody else ever would, the tragedy of his father's full, active, successful life; which had deteriorated into something empty and meretricious, and here reached an ignominous end, far from the scene of his achievements, far from ancestors, friends and homeland. He suddenly saw how the dead man's last years had been deprived of the things that make age tolerable: of recognition, tenderness, old companions; of public honour and private ease. And all this had happened — why?

It was as if he already knew the answer: he seemed to take one swift glance at it, and, in the same instant, to reject it in horror, slamming the doors of his mind. But the soundless interior crash came too late to exclude the thought he wished to repudiate; which was already inside his head, and would, however vehemently he disclaimed it, eventually find its way into consciousness. The knowledge of this struck him with a sense of disaster.

In his uneasy preoccupation, he hadn't even noticed the two men in blue working overalls, who had been watching him all along, leaning on their spades in the background. Evidently growing impatient, deciding that enough time had been wasted, they now advanced, dug their spades into a pile of dry brittle earth, and hurriedly started shovelling it into the gaping hole, small stones rattling like hail on the coffin lid. There seemed to Jeff something so insulting, both to the corpse and to himself, in their unseemly and careless haste, that he began shouting furiously at the pair; who paused with spades in mid-air, gazing at him silently out of their brown inscrutable peasants' eyes.

In spite of his anger, his smart clothes and assured bearing, the young man had at this moment a curious air of ineffectuality, which apparently made the gravediggers think they could safely ignore him. He felt it himself, and stopped abusing them, feeling humiliated and helpless, frustrated by something he didn't understand. Their disrespect seemed to augment the sense of catastrophe, which suddenly made the place horrible to him, so that he only wanted to get away.

A sudden gust set the dry palm leaves clapping with a sound of ironic applause. Small spirals of dust and dead leaves went whirling between the graves in a mad dervish dance — he stepped aside to avoid one, and saw Gerda, whose presence he had entirely forgotten.

Glad of the distraction, he fixed his attention upon her, noticing how she'd placed herself slightly apart, like a casual spectator, unrelated to what was happening. He wondered whether he'd given himself away to her—whether she realized his discomfiture. There she stood, with the vague absent look now habitual to her, which he resented as a trick by which she escaped him. Her face gave no clue to her thoughts, conveyed nothing to him. As if she were alone, she stood motionless, only the tips of her long whitish hair stirred by the wind. She might have been in a dream. But instead of being reassured by this vague farawayness, he suspected it of hiding thoughts unfavourable to himself. Baffled and bad-tempered, he called out roughly: "Come on — you needn't stand mooning there any longer," and then at once turned away.

Gerda barely caught a glimpse of his deliberately callous face before he strode off rapidly towards the iron gate, beyond which a long shiny car could be seen under the cypresses. She went after him immediately, walking as fast as she could along the weedy uneven path, knowing that, if she kept him waiting, he was likely to drive off without her; in which case, as she had no money, she'd have to walk all the way back to the hotel. But she wasn't consciously thinking about this, or about him; his voice had not made him any more real — he was still only a shadow-shape on the outskirts of her attention.

Her impassivity did not change, she took no notice of the staring gravediggers, or of anything; but, without one backward glance, slipped through the rusty gate, her tarnished silver hair floating behind her, lighter than the grey day, which seemed darkened and saddened by the black trees she was approaching. There was no thought in her head for the dead man they were abandoning so hurriedly in this dismal spot, almost as if running away from him. She was neither glad nor sorry about her step-father's death. It made no difference to her. Her life would go on just the same.

Arriving, breathless, at the car in which Jeff was already sitting, she started struggling with the chromium handle under his cold contemptuous gaze. There was a knack in opening the door which she'd never mastered. Instead of concentrating on what she was trying to do, she tugged and twisted at random, hoping to hit on the right movement by chance, embarrassed by the scornful, antagonistic young face, of which, now that it was divided from her only by a sheet of glass, she could no longer be unaware.

His lips tightly compressed, his whole expression set hard

110

in hostility, her step-brother surveyed her futile efforts, until, irritated past bearing, yet unable to bring himself either to open the door or explain its mechanism, he exclaimed furiously: "Press, idiot!"

At last she managed to slide in beside him. He immediately sent the car plunging forward so abruptly that she was thrown forward too; her head almost striking the windscreen. Glancing at her in silence, with a sour grimace, he wished she'd gone right through the glass, completely possessed by the wild rage which he had diverted from its true object to project upon her. He kept his foot pressed hard on the accelerator, driving headlong over the rough roads, deeply rutted by heavy traffic, so that his companion, too light to keep in her seat, was all the time thrown about from one side to the other. But she didn't protest: her expressionless face suggested that an immeasureable distance divided her real self from the discomfort he was inflicting upon her body — that he still hadn't reached *her*. Though she was not really the person he wanted to hurt, he grew increasingly infuriated by her elusiveness. And, suddenly, it occurred to him that he had a new grudge against her as the last remaining obstacle between his stepmother and himself. He drove the whole way like a madman, without speaking a word, intentionally running risks, inviting a crash; in the mood to smash up the car and Gerda with it; himself, too, perhaps, plagued by half-awareness of the thought he was repressing.

As soon as they reached the hotel, the two young people parted, still without exchanging a word or a look, Jeff going straight to the lift, Gerda prefering to walk the three flights to her room rather than spend a few more moments with him, but forgetting both him and the dangerous drive as she opened her own door.

As usual, she'd been given one of the cheap sunless rooms at the back of the hotel: but she liked it, feeling safe from her family there; knowing that neither her mother nor Jeff would be likely even to know its number. It was as if she'd arrived in another country, where, escaping from the life she lived with them, she could relax into the world of her imagination; reassured by the thought of all the stairs and corridors separating her from the people she regarded, not so much as enemies, as strangers, with whom no communication was possible for her.

Meanwhile, Jeff had left the lift, and was hurrying towards the private sitting room where he knew Regina would be waiting for him to come and tell her about the burial. He walked along the passage as fast as he could, hurrying back to her as

111

he always did after the briefest absence, rushing as if he couldn't get back to her fast enough. Today, however, his haste was automatic, and, in sight of the door, he stopped dead, arrested by the unprecedented realization that he didn't want to see her just then.

This was something so unheard-of, so incomprehensible, that he was almost dazed; hesitating for a moment, and then slowly turning towards his own room. Having shut himself in there alone, he stood staring out of the window while darkness fell lugubriously on the town below, the cafes showing as blotches of light, a string of flickering lights outlining the curve of the bay. It all looked dreary to him, dismal. At the thought of his father, abandoned forever here, unmitigated gloom filled him; beneath which the other suppressed thought clamoured for recognition. The effort of stifling it, thrusting it down, deeper still, into the obscure depths of himself, made him frown till his eyebrows met in a black line right across his forehead.

The three who were left continued to live as before, without ever mentioning the dead man. Even Jeff appeared to forget him. He was now alone with his stepmother most of the time; and Gerda, even when she was with them, was so unobtrusive that her presence hardly counted. Yet the pangs of his insatiable hunger seemed to increase, as though having so nearly got Regina to himself only emphasized the fact that she was still just out of his reach. She always would be, of course. But, not knowing what it was he wanted so badly, he didn't see this. In his bemused brain there was only the craving for some undefined state of finality, where she would be his absolutely. So he concentrated on the idea of getting rid of Gerda, since she alone seemed to stand in the way of his wish's fulfiilment.

The girl rarely appeared except at meals, when she seldom spoke, and often seemed not to be listening, lost in some dream of her own. Nevertheless, her inoffensive presence got on his nerves to such an extent that he felt awkward and constrained so that a silence of resentful frustration descended upon him. He would stare at the quiet dreamy girl opposite; and, if looks could have done it, she'd have been pardoned of his wish's fulfilment.

He went about for days, heavily brooding, unable to decide how to dispose of the irritating little creature. If only she'd been as vulnerable as in the past, he might have driven her to flight by making her life intolerable. Now, he told himself, in exasperation, she was too timid, too unenterprising, to go away by herself, even if he were to bribe her. To marry her off seemed the only hope. And what a hope! Nobody would look at her beside Regina.

It was true that the girl was so eclipsed by her mother that she might have been invisible. Tall, magnetic, arresting, with her wonderful clothes and jewels, Regina compelled attention, possessing a sense of theatre which dramatized her simplest actions. Jeff himself added much to her effectiveness, playing up admirably to her regal role.

This acting was a serious game they played between them without ever mentioning it. The young man knew that his step-mother did not distinguish clearly between her real self and the part she was playing, and he never referred to their act, except in indirect terms. So now, though it didn't strike him as odd for a grown-up woman to spend her life in a self-dramatizing charade, a delicate situation arose.

He couldn't see how it was possible to suggest that Regina should modify her performance to give her daughter a share of the limelight. But he'd decided that Gerda's fragile pallor, contrasted with her vividness, and emphasized by the right clothes and make-up, had a certain appeal, and stuck to the idea of getting her married off. The problem was, how to introduce the subject to his stepmother. It would be difficult, too, to get her a few decent dresses. What would be the best procedure?

He hadn't arrived at any conclusion when he drove away from the hairdresser's, where he had left Regina, and where he was to pick her up again in about an hour. The day was warm, so he decided to have a swim. But, when he got to the beach, it hardly seemed worth while undressing and having to get dressed again in a hurry in order to be on time. He strolled along to the quiet end of the bay, where only a few groups of people were scattered over the sand and under the pines, that here grew almost to the water's edge. Leaning against a tree trunk, he sat down in the shade, on the fallen pine needles, that made a cool, aromatic brown carpet, pleasant after his walk in the sun.

Only two figures were moving in his field of vision; automatically, idly, he watched their approach, the little girl carrying the usual beach paraphernalia, which the young man kept trying to take from her. When he finally succeeded in doing so, the on-looker had a better view of her. She was older than he'd thought; her smallness and slimness had misled him into taking her for a child. Now something familiar about her movements made him watch more intently, as the pair crossed the beach diagonally, towards the water. The man, brown and well-built, seemed good-looking, but kept his head turned away, towards his companion, to whom he was talking with animation, occasionally bending down to her in his solicitude, or exchanging with her a long smiling look of intimacy.

Jeff's face gradually assumed an expression of incredulous amazement, his eyes so wide and round that they seemed to be jumping out of his head. He'd seldom gone swimming with Gerda, and so hardly ever saw her like this, her hair hidden under a scarf; that was why he hadn't recognised her at once. There wasn't the slightest doubt now in his mind that it was she, moving over the sand with her characteristic straying walk. Astounded, he watched the pair of them in the water together, the man all the time protecting her, taking such care of her, and also showing off slightly before her, his wet brown glistening arm cleaving air and sea as strongly and regularly as a piston.

Utterly astonished, Jeff sat on the pine needles, simply staring at them. Gerda seemed a different being, attractive and lively, quite unlike the dim little thing he'd always known, as she swam and played and splashed in the transparent waves. And she'd done it all by herself. Astounding, it was to him, absolutely. While he'd been thinking how she'd have to be dressed up and presented to catch the eye, so that he could shanghai some young ass into marrying her, she'd quietly gone out on her own, and, with no help from anyone, got herself this very presentable young man, who was obviously crazy about her. She was a deep one, all right, sitting with them day after day, scarcely speaking a word, and then coming away to *this*. He felt a grudging admiration, mixed with resentment, because she seemed to have tricked him again. Then, with a rush of relief, he realized that, from his point of view, this was the very best thing that could have happened, not only sparing him the trouble of arranging the whole affair, but also letting him off the tricky business of tackling Regina — there would be no need now to mention their acting game.

But how on earth had the girl done it? Wonder overwhelmed him again, he stared and stared, and could never have enough of the marvel. When it was time for him to go back to the hairdresser's, he could hardly tear himself away.

Changing much earlier than usual that same evening, Jeff strolled through the hotel in search of his step-sister, coming upon her apparently by accident. She too was dressed for dinner, and he amazed her by suggesting that, as they were both ready so early, they should have a drink together before he went to help Regina dress, as he did every night. Without waiting for a reply, he fetched the glasses himself from the bar, and carried them out into the darkening garden.

Gerda didn't want to go with him, but, astonished by this sudden unexpected amiability, felt unable to refuse. Jeff's big, handsome face, tanned red rather than brown, affably incomprehensibly, smiling, and full of assurance, seemed to drag her along with him against her will. He was so sure of himself and of everything. It was his sureness mainly that made her go.

He led her to a secluded seat with a table beside it, set in a sort of alcove of foliage. Coloured lights, strung from trees and bushes, grew brighter each moment, as the dark wash of night painted sunset out of the sky. "It's cool here, and no one's likely to come, so we can have a nice quiet chat," he said, grinning, as they sat down.

Gerda remained silent. She had reverted to her usual subdued, almost quenched manner, gazing at him dubiously, her wide dilated eyes searching his face for a clue to what this unprecedented friendliness might portend. The suggestion that he had something to say in private disturbed her: but she was totally unprepared for his next words.

"You're a dark horse, aren't you?" His smile broadened, and he lifted his glass. "Well, here's to romance."

The girl made a quick convulsive movement and then went very still, sitting there as if frozen, silent, just staring at him with enormous eyes. He felt a familiar impatience; but his mood was too good to be easily ruffled and, even in this uncertain light, he had seen how her face turned white; so he tried to reassure her, grateful because she'd simplified matters for him.

"What's up? Why so scared?" he asked, with the imitation of his father's hearty good nature that was his nearest approach to kindness. "Come on, now — tell me what's the trouble."

Gerda took a long time to answer. She was trying to decide whether his extraordinary display of friendliness could be genuine. His ruddy face reminded her of a Halloween lantern hanging against the dusk, with its grin and its empty look. But he seemed to mean to be kind — he *might* be sincere. She had little cause to trust him, God knows. But she wanted so much to believe the best: being in desperate need of his help, she was tempted to give him the benefit of the doubt. She had scarcely dared to believe the unfolding promise, which, in the last few days, had opened a door from her lonely and empty life to a world of incredible beauty and happiness. She'd never hoped to enter that world of dream-happiness, from which her mother had exiled her. But Jeff could influence her mother, who would listen to him as to no one else. She couldn't help hoping that, if only he would help her, in

115

spite of her own profound sense of exclusion, the dream might come true. Groping for words, her head lowered, she murmered: "I thought nobody knew . . . "

"Why shouldn't they know? They'll have to know sometime," he said reasonably, trying in vain to connect the drooping dejected figure before him with the laughing girl on the beach.

This time, almost in a whisper, she answered at once: "I didn't want mother to know . . . because she won't allow it . . . as soon as she finds out she'll separate us . . . insist on moving from here — " Suddenly she was in despair, convinced that her hopes were doomed. She told herself it was better to let her dream end now, since every day it became more precious, the prospect of losing it harder to bear. Even Jeff, even if he agreed to help her, wouldn't be able to stop her mother resenting her love affair as though it were a personal insult. Never, never, would she put up with a situation of which she wasn't the centre. As if weighed down by the heavy tears in her eyes, the girl's head sank still lower: but it no more occurred to her than to the young man beside her, to criticize her mother; whose peculiarities they both took for granted, so accustomed to them that they seemed normal. However, where Gerda's fatalistic resignation made her regard their consequences as inescapable, Jeff's equally uncritical attitude was less passive. He knew that what she had said was quite true. He couldn't think how he'd overlooked his step-mother's jealousy and its bearing upon his plan. But the plan remained unaffected. To him, Regina's inevitable obstruction of her daughter's happiness didn't mean, as it did to the girl herself, the end of her dream; it was merely a difficulty to be surmounted. To make sure that there were no other more concrete impediments, he now inquired: "Could she bring up any real objections? I mean, is the chap married already? Or a crook, or anything?"

"Good heavens, no!" Seeing a pale shimmer of hair, as Gerda looked up wonderingly, he asked: "And you both want to get married?"

"Yes — oh, yes!" She gave the words the ardent sound of a prayer, gazing at him with her great eyes, her face beginning to shine with a delicate, tender look he had never before seen, there or anywhere else — moved by it to a sort of clumsy benevolence, he said: "Well, then, don't worry," and dropped his hand on her bare shoulder, surprised to find it so smooth and cool. To be touching the girl's flesh gave him an odd little shock. He was twenty-five and a fine specimen physically; and he'd never so much as glanced at any woman except Regina.

"But you know she won't allow it," Gerda said wistfully, the light dying out of her face. She was confused by the weight of his hand on her shoulder; such a huge, hot, dry, heavy, masculine hand — that it should belong to Jeff, of all people, seemed most extraordinary to her, most confusing. She couldn't decide, even now, whether he was to be trusted.

"She will — I'll get round her somehow," he said confidently, tightening his grip. "Let me handle this, I promise you everything will be all right." He hadn't yet got over the surprise of touching her skin, so soft and smooth and silky, so unlike a man's; it made him feel as if he'd just uncovered a secret; and also, to his astonishment, faintly ashamed of the way he'd treated her in the past, and (though the tough part of him jeered at this belated uprising of a kinder self), glad to do something to help her. In the gathering twilight, his ruddy smiling face hanging above her resembled more than ever a Halloween lantern. But it no longer seemed empty; it was full of a powerful assurance now, and even had a certain look of authority — the crude authority of his physical strength — to back up the words: "Just leave everything to me."

"Oh, Jeff — thank you!" Suddenly she knew she could trust him. It was as if a message had reached her, straight from his physical being, through his hand, through his muscular arm, telling her that he would support her with all his animal strength and stubbornness and vitality. A tremulous smile came on her face, her eyes were brilliant with such gratitude that he felt strong enough to move mountains. He had suddenly caught his first glimpse of what was attractive in her: of her modest, simple spontaneousness, her generous appreciation; a gift, it amounted to, of making a man feel big and important. He felt about six inches taller than usual, strong, wise and protective, as he said: "Just leave it all to me, and you'll be married by the end of the month." Whereupon, she repeated with great sincerity: "Thank you, thank you!"

He was a magnificent great stubborn animal, he would never give in. So she felt that her dream was safe. She had no idea why he was going to help her. He had his own reasons of course, she knew he wasn't doing it out of affection for her, but because it happened to suit his plans. But that didn't matter. She didn't even wonder what the reasons were. All her life she'd been kept in ignorance of the reasons for what was happening, sent here or there, without being consulted or told in advance, like a dog in a box. No one had explained anything to her, or told her anything: and her strange little

117

brain had closed in retaliation, not caring; not even thinking a question.

With a last encouraging grip, Jeff took his hand away and stood up; it was time for him to go to Regina. But for a few more moments he stood looking down at the girl, fascinated by her wide-eyed, tender, bright shining look, which seemed to reflect the radiance of some magic unknown to him. He wondered about it vaguely in his bewildered mind; what strange illumination could have such power to transfigure her? Was there something in life he was missing and knew nothing about?

Off and on, he continued to puzzle dimly through the ensuing days. He did not try to see Gerda alone again, but ra.her seemed to avoid her. It was essential that Regina should not suspect any sort of complicity between them. Perhaps that was why he kept away: or perhaps he was envious of his step-sister. But he made opportunities, while the elder woman was occupied with the beauty treatmen:s that took up so much of her time, to slip out and meet the young man.

From a worldly point of view, Val couldn't be considered much of a catch, being employed as secretary by some rich business man who rented a villa here for the season. Not that there was anything against the young fellow; his background was just dull middleclass and respectable. He himself had a lot of personal charm, and that was all he *did* have. He disclosed his circumstances at once and with perfect frankness, saying that he'd be glad for Gerda's sake if her people liked to make her an allowance, but that he would consider himself the luckiest man in the world to get her without a penny. Jeff felt drawn towards him at first; more than once, he became aware of an inexplicable yearning sensation when they were together. But Val was always in a hurry to escape from him and to find Gerda. He had eyes for nobody else. The two of them were quite madly in love. And soon the sight of their moon-struck state became irritating. Jeff began to long for the whole thing to be over and done with — for them both to be out of the way.

He increased the pressure of his campaign to win the mother's consent. His aim was simply to make Regina see the girl as a nuisance wherever she looked; a perpetual reminder of her age, as well as an expense, and a threat to her peace of mind. He never spoke openly, but, by sly hints and cunning insinuations, managed to keep the subject constantly before her. Now, in his impatience, sick of it all, he launched, perhaps prematurely, his one and only direct attack. "A grownup daughter about the place is — let's face it — just a *tiny* bit ageing." Never before had he dared to refer to her age, and he could never do so again; by this single assault he must stand or fall.

Against a background of ominous silence, he hurried on to describe how he'd seen the pair on the beach, speaking as if it had only just happened; explaining that Gerda had kept the affair secret for fear of objections being raised. "It didn't seem to have struck her that you might be glad to get her off your hands," he concluded; and waited, in fear and trembling, throughout a dead pause.

Regina was engaged in an interior struggle of her own. For a man to be in love with someone other than herself was an affront she simply couldn't endure; that the woman should be her daughter, made it still worse. Yet, though the insult was not to be borne, the prospect of getting rid of Gerda for good shone ahead of her like a door opening to sunshine at the end of a dark passage. The obstacle she couldn't get past was her jealousy, blocking the way like a great boulder — at last, with a tremendous effort, she hurled it aside; and at once she was bathed in sunshine. As she turned to tell Jeff this was a stroke of luck she certainly had *not* expected, it would have been hard to say which of the two was the more relieved.

* * *

The marriage took place before the end of the month, just as Jeff had foretold. He'd got what he wanted; at last he was alone with Regina. But he felt a certain foreboding, as he looked at the woman, who seemed to have blossomed suddenly with a new radiance, younger, gayer, more beautiful than ever before. He could do nothing more; there was no one else to get rid of. If his craving for her wasn't satisfied now, it never would be. He told himself that she was really his now —his alone. But really she seemed to be his less than ever.

Gerda had gone off on her honeymoon. And the two elders also started on a new journey, to a place not yet visited in their travels. To Regina, this trip was different from all the others. She felt she was starting an exciting adventure; a new life. Her daughter's marriage had affected her in a way Jeff couldn't have foreseen, very unfavourable to him.

She should never have had a child. As long as she'd been connected with Gerda, something of the darkness and horror of her first marriage and of the birth had remained with her, like a shadow upon her existence, imprisoning her in influences from the past. She had not been aware of this; only now, suddenly, she felt released, as if something dark and oppressive had been lifted from her. Now that Gerda was gone for good, she could start life again, as if there had been no child.

Looking back, she seemed to have been sleep-walking through the years, not fully alive, moving between two massive shapes that were her constant companions; a bodyguard indistinguishable from a pair of jailers. Now she had come to life all of a sudden. She was free and eager to make up for lost time. Coming to this new place, she felt a new woman, and looked round with new eyes at the men; who were already looking at her admiringly. Change, adventure, excitement, were what she wanted; it seemed high time she had a new admirer.

This didn't mean that she had no further use for Jeff, who, during the years of her marriage to his father, had become an integral part of her existence. She still couldn't imagine a life without him; his devotion was still her essential emotional food. At the back of her mind she knew dimly that this would not always be so; that a time would come when she would be ready to discard him. But it hadn't come yet. He was still necessary for the present; in the endless act of self-dramatization he was her vital support; and, as a factotum, indispensable in many ways. She was even attached to him, after her fashion; she felt he knew more about her than she could bear anyone else to know. Out of their long acting-association had grown an odd intuitive understanding, not of the mind but of the blood cells, such as might be expected to exist between identical twins. His massive presence in the background gave her a sense of security. But she didn't want him to emerge from the background, resenting, in her unclear subconsciousness, his jailer's part in the shadow that had darkened her life so long.

She wanted to talk to new people, with whom her dramatic powers would have wider scope. Nothing could have been easier: the hotel was filled with rich people, including a number of unattached men of various ages, some charming, some intelligent, some romantic, all prepared to orient themselves, like so many sensitive needles, towards her magnetic north. Besides her other charms, she radiated an indescribable aura of experience, which, since she looked the same age as her step-son, had a peculiar perverse appeal, attracting every man within range. She amused herself trying out the different candidates, finally choosing one who was especially gallant as her chief companion, though without entirely discouraging the rest.

Jeff was left more and more to himself; instead of attaining the closer intimacy he longed for, he was pushed out on to the periphery of her being. For the first time now, on the fringes of his own consciousness, appeared the horrid possibility that she might ultimately push him out altogether. He was hurt and alarmed; then, growing indignant, retaliated by flirting with the gay young things of the place. Gerda's shining look, and his own mysterious feeling for Val, had unsettled him emotionally, half convincing him that he was missing some valuable experience. So he set about looking for it with various pretty girls, who were quite ready to help in the search. But he found nothing, and got nowhere. His advances led only to frustration and ultimate boredom: he soon left the girls alone. Of course, it was Regina he was thinking about all the time. Fatally and for ever she had bewitched him; spoilt all the girls in the world for him. How could he flirt with some baby-faced blonde, when he was preoccupied the whole time with his Gloriana, so much more wonderful in every way, wondering what she was up to with that gigolo chap, with his histrionic profile and big brown spaniel eyes?

Jeff had never got over his boyhood's dazzled amazement when Regina first broke into his life like a shooting star. His own mother he'd almost forgotten; it seemed like magic to come home from school to this marvellous being, who let him pick out her dress from deliciously scented and rustling cup-boards, and choose from sparkling treasure-cases the jewels to wear with it. He'd loved to prepare her bath, gravely testing the heat of the water, and measuring perfumed essences, serious as a young acolyte. And he still loved to do these things, feeling that he shared in the magic creation of beauty, participating with her in a solemn rite. The ritual re-creation of her own beauty was the one thing Regina took really seri-ously, by far the most important thing in her life. So, though she might be out all day and half the night with her new admirer, stimulated by all the novelty and excitement and admiration, she never failed to return for the evening ritual, in which Jeff played his for-the-moment essential part. It was still an obsession which she could not break.

The young man was gradually turning sullen, resentful, as things got worse and not better for him. Like a charming bird, she darted in and out of the hotel, in and out of his orbit, leaving him profoundly injured by her neglect. It came to the point where he could only be sure of seeing her at this obsessional nightly ritual, when she dressed for dinner. Ten-sion was growing between them from one night to the next. He now scarcely opened his mouth while they were together, carrying out his appointed tasks with scrupulous, meticulous care, never omitting the least detail, but stubbornly silent, glum.

121

Regina seemed to enjoy this tense atmosphere, floating through the evening routine with a half-smiling witchlike look, derisive and rather sinister, as if by deriding him she avenged the shadow-years she had lost. Excitement and admiration had gone to her head a little. She was slightly intoxicated by her own power. She would glance at Jeff, standing stiff with resentment, handing the jewels to her one by one, his big hands holding them with unexpected delicacy, a black thundercloud on his brow. His black eyebrows, drawn together in a constant frown, ruled a thick black line across his forehead. In the mirror, where her beauty flourished and flowered, his scowling face behind her seemed as irrelevant as if it belonged to a bull on the other side of a stout fence; and she glanced at it as carelessly, with the same mocking contempt for his foolish, sulky bad temper; before floating away again, airily unconcerned.

There was no set time for the ritual to begin. Bringing a paper with him, he would sit down, an incongruous heavy shape, in the scented feminine room, stolidly, stubbornly, waiting. He was unaware of time, heavily, sullenly, ruminating, the projecting black eyebrow ridge giving him the look of some primeval man, who darkly ponders his barbaric acts, caught between animal impulse and human pain. Two maids came in to turn down the bed, which they did last thing before going off duty, forcing upon his notice the fact that Regina was much later than usual. She'd never kept him waiting so long before. The girls' concealed smiles and inquisitive glances irritated him: even after they'd gone he could hear their voices and smothered giggles all the way down the corridor; and his expression became still grimmer — he furiously resented being exposed to their ridicule.

It was Regina who had exposed him to it. With this realization, the unwelcome thought his mind had harboured unwillingly ever since the day of the funeral, suddenly burst through to the surface. Regina was to blame for all that had happened, from his father's death to the mockery of these nitwit girls — everything was her fault. At long last his resentment found its true object. But he still sat there, blankly, blackly, brooding, the heavy lowering look on his face making him less handsome, more like some big bad-tempered animal.

The premonitory sensation came that always told him Regina was approaching; a part of the blood-understanding between them, it was never wrong. Normally, he would have begun to prepare her bath. But he didn't budge now, sombrely watching her float into the room, lovely, complacent, moving in an almost visible aura of delightful compliments and events he knew nothing about — she reached the middle of the room before noticing that there was anything wrong.

For days she'd been living as a queen in her imagination, so absorbed in the excitement of her new life that she had hardly given her stepson a thought: he'd been a part of the rite and no more; she'd forgotten him as an individual. Seeing him stand there now, an ominous massive shape, black-browed, hostile, aggressive, she saw how the hard core of his individuality had set against her. Though it was difficult for her to descend from her pedestal to the level of everyday life, she was not yet beyond doing so, if necessary; and the vicious glint in Jeff's eyes under that heavy black brow-line showed her how necessary it was. Instead of the devoted factotum she hardly noticed, she suddenly confronted an antagonistic individual, who could not be ignored.

"I'm sorry to be so late; you shouldn't have waited," she said quickly and as charmingly as she could, trying to charm him back to her. But she saw that he was already far beyond coaxing: things had gone too far. The bull, no longer on the other side of the fence, was facing her in the open field.

She had come closer to him, her well-known perfume enveloped him like a spell. It was impossible for him to be near her without falling under her spell. But he hated it suddenly; hated the arrogance that made her so sure she could charm him; hated the assurance she wore as her natural air. He felt a sudden wild anger — he must shake her assurance. His resentment rose up from all sources, old and new, to demand satisfaction. He said: "I waited to say goodbye." The words were quite unpremeditated, he hadn't known he was going to speak them: but, once uttered, they seemed to voice a decision made long ago.

"Goodbye?" He was glad to see that he had succeeded at least in surprising her.

"Yes, I'm going away. It's been perfectly obvious lately that you've no time for me, so I'm leaving."

Amazing this, from her devoted factotum. She gazed in astonishment at the dark, bewitched, sullen face, turned stubbornly from her. Then, with the devastating sureness he so detested, she said: "But you can't do that."

"Oh — why not?" he asked, cool.

She was staring at him, blankly incredulous; but aware of a faint, distant uneasiness she refused to acknowledge. The situation was incredible, simply. She just didn't believe Jeff could be standing there talking to her with this hostile detachment. Suddenly impatient, she made a sweeping gesture as if sweeping away a child's nonsensical showing-off that had

gone on too long and become boring. "Because you can't —
it's quite impossible — " He smiled faintly, grimly, at the
refusal of her relentless egoism to believe it could be thwarted.
And she, seeing the smile, without stopping to think, replied in
the deflating tone she used to keep her inferiors in their place.
"Don't try to be melodramatic. You know you can't possibly go at this hour of the night. It's out of the question,
so let's hear no more about it."

"But I *am* going."

In spite of herself, Regina was beginning to feel disconcerted by his cool unemotional persistence. Her uneasiness
could no longer be denied. Yet she still didn't really believe
he would go. Though the situation seemed to have got out of
hand, she never doubted her ability, finally, to control it.
Reverting now to her winning manner, she asked reproach-
fully, "But why, Jeff?" intensifying her charm to no purpose,
since he wouldn't look at her. His obstinate closed face, staring away, reminded her of some stubborn bad-tempered beast,
avoiding the human eye.

"I should have thought that was obvious. Why should I
stay here just to be your chauffeur? And, incidentally, to be
the laughing stock of the place . . . " The giggling servant
girls had been in his mind. But now his father's remembered
glances returned to him with awful unanswerable reproach.
"I saw what happened to my father — he gave up his whole
life to you . . . lived to please you . . . and you couldn't even
bother to see him buried — " A sullen inarticulate Hamlet,
he let these words explode with peculiar emphasis in the quiet
room; then, coming back to himself, reverted to his former
expressionless, impersonal tone: "Having been warned what
to expect, I've decided to live *my* life as *I* please."

Regina couldn't believe her ears. Nobody had dared to
stand up to her for years, she had always had her own way
over everything. That Jeff, of all people, should revolt against
her supremacy seemed a blasphemous impertinence: an out-
rage she couldn't fathom. He was like a stranger to her at
this moment. The projecting black ridge of brow made his
face seem both brutal and impenetrable, like a masked face.
The power of her charm did not extend to the owner of such a
face, which seemed set immovably in barbaric antagonism.
For once in her life, she felt helpless, and had nothing to say.

He had silenced her. But he felt no satisfaction — no anything. His anger was dead. The echo of his own voice
sounded unreal in his ears; it surely could not really have been
saying those things to his Gloriana? Her perfume now seemed
to cast a spell over both mind and emotions, so that he could

124

neither think nor feel. As if dazed, he walked past without looking at her, out of her room and into his own; where he collected a few things almost at random, and threw them into a suitcase, which he carried hurriedly through the hotel and out to the car in the garage, taking no notice of anybody. Crouching heavily over the wheel, he drove rapidly, automatically, through the night, his reflexes operating, but his mind blank, less like a man than an extension of the powerful machine he controlled.

Regina was shaken by the incredible interview, and, still more, by the exit in which it terminated. Right up to the time Jeff went out of the door, she had not believed he really meant to go. His departure left her with an unpleasant and most unfamiliar sense of insecurity. She couldn't get rid of the thought that, if he could go off and leave her like that, anything might happen; though she tried to hide it behind other thoughts; telling herself she was glad she'd withstood his attempt to bully her into imploring him to stay. She had showed him that she wasn't going to be intimidated — that he couldn't browbeat her in that outrageous fashion. His conduct had been unpardonable, absolutely. Never, never, would she have believed it of him.

Resentment and pride carried her through the evening; she danced until very late, needing the reassurance of her many admirers. She had to keep making sure that her charm still worked; her unacknowledged superstitious fear being that Jeff's rebellion had somehow weakened its power. On her way to bed in the small hours she looked into his room, which was empty. Yes, he would make a point of staying out all night, hoping to alarm her. Tomorrow, doubtless, he would be back.

She slept badly, troubled by vague apprehensions, and got up towards lunchtime to find him still absent. Her face seemed haggard after the bad night; when she looked in the glass, she fancied her reflexion showed several new signs of age; and there was indisputably a grey hair.

As the day dragged on, she could not keep away from her step-son's room, though each time she surveyed its unnatural neatness, its unchanged emptiness, she grew more worried, restless, uneasy. The chambermaids' story of Jeff waiting for her had started various rumours among the staff; wherever she went in the hotel, she felt pursued by inquisitive glances. To escape them, she went out in the admirer's car; and he too, despite his urbane politeness, seemed to look at her with veiled curiosity — or so she imagined. Not until she had drunk several cocktails with him could she persuade herself that Jeff would have come back when they returned to the hotel for dinner. And even then, not entirely convinced, she tried to prepare herself to be disappointed.

She thought she was equal to facing the emptiness of his room. But, when she found that it really was empty still, her heart failed her, and she at last admitted the possibility that he might not come back at all. Quickly shutting the door on that demoralizing vacancy, she took a few random steps along the passage and stopped in front of a window, staring out as if some fatal message were written in the sunset sky, her hands clenched on the sill, her eyes wide and frightened. It was too soon, was the thought uppermost in her mind. She couldn't manage as yet without her factotum. Who would attend to life's practical details, who would protect her from the dangerous world, if he weren't there?

What a fool she had been not to provide herself with a substitute, when the whole world was full of men longing to replace him. A sudden vision of the race of men as a wolf pack, pressing round her with slavering jaws, made her shrink nervously from all the idea involved; the inevitable fight against sex, the long struggle for dominance. And then came a more obscure and unreasoning dread, approaching, still more deeply hidden within herself, a fear she did not dare to acknowledge, because it magically involved the thing she dreaded more than anything in the world — the loss of her power to charm: which seemed, at this moment, to the obsessional and superstitious elements in her nature, to depend on the ritual; now impossible to perform without her step-son's essential participation. Looking down at her hands, she interlocked the fingers more tightly to stop their trembling.

A less obscure possibility began to agitate her: suppose something had happened? Suppose there had been an accident? She ought to do something . . . tell someone that Jeff was missing . . . the manager . . . the police . . . But the mere thought of such an interview made her shudder. She, who was always so efficient and confident when giving orders to others, now that she had no one to command and must act for herself, felt almost panic-stricken. Other people had always relieved her of the prosaic practical business of life, she had come to think of herself as set apart, on a higher plane, far, far above the heads of the common herd. She'd always had a horror of meeting strangers, except on her own terms, and suitably dramatized, presenting herself as an object of admiration. Suddenly now she felt cornered, exposed; at the mercy of the world of coarse, common people, as if an invisible protective cloak had been torn away. Vulgar reality impinged too sharply upon her; life struck at her too directly, she was wincing beneath its blows. Why, oh why, had she allowed Jeff to go? She'd never meant to drive him to desperation by her neglect. It would have been so easy to give him a little attention. Why hadn't she done it? Willingly now she would have begged him to stay.

She was becoming more and more unnerved as she stood at the window, held there by an aversion to her own room which it had seemed safer not to investigate. But gradually, and against her will, she was being made aware that this reluctance sprang from a dread of confronting there the consequences of the breakdown of the ritual, which all these years had continued uninterrupted. Now she could no longer remain unconscious of her fear that, with the breaking of the ritual, the spell of her power would break, and she be thrown helpless upon the world.

She heard footsteps approaching, and, feeling that she could face no one just then, was forced to face whatever was awaiting her in her room, hurrying along the corridor and quickly shutting herself in.

The first thing she saw as the door closed behind her was Jeff, standing with his hand on the back of a chair, straight in front of her. She could hardly believe her eyes. She had been humbled and frightened by these last humiliating moments, and the shock of coming upon him so unexpectedly left her speechless. Her heart seemed unable to beat. He, too, remained motionless, silent. For some seconds they faced one another like statues across the narrow intervening space.

The young man was exhausted from driving for many hours. The endless ribbon of road, still unrolling behind his eyes, made everything seem slightly unreal. All night he had driven on, like an automaton; till suddenly, in bright morning light, it had dawned on him that he couldn't drive forever; sometime he must stop; face the emptiness of an existence without Regina. Without her he was nothing; there was nothing ahead of him; he seemed to be driving into pure nothingness. Like a sorceress, she had stolen his identity, making him a receptacle for her magic, deprived of which he was an emptiness filled with nothing.

Feeling only that it was impossible to go on, he had turned and driven back, all the miles he had come. He had to be with her, otherwise he didn't exist. In some obscure compartment of mind or sense, he was aware now of her perfidiousness; he knew she might at any time cast him off. Yet her spell was still stronger than he; he had fought it and been conquered, and now he would fight no more.

Seeing her again, through his tiredness and the road's unravelling, she seemed unreal; doubt on her face couldn't be real. It didn't matter; all that mattered was that the magic should be renewed; his weariness slurred over the other discrepancy. The compulsion that had brought him back all this way couldn't wait. She had turned him into a helpless creature, hopelessly in her power: he was her thing — almost a part of her. To his muddled brain, confused by exhaustion, it seemed that she must accept him; that she could no more refuse to accept him than her own arm. With a curious blurred look on his face, almost sightless, senseless, he went close, but without touching her, without speaking. With bowed head, he stood before her, waiting, strangely demanding in his total submission.

She hadn't quite dared to believe that he'd come back in humility to her. But now she knew it was so, and something went through her like an electric flash, instantly consuming all doubts and fears. There would be no need for her to conciliate him: she would not have to plead with him, or concede anything. Instantaneously, she was a queen again in the world of imagination, safely back on her throne. She put out her hand and laid it upon his hair.

And he at once felt her magic starting to flow into him, through the hand, filling his emptiness. He could feel the power that had enslaved his boyhood taking possession of him again, laying hold of him down to the roots of his being. There was no trace of resistance left in him now: his old craving was like a kind of agony, tearing him wide open, letting her magic pour in and fill him to overflowing. Inarticulately he muttered some fragmentary phrases: "Forgive me . . . I didn't . . . don't . . . I must have been mad . . . "

For the woman, this was a moment of pure triumph, the vindication of her fantasy-life. The thoughts and feelings of the last twenty-four hours had already evaporated like a bad dream. She was once more wrapped securely in the cloak of imagination, impermeable to reality. The rebellion put down, she was reinstated, more powerful than ever, supreme ruler and queen. She really felt like a magnanimous queen pardoning a conquered rebel chief, saying rather superbly: "Hush! It's all over now — all forgotten." Looking into the mirror across the room, her reflected face now appeared ageless to her, as if the years could not touch it and she must be immortal.

She let her hand fall. Her step-son caught and held it,

128

gazing into her eyes, fascinated, even in his befogged state, by the calm unyielding dominance looking out at him between her very long, very black lashes — the transcendant power that had always entranced him. Stooping over her hand then, he began to kiss her wrist, her fingers, her palm, her rings, in a kind of rapture, again and again; while above his bent head, she watched her reflection, exalted by her own magic. He did not see the oblique, mysterious look, slightly sinister, that came on her face; a look of sensuality, witchlike, her lustrous eyes brilliant with triumphant power.

Exalted by Jeff's adoration, she felt herself lifted higher than ever before, unapproachable and secure. It did not strike her as at all extravagant that he should be kissing her hand so adoringly, almost worshipping her. This was the only kind of love she wanted, and she accepted it as her right, as a queen. The witchlook of pleasure intensified on her face, as in a peculiar transport, half anguish, half ecstacy, he murmured: "I wish I could die for you . . . " Releasing her hand then, he stood back a little from her, staring at her adoringly, but with the curious blurred look of his extreme tiredness, as if he couldn't quite see her; as if she were an apparition, too bright for his eyes.

Smiling faintly, she was resolving to get rid of him as soon as she found another subject, more fanatically devoted, prepared to dedicate his life to her loyal service; Jeff himself having conveniently provided the pretext for his congé — she could always charge him with being unreliable and likely to leave his post . . .

Now, however, since no unpleasantness could approach or be evoked by the least allusion, she calmly watched the devotee she was already discarding, quite naturally, and as if nothing unusual had happened since yesterday, set about the preliminaries to the evening rite. Through the open door of the bathroom, he could be seen, his methodical movements only slightly slowed and stiffened by his fatigue, removing his jacket, rolling up his shirt sleeves, carefully, gravely, measuring scented essence into the water, and testing its heat with his bare elbow.

6

THE END OF SOMETHING

GERDA thought this night, the last night of the voyage, would never end. And, indeed, the whole trip had seemed outside normal time; day after day hot, monotonous, void; gentle blue heaving emptiness stretching in every direction, from nowhere to nowhere. Never another ship. Only the sequined explosions of flying fish, eternally scattering over the glassy swells. Or an occasional school of porpoises, rising and falling, curvetting effortlessly round the battered old ship, which, ignoring their agile antics, plodded steadily on. Rusty and salt-encrusted, the liner had made the trip countless times before, and seemed to be sleepwalking the invisible waterways it knew by heart. The engines' unvarying thump, day and night, sounded mesmeric.

Drowsing through the tropical hours in a not-unpleasant trance of exhaustion, she felt the liner, too, was entranced, and would never arrive anywhere. There could be no end to the rhythmic throb beating through the deck, through her body, indistinguishable from the pulsing of her own blood. Time and space converged and combined in the endless dissolving trail of the moving ship. Nothing seemed real to her imagination, slightly fevered in equatorial heat, and gripped by this fantasy of non-arrival. Having no friends on board, she could imagine herself a ghost, isolated in the midst of the little ship-world — itself isolated in the enormous blue wastes — moving among the people unseen, soundless, light as a leaf in the wind.

But now the voyage was ending, it was time to wake up. Thinking that she'd already stayed too long in her dream-lethargy, she looked out of the open porthole at the rising sun. And suddenly, under the gliding rays, her face turned white with the shock of realizing that this day, now breaking, was the day when she was to meet Val.

It was a hopeless understatement to say that Gerda was deeply in love with this rather superb young man of much personal charm, who, in the improbable way of a prince in a fairy tale, had transported her from an empty unloved existence to one of magnificent happiness — Val was her life's centre and its whole reason; without him it was worthless. She could imagine nothing more disastrous than separation. The worst possible thing that could have happened was the discovery of her illness, just before he was due to leave for a new post abroad; so that instead of sailing with him, she'd been rushed into a sanatorium, where, at the last minute, he'd barely had time to instal her.

Throughout the journey to that remote institution, she'd felt a growing terror of the speed with which the seconds were flying past, relentlessly bringing nearer their final parting, the amputation-like pain of which was already so violently present in her that, in spite of the rugs wrapped around her, she kept shivering like a sick animal.

It was all she could do to keep back her tears; to reply to Val's attempts at encouragement was quite beyond her. Though she couldn't bear to see his lively good looking face so overshadowed by worry and tiredness—though she blamed herself for failing him just when he needed her help — she was unable to speak the words of hope she knew he was longing to hear. And when, finally, he came to say goodbye to her in the cold cell-like room where she'd been put to bed, begging her to be brave and to get well quickly so that they could be together again, she simply could not respond. At this dreaded moment, utter despair overwhelmed her; incapable of restraining her tears any longer, she turned her face away and buried it in the pillow, really feeling her heart must break. How could she be expected to go on living without the person on whom her whole life depended — who *was* her whole life? Weeping bitterly, desperate and distraught, she didn't even turn her head to look up at the man she adored; but, agonized and absolutely beside herself, only gasped hopelessly: "You can't really love me, or you wouldn't leave me like this — I wish I were dead! I hope I shall die very soon . . ."

Completely shattered then, she allowed the tide of grief to sweep her through the intolerable situation almost unconscious, neither hearing Val's last words, nor aware of the precise instant when she was left alone. As she lay there sobbing, wounded to the quick of her being, exhausted emotionally and physically, her childish mind held only the one terrifying thought that this was the end. She had never had any right, she believed, to enter Val's bright happy world, from which she had now been thrown back to her proper place in darkness and isolation — that was where she belonged. Already an immeasureable distance seemed to separate her from the man she loved; she could not extend her thoughts as far as the other side of that vast expanse, but felt he had gone from her for ever.

During the days immediately after Val's departure, time's whole function seemed to be to torment her with the thought of him travelling further away every moment, towards an unimagineable strangeness, into which she'd let him go without even saying goodbye. Guilt increased the pain of her ever-present consciousness of separation. When she thought how she'd not only denied him the comfort of even a glance, but actually spoken words that must have added to his distress, she saw herself as a monster of selfishness, too engrossed in her own sufferings to consider what Val must have endured. At no time had she ever thought she was worthy of him or of his love; now she seemed to have failed him in every possible way, and began to believe that she only deserved to lose him.

Weeks passed before she slowly emerged from a state of alternating apathy and tearful despair, gradually coming back to life, encouraged by the friendliness of the people around her. The story of the young lovers and their tragic parting had aroused much sympathy. And nobody could help liking Gerda, who, as a result of illness and grief, looked more child-like than ever in the high hospital bed, her pale straight hair falling about her in little-girl disorder, so pale it had almost a green tinge, like the fine limp silk of a young corn-cob. There was something touching in her shy, modest gratitude for any attention. Her simplicity and appreciativeness had a special charm that appealed to everyone, as she began timidly to participate in the life of the place. But she had never learnt how to make friends, and she made no real friends now, becoming, instead, a kind of pet of the whole sanatorium. Staff and patients alike treated her, once she was able to be up and about, as they would have treated a charming child; and she took a child's pleasure in their attentions, enjoying the spoiling she'd been denied at an earlier age. Slight and small-boned, with her soft long colourless hair, and wearing the simple, becoming clothes Val had chosen, she had the delicate grace and the fascination of an enchanting puppet, a beautifully-made doll. But she seemed not to notice any advances that were made towards her; despite her attractiveness, she remained unattached, impervious, seemingly, to the sanatorium's febrile emotional atmosphere, on the edge of which she moved, vague and abstracted, between her room and the dining-hall, and the walks in the grounds. The real part of her consciousness seemed to be somewhere else — with Val, presumably.

Yet, though her health continued to improve steadily, she did not ask to be allowed to leave. Never having known the secure, happy background of an affectionate home, she was quite content here, once she had got over the acute pain of separation. She had learned that happiness was not to be trusted, and now instinctively feared any change, suspecting that it would prove for the worse.

She had implored Val to forget what she'd said in the stress of parting, and he appeared to have done so. From his reassuring letters she gathered that he'd settled down to a life without her, and felt glad she wasn't urgently needed; her inaction was thus excused. He was evidently quite comfortable in the cottage that went with the job. He had an office in the big house near by, and Louis Mombello, his rich employer, often asked him to meals there. In almost every letter Gerda was urged to go through with the cure patiently — on no account to leave until she was pronounced absolutely cured. So she was shocked and astonished when her husband suddenly wrote begging her to come at once; for a visit, if she wasn't well enough to join him permanently. He gave no reason, the letter ending abruptly: "You must come. I need you here. It's urgent."

She was alone in her room. What she'd just read, breaking through her abstraction, threw her into a state of alarm. What could it mean? What could be the matter? Without knowing what she was afraid of, she felt threatened, personally, by some nameless danger; and, feeling she must have support from someone, she went to the Superintendent, to show the letter to him. While he read it, she sat in the chair she'd occupied many times, beside the desk, on which stood photographs of his wife and children. It was early January, and a kind of New Year brightness and barrenness of good resolutions was everywhere visible; a clean sweep had been made of the past, on the uncluttered desk, as in the empty flowerbeds outside. There could be no frightening secrets in this room. Already the girl was calming down. And when, very calmly, the doctor said: "An emotional letter — have you any idea what's behind it?" she shook her head slowly, looking at him with her big violet eyes. She could feel herself going vague and absent again, wondering what all the fuss was about: and she felt like a person who, half asleep, hears an alarm clock supposed to wake him, and determinedly will not hear.

"Well, then" — the Superintendent placed a paternal hand on her shoulder, — "my advice is, take no notice. Your husband probably wrote on the spur of the moment — some temporary upset — very likely, he's forgotten all about it by now. He's been very sensible so far."

Gerda became almost peaceful again, backed up by the father figure. But, though she wanted everything to be as

133

before, she couldn't quite forget the unanswered letter, which seemed to have entered into her somehow. She didn't think about it; but, as she performed the repetitious moves of the day, she carried it always within her, a vague uneasiness, preventing her complete identification with the life of the place and the routine she was following.

In unconscious suspense she waited for her suppressed fears to be confirmed or dissolved. A much longer period than usual elapsed before Val wrote again. But his next letter, when it did come, immediately reassured her: it was the same as all his letters had been, except the last; cheerful, affectionate, optimistic. In a cramped little postscript he told her not to take any notice of what he'd written last time. "— I was a bit under the weather. Of course you mustn't on any account interrupt the cure."

So everything was all right. The relief was so great that she wanted to cry; then, the next second, she was taking dancing steps across the room, like a child. Now she could belong to the sanatorium again, without reservation. Suddenly the disturbing letter seemed like a bad dream. How lucky she hadn't answered it.

For a few days she was gay, flitting about like a little delicate dancing doll, her eyes wide and violet-coloured, and her pale, pale hair floating, thinking no more of the letter than of the man in the moon. She was lapsing into her semi-abstraction again when another letter came, not addressed in Val's handwriting, though the stamp and postmark were the same. It was much too soon for him to have written again; and in any case, he never typed his letters to her — yet she knew no one else in that foreign country. So it must be about him, she told herself, as if trying to wake into consciousness, or perhaps trying not to — suppose he were ill?

She sat on the edge of her bed, trembling, as she extracted the single sheet from the envelope. On it was typed:

"Have you no moral sense? Don't you care what happens to your husband? Or don't you know what's going on? This is to warn you that you'll lose him body and soul unless you come soon."

No more; no signature; nothing.

Gerda turned her head aside, as if she couldn't look at the thing, her expression frightened, but her consciousness dim. The fright was in her nerves, her consciousness remained vague, as if she knew nothing about it at all. Gradually, however, the realization began to come through: someone had sent her an anonymous letter about Val. What it meant, she hadn't the least idea. Reluctantly, she forced herself to read the message again, without being much the wiser; though she understood the meaning of each separate word, together they made no sense. But now its sordid, melodramatic nastiness crashed through her dream-screen, striking her sheltered fragility like a lump of mud. With a queer little stifled cry she fell back on the bed, her thin limbs oddly sprawling, so that she looked like a delicate walking doll, broken by rough children, lying in the midst of her pale silky hair and disordered clothes.

However, she had inherited some of her mother's determination; that frail appearance hid an unlikely will-power. Her love for her husband, which had seemed dormant of late, revived again now in all its strength. As long as he'd seemed content, she'd relaxed in the security of the sanatorium regime, telling herself she must get well for his sake: that he wanted a healthy, live wife; not an idealized marble girl on a tombstone. So she'd justified her non-action. But now, when she felt that he needed her, as soon as she'd recovered a little from the shock of the anonymous letter, striking her like a handful of primordial slime scooped up from the savage hidden under-side of existence, she knew she must go to him. She did not understand what it was all about. How could she, poor little pale innocent, understand anything belonging to that dark fearful under-side of life, to which this was her first introduction? But she knew Val was in danger; which was all she needed to know. She did not waste time trying to think further. Far too much time had already been wasted. To reach Val with all possible speed became, during these few moments, her simple, unshakeable determination.

She went straight to the Superintendent to ask for her discharge; which he was unwilling to grant; the more so since he suspected renewed pressure from Val, and resented having his hand forced by the impatient young man. But she paid no attention to his arguments, not even listening, already gone from the sanatorium in everything but the flesh. The Superintendent felt her soft, everlasting obstinacy, and wondered what had come over the girl, hitherto always so mild and biddable, now looking at him out of wide eyes full of an endless stubborn resolve that made all arguments seem futile.

"All right, then, go!" he exclaimed, giving in with a very bad grace, seeing that she would go anyhow, with or without his consent; angry because she'd challenged his power and made him lose his temper. "But understand that you go at your own risk and against my advice."

Gerda was quite indifferent to his threatening tone. Her one fear was that Val might hear she was coming and try to stop her. She must hurry, hurry. How she managed to arrange everything, she never knew. Shy and inexperienced, she had lived for over a year completely cut off from the world. To organize the long trip unaided was an appalling task. But she was absolutely determined to get to Val, and so it was all arranged somehow.

Only when she was safely on board the liner, listening to the opening beat of its rhythmic pulse, which would continue without pause until it brought her to him, could she relax at last, thankful to let the ship carry her to the point from which her inner consciousness had never deviated for an instant. Only then did she realize how much had been taken out of her by the effort, the magnitude of which no one, not even she herself, would ever appreciate. Her body felt drained and useless; her mind dazed and shut-off. She would sometimes look round the decks in amazement, unable to believe she had really got herself on to the ship — it seemed impossible that she should have done it. Then, to escape the thought of the greater effort before her, she would relapse into her daze of tiredness, not wanting to do anything, or to talk to anybody.

* * *

She had been grateful for this respite, but now it was over. Now she must start struggling again; this time against some alien horror she couldn't even imagine.

As she dressed and packed her night things, she tried to think calmly about meeting Val. But, though the prospect no longer filled her with delirious joy, she still seemed unable to take it in. She told herself: "I'm his wife, and I'm going to be with him. We'll be happy together again as we used to be." But she knew she wasn't free to follow her natural impulse to love and happiness. The other hateful thing cast its shadow on her spontaneous feelings and clouded her face — a face without secrets, and, partly for that reason, singularly defenceless. Now, as she finished dressing, it suddenly became frightened.

The anonymous letter became suddenly horribly and vividly present to her, with all its abominable, mysterious implications, a responsibility too heavy for her to bear. She was so tired still, she knew so little of life, she was unequal to the appalling burden — she would fail Val, just as she'd failed him at the time of their parting. Crushed by the weight of her fears, and by her excessive humility, she sank down on the edge of her berth, under the open porthole.

Sitting there, she gradually grew aware of steps and voices on the deck above; the ship moved in a curious stillness, without sound of waves or wind. Looking out, she saw flat land-locked water. the end of a long grey mole gliding past, and realized that they were already in the harbour. It seemed only a few minutes since sunrise. Now, although she was dressed and ready, she still sat in the airless cabin, hearing the new noises above, but remembering only the swish of water as the sailors hosed down the decks, which would have been the normal sound at this hour.

Afraid to advance into the future, she clung to yesterday's shipboard routine, which, having lasted the voyage, was now dissolving, like a pattern of beads shaken apart for re-grouping. She wanted the voyage to last for ever, as in her fantasy-thinking it had seemed it must do, so that she need not meet the terrifying new factor which had entered her relationship with her husband, and which she feared might prove stronger than her adoring love. She loved him as much as ever, she wanted him only, but suddenly she was afraid he might now want something else.

At the back of all she had endured and achieved, had always been the belief that the happiness they had known together would be restored. But suppose it wasn't? What could she do? — Nothing. She might wear herself out loving him; but she could not force happiness to return. And, without it, or the eventual hope of it, she couldn't go on; she would be finished, the driving-force gone — there would be nothing to go on for.

At this point, with disconcerting abruptness, Gerda awoke to the fact that the ship was no longer moving; the eternal-seeming pulse of the engines had stopped — how could it have happened without her notice? Hurriedly she combed her hair and powdered her face and went up on deck.

The gangway was down already, but there was some delay before passengers could leave the ship. Emerging, she caught sight, between crowding heads, of the inevitable officials coming aboard. Everyone wanted to get close to the rails, to see what was happening; behind the tightly packed mass of people the rest of the deck was deserted, the girl had this space to herself. Nobody took any notice of her. She looked enviously at the excited crowd. She alone felt nervous and lost, bewildered by the noise and confusion, full of apprehension as to the future. Suppose Val didn't come to meet her? A sudden unsteadiness forced her to lean on a pile of chairs for support.

All at once then, with something between terror and ecstacy, she heard Val call her name. She looked up and saw him. Val, whom she'd expected to see, if at all, much later, somewhere on the quayside, was miraculously coming towards her, dressed in a light suit accentuating his deep tan, hatless, the tips of his warm brown hair sun-bleached and

137

glinting, so handsome that, even here and now, at this moment of general preoccupation, several heads turned to follow his progress. To her immense relief, she saw that his face wore its usual gay, lively expression, smiling and easy, with an amused look in the eyes. And now she could no longer see all this remembered yet not-quite-realized charm; all the adorable qualities she seemed never to have appreciated in full until now. She felt his arms round her shoulders, his sun-warmed, faintly rough cheek against hers; together with the sudden wetness of her own tears, which she forgot instantly, trying to say something to bridge the lost year and more she had somehow survived without him.

"You're here . . . " There were no words long enough to stretch over the endless months, or ecstatic enough to describe this re-union. If only he could hold her like this for ever; hold her tighter, tighter, to crush out memory, crush out past and future — if there could be nothing except this rapture that made everything seem worthwhile . . .

Far too soon, his arms loosened and let her go. "Why were you hiding behind all those chairs, darling? I was beginning to think you hadn't come after all . . . " It was his well-known, seldom quite serious voice, humorous and engaging. And yet it was not quite the same, there was a difference, or perhaps merely an accentuation of something not noticeable before — a subtly suggested assurance, that was surely new.

"You're not angry with me for coming . . . ? You don't mind . . . ?" She hardly knew what she was saying, or what she was looking for in his face, searching there hungrily for something she did not find; for some assurance that the year had not changed him. But though she tried to believe it was only the unfamiliar tan and the smart unfamiliar clothes, there did seem to be a difference somewhere, which she couldn't place . . .

"You didn't give me much chance to mind, did you?" Although he seemed to be joking, she felt a cold touch of fear. It was as though, for an instant, she caught sight of another face, sullen, spoiled and aggrieved, behind his splendid bronze handsomeness: as though, for a second, the mask had slipped. Then, the illusion gone, he was looking her up and down from her feet to her hair, falling soft and colourless in the strong sun. "You look younger than ever — about fourteen-and-a-half." He spoke in the teasing voice of unsentimental affection she'd never been able to resist; she didn't try to resist it now, but gave herself up to his charm, deferring all serious thoughts, bothering no more about possible differences.

Yet the faint impression of change haunted the back of her

mind, beyond her wondering admiration, as, obstacles melting out of Val's path, they were first down the gangway, before the other passengers had even begun to disembark. Looking back at the ship, shrunk to the insignificance of a battered toy-boat among giant derricks and cranes, she was aware of watching faces, familiar until a few minutes before, now fading into oblivion. The voyage had vanished already into the limbo of shadowy half-forgotten things, ghostly beside the vivid reality of her husband; in whose bronzed body and faintly bleached hair all the dynamic vital force of sunshine seemed to reside — if before he had been a prince, he'd been promoted now to a demi-god.

How far Val had in fact travelled from their former modest style of living became evident in his casual manner of sliding into the driving seat of a huge car, as if he'd always been used to such powerful, streamlined, vaguely sinister-looking machines. Gerda commented on its splendour as they drove off, sitting almost nervously at his side, watching his expert off-hand skill in handling it with adoring eyes.

"Yes, it's in good shape, even if it is four years old. Louis has three newer models — that's why he gave this one to me."

"Do you mean to say this great thing belongs to you?"

"To *us*." Val took one hand off the wheel to pat hers. "What an angelic infant you are still — I'm glad you haven't grown up."

Leaving the town behind, the car settled into a steady flight along the gentle switchbacks of the deserted road. While the girl leaned against him, relaxing contentedly, as she always did at his touch, which seemed to deprive her of the power to think.

* * *

Though Gerda had paid little attention to the country through which they'd been driving, she had received an impression of endless, parched, rolling hills, piling up behind one another, stark, barren, bone-dry, colourless, under the blazing sun. In spite of the car's cooling device, she'd begun to be oppressed by the heat and glare. It was the greatest relief to come to the cottage which was to be her home; she recognized the garden at once from Val's descriptions: a pleasant place, green and cool and flowery, like an oasis, after those miles of parched earth, not a glimpse of which was now to be seen. Tall eucalyptus trees formed a shady screen, completely encircling the white one-storey house, which seemed secluded and shut-away, enclosed by this plantation of graceful trees, and by inner hedges of hibiscus and oleander.

Forgetting the tiredness that had been threatening her, she jumped out of the car, and stood looking round her, enchanted.

"Heavenly — quite heavenly!" she exclaimed in rapture, not knowing where to look first — at the great vine, wound round the verandah posts and roofing it with thick leaves, or at the neat dark-skinned servants, who wanted to present her with creamy sweet-scented flowers "for luck and happiness."

Too excited to sit down at the table laid ready on the verandah, she insisted on seeing the inside of the house. "It's beautiful," she kept repeating, as Val carelessly flung open one door after another. And the rooms really were beautiful; spacious, pale, sparsely furnished, with lustrous bare polished floors. But, though an excellent background for his warm brown masculine comeliness, they were not the right rooms for Gerda, whose subtle charm needed a softer frame. Against their cool uncompromising austerity she appeared rather forlorn, her fragility and her almost transparent pallor now emphasized by fatigue.

Her face appeared much more luminous and alive when they sat down to lunch on the verandah, on which the strong sunshine filtered through dark green leaves, cast a watery mosaic, shot through with brilliant unstable beams, now and then touching a strand of her hair, or illuminating its highlights of dim gold. The girl could imagine no more idyllic situation. It seemed to her that she should have been perfectly happy. Yet she couldn't stifle a growing uneasiness, an increasing awareness of some change in Val. By the time they were left alone at the end of the meal, she had come to the point of admitting that all was not well between them; a barrier of unknown events separated them by far more than a year's distance. Remembering the lovely simple intimacy of the past, when they had seemed to share one another's thoughts, she wondered rather wistfully whether it would ever be like that again. What was Val thinking about at this moment, as, lighting a cigarette, he gazed idly away from her across the garden with a preoccupied look? Suddenly she felt shut out of his thoughts; he seemed to have left her alone. It was something she'd never felt before; a sensation so unexpected and so disturbing that she found herself staring blankly at him. He had taken off his jacket and slung it over the back of the chair; now for the first time she noticed the beautiful silk shirt he was wearing, which had obviously been made for him, a small monogram embroidered on the pocket, matching the one on his cufflinks, which, like his wristwatch, were new to her, and much more elegant than those he'd been accustomed to wearing.

These observations, undertaken in unconscious hope of distraction, led to a new uneasiness, as she began wondering how he could afford to be so much more expensively turned out than she'd ever seen him, when all this time he'd been paying her sanatorium fees. But then, hurriedly accusing herself of disloyalty, she decided that things must cost far less here than at home; an explanation she, in her innocent unworldliness, could accept the more readily for having already become affected by Val's unspoken suggestion that luxury belonged naturally to his way of life, and was to be taken for granted. Suddenly unable to bear the silence any longer, she asked, "What are you thinking about?" in a hurried, low voice, as if hoping he wouldn't hear. At the same time, she opened her bag nervously, and brought out a powder compact, holding it up like a screen, while she dabbed ineffectively at her face, which, in the greenish light, looked almost ghastly to her, far too thin, and utterly unattractive.

"Why cover your face with that stuff, darling?" Instead of answering her, Val reached out and took the compact from her. "It's a very sweet face just as it is."

She said nothing, but, overcome by inferiority-feeling, shook her head so violently that two locks of hair fell forward across her cheeks, making a screen between them. She half believed he must be laughing at her; a suspicion that strengthened when he did actually laugh, saying: "I like it that way, anyhow."

Another silence fell. Through her hair, she could see him already resuming his private preoccupation, retiring to a mysterious distance again. The sinister matters she'd wished to ignore seemed to have gathered round like a circle of ominous faceless forms: the few hours of happiness she'd hoped to snatch from them had already escaped her — as Val himself had done. Timidly trying to recall him, she murmured: "There's nothing wrong, is there?" Frightened of precipitating some crisis, she let her head fall forward, looking down at her nervously twisting hands.

No crisis was provoked. He said simply: "No, nothing's wrong." He had not looked at her. His pose and expression remained unchanged, fixed and private. If he had spoken the truth he would have said: "Nothing except that you're here." The news of her imminent arrival had come as an unpleasant shock; but, since he couldn't prevent it, his easy-going nature, which disliked hurting people or seeing them unhappy, moved him to make the best of the situation. His first glimpse of her after so long, and of the childish charm he had almost forgotten, had awakened associations of tenderness. Now, however, his affectionate impulse spent, he was beginning to feel bored, and to wonder how soon he could get away.

"Are you sure there's nothing the matter?"

His attention caught at last, he looked at the girl, quite unaware that for her this was a serious moment. "What is it? Haven't I made enough fuss of you?" Smiling, leaning across the table, he put his hand under her chin and tried to raise her head, drooping with all the weight of its hanging hair.

She flushed, refusing to look at him, stammering: "You seem . . . you're so quiet . . . " unable to say: "You haven't kissed me properly yet." She felt a confused sense of unhappy embarrassment, shrinking back in her chair, when he got up and came to her side.

"I say, you're not going all temperamental, are you?" he asked, his hand on her shoulder, simulating alarm. "You won't start imagining some tragedy every time I keep my mouth shut for two seconds, will you?"

It seemed like the same affectionate teasing voice that, in the past, had never failed to entice her back to cheerfulness, out of any bad mood: she wanted to believe it was the same, with the same note of humorous diffidence; the same underlying tenderness. It was quite against her will that she persistently felt it was *not* the same, sensing a difference in its very sameness; the difference between the real and the recorded voice; almost as though he were reproducing it from memory . . .

"I'm sorry . . . I'm afraid I must be a bit tired . . . " she murmured, in bewilderment and distress, still without looking at him.

"My poor angel — of course you must be — I ought to have thought — " He seized upon her excuse with eager relief, suddenly seeing a path clear, where before there had been only obstacles and obscurity. "You lie down and rest while I clear up one or two things at the office — it won't take long. Try and have a nap while I'm gone." Relief revived his affection: he took her hands, and pulled her on to her feet, holding her as he had on the ship, pressed close to him, his cheek against hers.

Immediately, she felt the old magic of his touch coming over her like a spell, sending her brain to sleep. That, at any rate, was unchanged; a spell as powerful as it had ever been. "Now he will kiss me," was her only thought, as the pressure of his strong young body under the thin silk worked its enchantment; her eyelids dropped, helpless against the heavy insistent spell; her lips parted in tranced expectation of the dreamlike ecstasy so long awaited . . . the waiting forgotten now . . . everything forgotten. She began to feel his

142

mouth moving over her skin with an extraordinary soft lightness, touching her cheeks, her forehead, her throat, with the barely perceptible lightness of thistle-down, of those eyelash-flicker-caress children call "butterfly kisses," disembodied almost, hardly a touch at all. It was like being kissed by a ghost. Had he really kissed her, or had she imagined it? Really, she wasn't certain, when he suddenly let her go, and went bounding down the verandah steps, to the car standing under the trees. "Goodbye," he called, sliding behind the wheel, gaily waving his hand. A puff of exhaust fumes, a crunch of gravel, and he was gone.

Astonished, disappointed, Gerda didn't know what to think of this disappearance, and of the inconclusive embrace by which it had been preceded — if it could be called an embrace. By no means an unsatisfactory or half-hearted lover in the past, Val had left her bemused by the spell of his physical presence, she half expected him to come back to finish what he'd left incomplete. In the turmoil of her confused emotions, she stayed motionless for a minute or so, until it became evident that he would not return; when, once more aware of her tiredness, she entered the house to lie down.

Her luggage had already been unpacked, she discovered; the servants had dealt with her few possessions with the utmost neatness and efficiency, but with one preposterous error — they had hung up her dresses, arranged all her belongings, in the spare bedroom. It seemed incredible that they could have made such a fantastic mistake; and made at this particular moment, it aroused her rarely-stimulated indignation. In most uncharacteristic annoyance she rang the bell, determined to have her things moved into Val's room on the spot. But there was no reply: it was the time of the siesta, and the servants had retired to their own separate quarters. After going all through the house, finding no sign of life, the girl recovered her accustomed tolerance. Indeed, the mistake began to seem rather funny. "Who do they think I am, then?" she asked her reflection in Val's mirror, started to giggle at the thought of what an amusing story it would make to tell him when he got back.

Suddenly then, standing beside his bed, about to take off her shoes before lying down, she was overcome by a strange reluctance. Suddenly she felt like an intruder, looking round the impressive room, seeing nothing that was familiar among the attractive costly objects, not one of which belonged to the period of her life with him. Val would have to explain all this luxury — to introduce her to his new possessions, and to the room, before she could feel at ease in it. She couldn't use this bed as her own. But to rest in the spareroom like any casual visitor — that was something she couldn't do either. So she wandered out again to the verandah, where everything seemed to drowse in the afternoon heat. A grassy bank under the trees looked cool and inviting, and, taking a cushion for her head, she stretched herself out there in the shade.

Not quite awake and not quite asleep, she lay dreaming of Val, and of the embrace he had left unfinished. She had always loved his splendid physique, now more splendid than ever, the magic of his absent body was still at work in her nerves. Fascinating, the mould of his torso under the sliding silk . . . the broad, hard chest tapering to the low, narrow waist, fitting down into the socket of the pelvic bones . . . she lovingly traced its shape with her dreaming hands . . .

Footsteps entered her dream; steps that could have only one meaning to her dream-fixation — Val must have returned. For a few seconds after she was awake, she allowed the dream to go on, luxuriating in the anticipation of her love's fulfilment. Then the steps ceased, and she opened her eyes.

Not Val at all, but a thin, very tall man in pale clothes, with pale hair not unlike her own, and a pale, rather good-looking face of no special age, was watching her from a little way off. Gerda sat up hastily, disappointment and the too sudden loss of her dream stimulating for the second time that afternoon her rare aggressive impulse, making her say indignantly: "This is a private garden — Who are you and what do you want?"

The stranger took one step back, towards a gap in the hibiscus hedge through which he appeared to have come, and, after this token withdrawal, stood still, surrounded by scarlet flowers. "I beg your pardon," he said, in a low, oddly plangent voice. "I came to see whether I could do anything— to make sure everything was all right in the house. My name is Louis Mombello."

"Oh-h-h . . . " came Gerda's long-drawn exclamation of embarrassed surprise. Sitting on the grass, she stared up, wide-eyed, at her husband's employer — he was so different from the luxury-soft, middle-aged millionaire she'd expected. It was hard to guess this man's age: he might have been only a few years older than Val; but his exact correctness made him seem older. Lean and long-boned, he had a look of strength and hardness, all his lines smooth, straight and clean; hair, skin and clothes all the same neutral tint, like a figure sculptured in some pale stone. His eyes, unaffected by the strong sunlight, fixed on her in a long, straight stare, reminded her of pale marbles, as, recovering her wits, she apologized for the sharpness with which she'd just spoken.

"I should be apologizing to you," he said. "It was wrong of me to intrude. Please don't think it's a habit of mine — I promise you it shan't occur again."

Still slightly embarrassed, Gerda assured him that it didn't matter; and that the house was everything she could wish. Why didn't he go now? she wondered, seeing him still standing against that background of red flowers, all putting their tongues out at her, she'd just noticed. She asked if he wanted to see Val. But he answered, no; he'd just strolled down to see that she had all she needed. "And I'm glad I came," he added, smiling for the first time. "As I see something *is* needed badly." He had a pale, narrow mouth, which contributed to the general impression of hardness; but neither this, nor the almost predatory whiteness of his even teeth, detracted from the smile's surprising charm.

Gerda saw that, smiling, he was attractive. But she'd barely appreciated this fact before he turned away to give an incomprehensible order to the servant who had just come out on to the verandah. And when he looked back at her afterwards, his face was set in its hard unsmiling mould, as before.

"I'll wait, if you don't mind, to see that they do the job properly. But don't let me disturb your siesta." And off he went, to the other end of the garden, to show that she wasn't expected to entertain him. She could see him pacing about, extremely tall, statuesque, in the sun-speckled shade under the eucalyptus trees; a sun-impervious statue walking between the pink, peeling trunks, that were like pale flesh peeling from too much sun.

Very soon, with a tremendous chattering, a gang of dark workers appeared, carrying metal and canvas parts of what proved to be one of those garden swing-seats; a luxurious affair, with deep cushions and a canopy overhead. Louis, returning to supervise, had it set up not far from where she was sitting, and then sent the men away. "Won't you try it?" he invited, with a courtly gesture, as if offering her a throne.

Unaccustomed to such attentions, Gerda couldn't have been much more impressed if he had. To give him a cup of tea in return seemed the least she could do. To take such thought for her comfort, seemed to show that he must like her, and this gave her confidence. She sat beside him, becoming gradually quite at ease, while he explained in his slow, sonorous voice why she ought not to sit on the ground; telling her about the various dangerous creatures, snakes, spiders, scorpions, and how to distinguish between those that were poisonous and those that were harmless, like the great lizards, which looked so fierce that people were always killing them, though they were not only harmless but actually useful, living on insects that destroyed the crops. She remembered Val telling her he was writing a book on the country and that they made expeditions together into the wilds, and listened with the more interest on that account, concerned with whatever concerned her husband.

As soon as Louis' cup was empty he put it down on the grass and stood up to go, saying: "Please don't move. Let me take away a mental picture of you sitting there. You look charming — like a—" he mentioned some painter unknown to her.

Even Gerda, naive and apt to seem gauche in her inexperience, could hardly be embarrassed by a compliment so impersonally phrased. Nor was she impervious to the charm of the smile lingering on his pale lips, as he stood gazing at her, as though she were indeed a girl in a picture.

Actually, he was cogitating, not quite sure of his next move. His intentions were clear-cut and final: he had decided, some time before ever seeing her, that her presence was undesirable, that she would interfere with the smooth-running mechanism of his existence; she could not be allowed to stay, but must be got rid of as quickly as possible. She herself, however, was an unknown quantity; he had never had dealings with anyone like her. He saw that he must go cautiously, taking care not to frighten her at the start so that she shut her mind and her door against him and made everything more difficult. But he didn't want to waste time either, to risk other influences getting to work.

Much of his life had been lived in this country, saturated with the magic of the old days, of the old religion, which had never quite been stamped out — tribes were said to exist in the almost unexplored regions, practising the ancient rites and offering human sacrifices. To breathe this atmosphere for years and remain unaffected was an impossibility; and Louis, in his search for material for his book, had breathed it in more deeply than most white-skinned people. Almost unconsciously he had absorbed something of the dark mystery with which the air was charged. So now, while he was standing there perfectly still, uncertain how to proceed, he deliberately suspended for this moment his civilized western self, letting the local magic flow in and possess him.

He scarcely admitted what he was doing even to himself. It was a useful technique he practised occasionally; but never openly, in full awareness; always keeping the secret of his temporary nullification as a civilized westerner, which had to precede his identification with the other alien powers, and his drawing upon them. It was as if for a second he turned his back on himself, and knew nothing about it. His educated, civilized mind seemed to wait, in suspense and amazement. Then, immediately, came the strange thrill of the ancient, dark mystery, like a potent injected drug, circulating all through him, uplifting him with a sense of enormous power. He had only to let it take charge of him — of the situation. He felt exalted, and hugely strong, with the strength of all the countless other participants in the rite, dead and alive.

"I do so admire your courage in coming out here," he said to Gerda, as if impulsively. Suddenly, as when he smiled, he seemed younger to her, speaking with this young-seeming, natural-seeming spontaneousness. Surprised, she asked what he meant.

Looking down at her, he said: "You won't be angry?" in the same youthful voice, which he assumed like an actor, together with the appropriate expression of near-diffidence, quite unnatural to him, drawn from an invisible stock of disguises.

Mystified, she shook her head. What could be coming? Her unstable seat moved, revealing him from another angle; she felt a sudden uneasiness, like a premonition. And he, watching her wide, startled, vulnerable eyes, smiled inwardly and with faint contempt—he would soon finish her off—confident in his access of age-old power, sly and subtle. It made him feel almost a little drunk. But outwardly, to Gerda's eyes, he remained Val's wealthy, rather good-looking, very correct, employer, whose thoughtful kindness had provided the luxurious swingseat — absurd to feel nervous of him. Now he spoke again, and though his words seemed to have no connexion with what had gone before, they were guaranteed to overcome her doubts and evoke a friendly response.

"It's made a great difference having your husband with me this last year. I don't mean only because of my work, but as a companion — a friend. Being a rich man is a lonely business. I'd almost begun to believe it was impossible to have money *and* friends—until he proved to me that it wasn't. All those trips we've made together . . . to the forests and the mountains . . that's how you get to know a person. When you're alone with him at the back of beyond, not another soul, perhaps, for miles around. That's when you get to know the real man . . . Talking at night . . . when everything else has vanished into the dark, and there's only the pair of you, isolated in that enormous blackness." The sonorous voice paused, and when it went on the ghost of a smile hovered on the pale mouth. "I'm talking as though you and I were friends, too. I can't help it. And yet, as a rule, I never talk like this to anyone. Perhaps it's because I've heard so much about you that I feel I know you quite well already. I know I can trust you. Otherwise I wouldn't be saying these things." The smiling look disappeared, the voice became grave. "Because it's something one doesn't take chances with — something personal and very precious — the special kind of friendship that can grow between two men alone in this great savage country."

He was not eloquent. The girl was affected, not by his actual words, but by his almost uncanny powers of suggestion, making her feel the drama of the vast, alien land, full of dangers, full of wild beasts and poisonous things, difficult and unrewarding, and yet fascinating, with its own weird attraction of strangeness and mystery. She seemed to feel the bond between the two lonely midgets from far away, pitted against its hugeness, its ancient cunning and cruelty, alone in the hostile dark. And, more personally, she was flattered by the speaker's confidential manner, agreeably elevated in her self-esteem by his friendliness, with which she unconsciously compensated for her disappointment with Val.

Louis was watching her all the time, as he put the curious power of his voice over her, as though she were a kitten he stroked incorporeally with his flattering voice. He waited until he was quite sure she'd forgotten her moment's uneasiness. Then, when the unsuspecting kitten was contentedly purring, he administered a slight slap. "It explains why he showed me the letter."

"What letter?" she asked, not understanding, but with fright in her voice, thinking, for a bewildered instant, of the anonymous horror.

"The letter the doctor wrote when you left the sanatorium."

Hearing this, she was relieved: relief changing immediately to resentment because Val had said nothing to her about any letter from the Superintendent; resentment transferring itself to her companion — why on earth should he show it to Louis Mombello? She stared at the man, indignant, astounded, without a word.

Pleased with the reaction he had induced, Louis again felt the thrill, intoxicating almost, of the power in him. A triumphant quiver went through all his nerves: but he let his head fall forward as if sorrowfully, murmuring: "You *are* angry—I've offended you . . . " His voice sounded really hurt. Careful, now don't overdo it, he warned, hearing his voice make use of a simple phrase she herself might have uttered: "Now you'll hate me and send me away" — incompatible, indeed, with his sophistication.

However, he saw, glancing through his lashes, that she'd swallowed it all right, without getting suspicious. It was close enough, in fact, to her real feelings to soften the kind-hearted girl; seeing him apparently so upset, she was mollified. It seemed rather unfair to blame him. "No," she said, sighing: "I was just surprised;" and, distrust being utterly foreign to her nature, went on: "I don't know what was in the letter, or why he showed it to you; but it seems a queer thing for him to have done." Her big, grey-violet eyes looked straight at him, undefended, wide-open windows through which to strike at her heart.

He looked into them, and then quickly away, muttering as if to himself, "You're good and beautiful . . . " as if he were really moved. Perhaps he even *was* moved, transiently, by that look, childlike, or rather, unfinished, upon her face, due to the scarcity of love in her short life — a scarcity he meant to perpetuate, at least where Val was concerned. But the other dark force so possessed him that there might have been no such thing as pathos or innocence. The vast invisible hord of brother-participants pressed upon him, urging him towards the completion of the rite. There was no time to feel touched. .

"I wish I could make you understand how close to each other people can be in those lonely places," he said: "closer than brothers — they seem to think with one mind and feel with one heart." All this time he'd kept a distance from her. But now he suddenly came up and grasped the chains by which the swing was suspended, looking down closely into her face. "What your husband did wasn't in any way disloyal . . . or indelicate . . . you don't think that, surely?"

"Oh, I don't know what to think!" she exclaimed, suddenly fretful and plaintive, with a thread of impatience running through the words. She didn't like the way he was standing over her, feeling herself imprisoned between his arms. She turned her head away, twisting away from him. His proximity seemed overpowering, though all he did was to look down at her gently, with an air of solicitude. But she felt something else, something hidden. Though she wasn't certain, she seemed to have caught sight of something relentless and frightening in his curious pale eyes, which he'd concealed immediately by the gentleness. She searched his face now, making only trivial discoveries at such close quarters — a certain coarseness in the thick pale skin over the cheekbones, enlarged pores that might almost have been scars of long-ago smallpox; an inconspicuous wart near the edge of the rope-coloured hair; a fastidious masculine odour of expensive soap, cigarettes, perfumed Cologne. Her eyes, lowered now, came in line with his chest. A button of his jacket was undone, and in his present position, bent forward with extended arms, the fronts gaped open so that she saw the silk shirt underneath with its mono-

149

grammed pocket. "It's exactly like Val's," she thought, with unaccountable dismay; the initials of course different, but with the same embroidered design. Without trying to think why this should perturb her, and bring the anonymous letter vividly to her mind, feeling only that she must escape, she threw her weight back, meaning to swing the seat away from Louis. But she was unable to move it as long as he gripped the chains. Suddenly she felt helpless, as in a nightmare when the paralysed body can't stir. Suddenly he had taken control of the situation, and of her movements. His expression remained gentle and kind; but he seemed to radiate a hard confidence and assurance that undid the benevolent look. His eyes shone bright and elated, reflecting the bright day, so that they appeared to shine with a hard white light. Why didn't Val come to rescue her He must have been gone for hours . . . Abruptly, her resentment broke out in words: "I still don't see why he showed you the letter." The imperviousness of the man! was what she was really thinking. How could he not realize that she hated him standing so near?

"Well, you see, he was afraid," Louis answered patiently, as if unaware of any tension. "He wanted to be reassured." The calm, quiet voice spoke indulgently, as if to a child; and also it had the sound of a grown-up's superior knowledge and sureness that got on her nerves; suddenly she could bear no more.

"Afraid of *what?*" she cried, exasperated, on a faint rising note of hysteria, faintly shrill, throwing herself back again on the cushions with all her weight — this time, startled, he let go of the chains; the seat flew up in the air madly, and then hurtled down, out of control, swinging her up and down, to the accompaniment of a thin, mad squeaking; through which, remorselessly, came the pursuing voice. Nothing, she frantically thought, nothing would ever stop it.

"Afraid of you . . . of himself . . . of his love . . . of not being strong enough to resist temptation. Knowing your courage; knowing that you wouldn't hesitate to risk your health, your life even — he was afraid that, in a moment of weakness, he might accept your too-wonderful, too-generous offering . . . Even though the doctor had told him it would be dangerous for him to make love to you . . . "

An agonized flush spread slowly over Gerda's face as the meaning of what he had said dawned upon her. The swing was gradually slowing down; but she stayed in the prostrate position into which she'd been flung by its first violent plunging, speechless, absolutely dumbfounded. She looked small suddenly, like a child that had been hurt and left lying there, a pathetic bundle of clothes, as she gazed up at Louis as if

150

she hardly knew who he was, incapable of any more feeling.

And he, having achieved his object for the moment, wasted no more time or energy, but prepared to depart. She made an effort then, seeing him about to go: she sat up and said good-bye, and vaguely pushed back her hair. The flush had faded, and left her face very white, vague and strained.

For several minutes after her visitor had left, she remained where she was, shocked and stunned by the intimate revelation, that had come not from Val himself, but from this stranger she'd never seen before in her life. The whole thing was too extraordinary; it made her feel dazed, absolutely blank — beyond words. And also, as a result of the violent swinging, or the emotion, or both, she had begun to feel slightly sick: she wanted to get away from the swing to something more solid.

So presently she wandered vaguely into the house, cool and deserted beneath its awnings. The rooms looked bare, uninhabited to her, as if no one had ever lived there, or ever would. "So it wasn't a mistake, after all," she thought, opening the door of the one which was to be hers, looking round at her neatly arranged belongings; what a mercy she hadn't asked the servants to move them . . .

Shame swept over her in a sudden unreasoning wave, merging with a feeling of extreme desolation, such as she hadn't felt since her childhood, and had never expected to feel again. She let herself fall on the bed, and did not move, when a few minutes later, she heard the noise of a car, followed by Val's voice calling her. She neither answered nor moved when he opened the door, closing it with elaborate quiet, tiptoeing away.

She was left to herself now. She hadn't realized how tired she was; too tired to think any more. Half asleep, she wished she could stay for ever in this quiet room; safe from problems too difficult, responsibility too heavy for her; sleeping or half-sleeping her life away.

*   *   *

Long afterwards, as it seemed, Val re-appeared, saying in a tone of reproach that it was near dinner time. For the first time in her life, Gerda didn't want to look at him; he had wounded her too deeply by discussing the most intimate aspect of their love with an outsider — a thing she could never have done. And now his presence embarrassed her; too vigorous, its physical quality was too intense, reminding her too painfully of what was henceforth forbidden. She did not differentiate between love and passion, for her love was total — to cut off any part was to mutilate the whole. Instead of a splendid thing, proudly proclaimed, her love had been turned into a crippled secret, shameful, to be kept hidden.

Resenting her silence, Val stood frowning down at her. Months ago, when his relations with Louis first began to develop on unconventional lines, he'd sent for his wife in a panic, needing the protection her presence would give him. His attitude soon changed, the many advantages of his new relationship with his employer quickly outweighing his original faint aversion, so that, in fact, her failure to respond suited him very well. But he could not forgive her not answering his letter. Even though he now looked upon her arrival as a terrible bore, the old grievance remained, and her present unresponsiveness brought it to the surafce. Thinking of all the amusing things he might have done, had he not given up the evening to her, like a spoiled boy, he felt inclined to jump in the car and drive off and leave her. It was only what she deserved for taking no notice when he begged her to come, and then turning up when he *didn't* want her.

But once again his basic good-nature got the upper hand. He began to exert himself to coax her back to happiness; and of course he succeeded. Never, never, would she be able to withstand his charm. All the evening he was gay and amusing. It was almost like the old honeymoon days. But not quite. Those days had vanished beyond recall; she sensed the evanescent quality of his mood, even while she surrendered to it. When, quite early, she said that she wanted to go to bed, he didn't try to dissuade her, but, determined to make a success of things to the last, escorted her to her room, leaving the door open behind him, a way of escape.

"You'll be all right here — quite comfortable, I mean?"

It was the formula of politeness he'd have used with any guest. But what perverse demon, he wondered, after all the trouble he'd taken to get Gerda into a good mood, had made him speak the words now, endangering his whole evening's work. The topic of their separate rooms was the very last thing he should have brought up at the moment, as he well knew, attempting the hopeless task of diverting her thoughts; asking if she'd like something to read or drink, another pillow or blanket — questions which remained unanswered, because she simply could not speak.

The silence seemed to her to be loud with all the things that had not been said. She was painfully conscious that she herself had said nothing about the anonymous letter, or why she'd come now instead of when he'd sent for her. But it seemed too late to speak of these things, which should have been discussed earlier, when they first met on the ship, or at latest, on the way here. Besides, now that she thought about it, she realized that she was incapable of explaining why she'd ignored his letter. It really was incomprehensible to her that when he'd written "I need you," she should not have replied. Ashamed, almost frightened of her own inexplicable conduct, she hurriedly turned her attention from it to her grievances — like a dark flood, they instantly swamped her mind, leaving no room for anything else. How could Val show the Superintendent's letter about her to Louis Mombello? And, far worse, how could he exile her to this room, without telling her, even? She couldn't understand how he could go on as if nothing had happened. Coolly he banished her from his bed, and seemed to think no explanation was needed — he passed over the fact as though it were too trifling to mention. Her eyes hot and heavy with tears, she whispered, "What have I done to make you so cruel?" and then stood silently clutching the wound in her breast. For the moment, the pain of it obliterated everything else: she'd quite forgotten the anonymous letter and her own unaccountable silence. Genuinely unaware of anything blameworthy in her own conduct, she faced him with the deeply hurt, bewildered reproachfulness of a child which has received an undeserved blow.

Val had been glancing uneasily about the room, looking anywhere except at her. But now he was forced to turn to her, as she gazed at him fixedly, all her terribly-wounded love in her eyes; so that he received the full charge of her humble, adoring look, full of submissiveness, and yet possessive, as if asserting over him the power of the love he had ceased to return long ago.

Their love affair was to him such a thing of the past, that his first reaction was one of astonishment, seeing her watching him with that agonized, wistful reproach, as though he were still implicated. What had her emotions to do with him? She surely couldn't imagine that there was still anything between them? Incredulously, he saw, from her exposed intimate look, that she did; and at once he became resentful. The light of passionate love shining out of her face rather shocked him; no longer in the least attractive to him, it now actually repelled him slightly. He told himself indignantly that she had no right to look at him like that after the way she'd let him down; it was all her own fault that she'd lost his affection. To ignore his letter was as good as telling him she didn't care a damn for him any longer. He felt perfectly justified in his attitude, her anguished expression only increased his sense of grievance. He'd devoted the whole evening to amusing the girl, and here she was, starting a scene, defrauding him of the peace he had earned by his labours.

"I don't know what you mean," he said coldly, his heart hardened against her. "You must have realized that we couldn't share the same room."

"Why not? We always used to . . . " Her timid voice, starting on a note of simple surprise, faltered into embarrassed silence.

Glancing at her, he saw with distaste the delicate rose pink suffusing her face — in spite of it, she kept her eyes upon him, still importuning him with that awful humility and possessiveness, based on misunderstanding, that he couldn't bear. Why couldn't she see that he didn't want her devotion? — that it meant nothing to him? Recoiling from the naked love shining out of her face, he went to the window and started to play with the catch, keeping his eyes upon it while he was speaking.

"Because of your illness. I should have thought that was obvious." His mouth screwed up in a curious way, as if the words had a lemon-sourness. The whole situation was frightfully distasteful to him. He hated any sort of scene; hated to hurt anyone. He deeply resented being forced to put into words things which should have been tacitly understood. Yet, seeing how Gerda still lived in the past, living on a love that only existed in her imagination, he couldn't help being a little sorry for her. But he reminded himself that she was to blame for what had happened, and again thought what a confounded nuisance her presence was. He *must* make her see that he had no use for her adoring love. How his friends would laugh if they found out that he was the object of a sort of schoolgirl crush. Gerda's simple passion for him, which had once been his strength and pride, was an embarrassment in his new life; it seemed to make him more than a trifle ridiculous. If he wasn't careful, he would become the laughing stock of the worldly set in which he now moved.

The girl said no more. And he, now that he was no longer looking at her, out of range of those great shining eyes, gradually reverted to his usual optimism, beginning to view the position in a more hopeful light. Although having her here was a nuisance, it was not altogether a bad thing. It would automatically put a stop to certain rumours that had been going round. And doubtless there would be other ways of using the situation to his advantage. In her little-girl way, Gerda was rather charming, utterly unlike his smart women friends; her very difference could be rewarding, if properly handled. With her simplicity and her childish grace and her almost white hair, she could be quite a social sensation — he would turn her into an asset instead of a liability. But first, before anything else, he must straighten out the subject of their personal relations.

154

Turning to her, he now said much more cheerfully: "There's another point — Louis often works very late — we carry on till three and four in the morning when he's in the mood. Sometimes I sleep up there at the big house — on the office divan. Or I may walk back through the gardens. So you see, if we didn't have separate rooms you'd never get any rest."

"When do *you* rest?" she asked softly, without changing the focus of her steady defenceless eyes, which again started to unsettle him, so that he went back to his fiddling with the window. "Oh, I can sleep anywhere, any time," he said airily. "If I miss a night, I just sleep the next day."

For a while she was silent, digesting this and its implications. "It doesn't look as if I shall see much of you, then," she finally brought out, rather uncertainly.

"No, I'm afraid you won't," he said, cheerful as before. He felt a bit of a brute, hearing the little sound that escaped her, the murmur of an unhappy child. But he didn't want to go through this again; he was determined to impress upon her, once and for all, that he intended to live his life without interference — that he was no longer the insignificant youngster who had been at her beck and call. Besides, he told himself, it was the kindest way. One sharp tear and the break was made — it would all be over: far better than the long-drawn-out agony of breaking it gently. After giving his words time to sink in, he added: "I'd have explained all this before you came if you'd given me half a chance. You did rather take the law into your own hands, didn't you, darling" ending on a note of half-playful reproach, accusing and forgiving her in one breath.

She did not speak: but he suddenly had the impression that she was about to ask why he'd once felt so differently about her presence here. Although he condemned her for leaving his letter unanswered, he had no wish to discuss it, and, to distract her, said quickly: "I'll make time to be with you somehow — don't worry." Simultaneously, he came up and put his hands on her shoulders, attempting to draw her to him. But she shrank away, all the light in her face extinguished, her big eyes darkly shadowed.

Her small, white, helpless face, the face of a very young girl caught in an adult predicament, revived his feeling of mild sympathy. Having clarified the position, he felt a desire to pet her and make her happy again; instead of shrinking this time, she nestled against him, while he stroked her hair as he might have stroked a small, soft-furred animal. She really was rather a sweet child. He didn't want her to get hurt. If only she would accept his new life, without asking questions, there was no real reason why they should not live together quite happily.

155

Optimistically, he began to picture her as he wished her to be, gay, independent, popular, an envied possession and a shield from malicious gossip. In two seconds, he'd convinced himself that he'd solved the problem of their relationship in a way advantageous to both of them; that he was offering her a life any girl would jump at.

"The first thing is for you to learn to drive," he said, beginning to think aloud in his enthusiasm. "Then it won't matter if I have to go away occasionally. I'll arrange for the car always to be here so that you can take it whenever you like — I can use one of the others."

Gerda had gone very still, she hardly seemed to breathe, as though hoping that, if she kept absolutely quiet, he might forget to release her, and let her remain for ever resting against his heart. She tried not to listen to what he was saying. With all her will, she tried to be conscious of nothing but his magical nearness, the soft touch of his hand on her hair. There no longer seemed to be any understanding between them, so his bodily presence became all the more indispensable — nothing was quite unbearable as long as she could feel him pressed closely to her. But now, suddenly hearing him say something about buying her some new clothes, she felt cheapened; the whole situation seemed to become cheap and shoddy, as though, in compensation for her broken heart, he offered her a new dress. But, though she realized that the repetitive movement of his hand on her head was quite automatic, she still couldn't bear him to let her go. In an agony of helplessness, she felt the tears she couldn't keep back overflowing her eyes, not daring to move to wipe them away.

The curious sensation of warm wetness on his chest arrested Val's flow of ideas. He looked down; seeing only the colourless sleek curve of the head he'd been stroking, the slight girl's body resting against his, as if spellbound. How could she cry without moving or making a sound? But he couldn't doubt the reality of her tears, for which he felt no compassion, his mild affection having again given place to a sudden resentment. On the point of saying how ungrateful she was to involve him in a tearful scene at the very moment when he was planning her future happiness, he suddenly thought better of it, and pretended not to have noticed that she was crying. "Time little girls were in bed," he told her, with a very poor imitation of his former amiability, terribly afraid she would clutch him, cling to him, hold him back by force; his one aim being to get away before she could embroil him in her emotion. He turned round, and, taking care not to look at her, hurried out of the room in long strides, closing the door with a sense of deliverance.

He need not have been so anxious. Gerda had neither the will nor the strength to create the scene he so much feared. Watching him hurry away from her, pretending to be unaware of her tears, she didn't even want to detain him: to keep him there against his will would have been far too painful.

"So it's all over — he doesn't care about me at all any more," she thought, passively accepting as inevitable the doom that seemed to have been hanging over her for a long time. The idea of putting up a fight never entered her head. There seemed to be nothing she could do to change or even influence the course of events. Long ago, in the sanatorium, she'd anticipated this hopeless situation, knowing that to lose Val was only what she deserved. In her overwhelming sense of guilt, she somehow seemed to lose sight of the fact that she'd offered him no explanation of her behaviour; and this perhaps increased the confused distress that, long after she was in bed, kept her repeating: "I'm horrible . . . wicked . . . How he must hate me . . . " while the pillow gradually became soaked by her tears. A long time passed before, like a child too severely punished, she eventually sobbed herself to sleep in her lonely room.

How different was this reality from her dream of reunion: in the dreams that came to her now, she was always searching for Val, or following far behind, never able to come near him. And, like a connecting thread through them all, ran her sense of guilty unworthiness, leading her towards some unimagined catastrophe, as to a foregone conclusion.

*   *   *

By the time Gerda was dressed the next morning, Val had already left the house. That he should vanish like this on her first day, without leaving any message, reinforced the conclusion that had become fixed during the night: he didn't want her — wished she hadn't come. She was only a burden to him, and must go away again as soon as possible. To leave him his freedom would be her last act of love.

But first she must tell him about the anonymous letter, which, like a guilty secret, weighed on her bewildered mind, and seemed to incriminate her more deeply the longer she kept it to herself. Yet, because anything in the world seemed preferable to losing Val altogether, her eagerness to get rid of this burden was almost outweighed by her dread of having no further excuse to stay here.

She went through the day in a sort of trance of restless misery, waiting for the sound of the car, wondering when her husband usually returned, but not liking to ask the servants, whose curious dark inexpressive eyes followed her aimless comings and goings. For some reason she seemed unable to settle down anywhere in the little house. The bare gleaming floors reminded her of wet un-marked sand, just revealed by the tide, where no foot had trodden, and where her own feet were too light to leave any imprint. She could not have explained why this should seem so sad, incapable of formulating the idea that, here, as in the world at large, she was lost and unwanted, wandering in a place where the final order of things had been fixed by strangers, without reference to her wishes or well-being. Regressing in her unhappiness to the childhood she'd scarcely outgrown, she felt helplessly that life was, and always had been, beyond her control, and she merely its passive victim.

She left the house in which she could not feel at home, and went out into the garden. But here, instead of the idyllic scene that had so delighted her yesterday, she saw only a place from which she would soon be gone. Despair overcame her: how would she ever find courage to live alone? Although she had resigned herself to the total wreck of her marriage, she could not yet contemplate it in such concrete terms as parting and starting a new life by herself; rather than do so, her thoughts returned to the sinister letter — what would be the best way to introduce the subject to Val?

As it happened, she had no chance to speak about it that evening. The sudden chill of the short twilight had already driven her indoors, when she heard the soft crunch of tyres on the gravel outside; the sound for which she'd been listening all day long. Now that she heard it, her heart beat rapidly with apprehension; remembering how they had parted the night before, she stood silent and motionless, paralysed by uncertainty and the fear of rebuff.

Her humble diffident look, implying that to be left alone all day without a word was only what she deserved, caused the man some compunction, and also a vague annoyance — feelings he concealed behind a brisk cheerful manner, reminding her that they were to dine at the big house. What was she going to wear? They would have to start getting ready at once. In a friendly fashion, he came to examine the contents of her wardrobe and picked out a dress for her, before going off to change his own clothes. As last night, there was again the feeling of a temporary respite; of something pleasant but not quite real — to which Gerda surrendered the more easily because she didn't feel very real herself.

Her impressions of the grand house to which she was taken were hazy and feverish. She had a queer feeling of being without weight, small and flimsy, as though she were a moth that had fluttered in from the dark, attracted by all the lights, amazed at finding herself in the midst of so much splendour. It all seemed dreamlike, as if translated into another and larger dimension; the long lofty room, with its gallery and huge pieces of furniture, tremendous pictures, and great urnlike ornaments filled with tall-stemmed flowers; the acres of polished floor that divided them from what she saw as a crowd of magnificent, chattering people. The women were so resplendent that they made her feel she was in her nightgown; Val having decided that she should wear her wedding dress, which was white and perfectly plain. Walking beside him, feeling exactly as if she were dreaming, she was thankful for his protecting presence, without which she would have been frightened. Now, as they came near the group, the talk faded out, she glanced at him nervously, startled and surprised by this unexpected hush: and was surprised even more, made to feel still more dreamlike, by the beaming smile of approval that she received.

Val had, just then, had a moment of genuine fondness for her, gratified by the way she was impressing his fashionable friends, thanks to his simple trick of accentuating the difference between her and themselves. She seemed to be playing up to him just as he'd hoped she would, looking at him at just the right moment, and with exactly the right mixture of diffidence and devotion to win over the women, and to prevent them from regarding her as a potential rival. He answered with a complacent smile the question, "Why didn't you tell us you'd married an angel?" from his hostess, an imposing white-faced woman with a deep red vampire's mouth, who, having subjected Gerda to a prolonged stare all the while she was approaching, now began to lead her round, introducing her to the other guests.

In that plain white dress, with her long straight softly-shimmering hair, the girl really did look rather like an angel from a medieval painting. But the early years of disparagement and neglect had done their work thoroughly; her hair would never be anything but rats' tails to her; her legs matchsticks; her complexion washed-out. So, though she was vaguely pleased and flattered by the attention of these exotic looking people, she continued to feel as if it were all a hallucination; only a little less intimated by them, only slightly relaxed.

It was Val's unexpectedly affectionate look that, more than the compliments or the champagne, made her enormous eyes gleam softly bright, in spite of the way her head was now aching. She was grateful to Louis Mombello, at whose side she'd been placed, for telling the servants not to offer her any more dishes at the endless dinner, when she'd convinced him of her inability to swallow another mouthful. Altogether Louis was so kind, showing a special sort of concern for her, that she had to revise the unfavourable opinion with which she'd been left at the end of their previous meeting. It even occurred to her that he might have wanted to spare her the shock of hearing such cruel words from Val's lips, taking upon himself the burden of uttering them, so that he, rather than Val, should be the sufferer from her inevitable reaction.

A film was to be shown after dinner, and Gerda was thankful for the prospect of being allowed to sit quietly in the dark, with no further obligation to talk or try to look pretty. Already the temporary and unaccustomed stimulus of the alcohol was wearing off; her headache consequently was worse than ever. But it didn't prevent her thoughts from dwelling fondly, as they'd been doing throughout the interminable meal, on Val's warm glance; which — with the terrible determination of unrequited love, feeding upon the substance of every shadow — was all the encouragement she required for the building up of nebulous hopes. Now she looked round for him, wondering whether he would come to sit beside her in the great hall. But he'd already taken a chair next to a girl in red, into whose radiant face he was smiling, just as he'd been used to smile into her own, without ever glancing in her direction — he might have forgotten that she was there.

The foolish hope, built on such negligible foundations, which had been buoying her up all the evening, collapsed suddenly, and, deprived of its illusory support, she felt lost; what was she doing here among these sophisticated rich people? The men's tanned faces, the faces of the women, bright with cosmetics, all suddenly appeared similar, as though wearing identical masks; hard, smiling, decorative, devoid of feeling. Not one of them seemed capable of expressing affection or pity or any of the softer emotions. They frightened her, these gay, hard, animated, worldly masks; she would always be a stranger among them, lost, ill-at-ease, out of place.

Pressing her hands to her aching head, seized by a sudden longing to escape, she looked instinctively, from force of old habit, towards Val, before remembering that she must not now expect help from him. For a second she couldn't see him, he seemed to have vanished. And then, with a nightmare sensation, she realized that he, too, had a mask instead of a face; brown, handsome, indistinguishable from all the other masculine face-masks. Perfectly at home here, as if he'd never known any other environment, he'd turned into a perfect stranger to her, just like the rest.

In sudden horror she turned away, blinded by dizziness, uncertain whether the darkness was in her head or in the room, where the mechanized voices boomed so horribly.

"Come outside a minute." A softer, closer voice spoke; she felt the support of an arm. Miraculously then, she was out in the cool, dark garden, scents of flowers and of foreign earth all about her, stars clustering between black masses of foliage overhead. In childish wonder her fingers explored the stone seat on which she was sitting, feeling it still faintly warm from the sun which had set hours ago — this seemed magical to her. Just for a moment she seemed to catch a glimpse of the great, mysterious, dark country all round, of which she had seen so little; and then, like a wall, her predicament closed it out. Slowly she lifted her eyes to the tall figure beside her. She had known all the time it was Louis Mombello; yet somehow she seemed only now to recognise him.

"What happened?" she asked nervously, peering at his indistinct face. Though it was becoming fainter each second, the memory of the rows of masks still made her shudder.

"Nothing," he calmly answered. "Nothing happened. Nobody even noticed." It was true that their unobtrusive exit through the long windows had aroused no interest, drawn no eyes from the screen, with the exception of one pair, which Louis had attracted deliberately, making sure Val had noticed what was going on. "I saw you weren't feeling well — it was hot in there with all the curtains drawn, and you aren't used to it." His calm, monumental shape towering above her, again made the girl feel small and weightless, an insignificant, fluttering thing, beside him. Partly reassured now, knowing how foolish it was, she still couldn't quite forget those frightening masks. She might have been eight years old, asking quickly:

"I needn't go back in there, need I?"

"No, of course not." She saw the brief white gleam of his smile. "I'll run you home in my car. Or, if you feel up to it, we might stroll down through the garden — there's a short cut, it's no distance at all."

She stood up hurriedly, saying he mustn't bother about her; she'd find her own way — she wouldn't dream of taking him away from his guests. Waving her apologetic protests aside, he quietly took her arm and began to guide her through the cool darkness. "You'd get lost alone. And anyway it only takes a few minutes." Placidly, as though the situation were perfectly natural, he talked to her about the various trees and plants they were passing. It was too dark to see very much, walking down the gentle slope, between terraces

161

of massed flowers, from which, as they passed, varied sweet-
nesses floated towards them, like ghosts inhabiting this dim
black and grey night-time world.

"Do you want to go straight in?" Louis asked, when they
reached the dividing hedge, the boundary of the cottage
garden. If she wasn't too tired, he would like to show her
a cool quiet place where she could sit sometimes. "It's close
to you, and quite private. No one ever goes there."

Although Gerda would have preferred not to go with him,
she found it impossible to resist his queer clanging voice, so
strangely persuasive, that seemed to sound somewhere within
her head. The soft, penetrating insistence of it made her move
with him through the darkness, as if she had no will of her
own.

All she could see was the black bulk of dense foliage like
the outline of a mountain range, and below, the dark glint
of water. Long drooping branches swayed, light as feathers,
brushing her hair as they strolled beneath. There was a cool,
leafy smell, and the smell of water on which the sun never
falls.

Louis paused. Standing beside him, she saw water at their
feet. "It's always cool under the willows," he said. "And
there's a little boat. I put it there for my wife — years ago,
when we were first married, to remind her of home. But
somehow it wasn't a success. She never cared for the place,
I don't know why. Too far from the house, perhaps. Anyway, she never comes near it now. It must be years since
she was here last. But I've always kept the boat painted
and watertight. Will you sit in it sometimes? I'd like to
think it gave pleasure to somebody."

Gerda consented at once. She had forgotten her unwilling-
ness of a minute ago, listening to these confidences with a
feeling of fascination. Once again he had put over her the
peculiar power of his voice, which now had an almost impersonal sound, as if the night itself were speaking to her.
At the same time, with its queer evocative quality, it called
up a picture of long-drawn-out disillusionment; misunderstanding; the lingering death of some human relationship,
which obscurely inclined her in the speaker's favour. She
waited for him to say something more: but now he was
silent; and, after a few seconds, turned away from the pool.
Feeling vaguely disappointed, she walked back to the cottage
with him.

The vine leaves were a startling theatrical green in the
light of a lamp burning inside, the verandah itself seemed
very bright after the darkness in which they'd been walking.
Instead of following her up the steps, Louis stopped on the

grass, while she paused on the verandah to say good-night and thank him for bringing her back. She didn't look at him, suddenly shy in the light; but he, just outside its radius, had his face lifted, watching her.

"Don't go for a moment," he said softly. She gave him a rapid glancing look of surprise; and yet she wasn't really surprised, she almost seemed to know what was coming. "I just want to say" — his voice became very soft and cajoling — "that, if I can do anything for you at any time, I hope you will let me." In apparently spontaneous appeal, he flung out his arm, stretching his hand towards her. "Will you promise me that . . . please . . . ?" Shadowy in the dimness beyond the light, he stood with his arm extended towards her, making no attempt to approach: while she gazed at him as if in startled wonder, and also as if miles away. A strange notion had just entered her head as though inserted by some-one else — as though it didn't belong to her at all — making her feel she had lost control of herself, of her own thoughts. With some part of her she knew she ought to regain control; but she didn't want to fight that soft voice, so extraordinarily soft and suggestive, it seemed to be speaking right into her ear, or even closer, in spite of the distance between them.

"Sometimes it's easier to discuss things with a comparative stranger than with somebody one loves." Always it spoke with that same softness, and now brought out the cliché with a subtle sound of sympathy, understanding. "Don't think I'm being intrusive. I only want you to know I'm there, if you ever need me."

Still she didn't answer; but, reassured because he came no nearer, she was all the time getting used to the strange idea; it was beginning to seem less alien.

"Things can be difficult at first in a strange country. It isn't always easy to know who's trustworthy — I hope you feel you can trust me."

Listening, not listening, to that soft, lingering voice, she felt herself falling hopelessly under its spell. Had Louis put the idea into her head? Or was he trying to draw something out? Aware of the foolish fluttering of her thoughts, she wondered if their foolishness mattered.

"You do trust me, don't you?" The soft, persistent voice seemed to be in her brain. The speaker was watching her all the time with a fixed upward gaze. Though she couldn't see them, she was extremely conscious of his pellucid eyes, wide open, intensely bright, fastened upon her. She was fascinated by his unseen stare, as by his softly suggestive voice, which seemed to wander about inside her head, going through her thoughts as it pleased.

163

"Yes," she whispered, helpless, throwing herself on his mercy. She could do nothing. She was in his power, gazing at him with vague, childish, dilated eyes, at once victimized and enthralled. He wanted something from her — what was it? She could feel the power of his will upon her, like sorcery, and she was frightened; but also she was fascinated, as though something strange and secret had passed between them, something as strong as love. Her eyes had a tranced look; and in a tranced, scarcely audible voice she whispered: "There is something you could help me about now . . . a letter . . . " She could feel his will drawing the words out of her mouth: she knew she ought to resist. But the fascination was much too strong. She could almost see the commanding, determined will emanating from him, coming towards her, from the black tall shadow he had become, a little larger than life, rather dreadful. Whispering, "I'll fetch it," she turned away, her knees shaking, and went into the house.

Hardly knowing how she got there, she reached her room. The idea of showing the anonymous letter to Louis, coming to her like a message from outside herself, had grown into a definite need, connected obscurely with Val's action in showing him the Superintendent's letter. She believed that, in some mysterious, unclear fashion, beyond all reason, the two things would cancel out; the wound she had suffered would be assuaged. She did not ask herself why Louis should want her to do this thing. Under his influence, again feeling his implacable will reaching out to her, like something secret and fascinating that moved between them, not thinking of anything definite, she went to the drawer where the letter was hidden, returning with it to the verandah, and holding it out to the inscrutable shadow that waited there. She seemed to have no thoughts about what she was doing. She had gone into that vague, absent state where she seemed not to be there, her ordinary everyday consciousness as if suspended. When Louis asked, "Am I to read it?" she nodded in a slow assent, as if under hypnosis.

He came closer, holding the paper towards the light. She saw his face bright with a curious smiling look, that was not an exterior smile, for no muscle moved. Still as a statue, he stood there reading, his face bright and remote. It didn't matter to him what was in the letter; the important point was that he should possess it. He was somewhat amused, however, by what he read. It was not the first time such a letter had been in his hands, and he didn't suppose it would be the last, having a shrewd idea of who had written it; or rather, caused it to be written, since he believed his wife could not use a typewriter. In his slightly macabre way, he found it amusing; his gleaming triumphant look became almost an open smile.

Looking up from the letter, he saw the girl's small pathetic figure in darkness against the light, only her hair edged with pale luminous gold. She was watching him, fascinated. As their eyes met, some spark seemed to leap from his into her own, as his voice had entered her head. Now she was doubly in his power, twice under his spell. Wide-eyed, fascinated, she watched his face, bright with triumph, and now smiling at her outwardly.

"Don't worry about this — it's not worth it. There's only one way to treat nastiness of this kind — " His voice at its most reassuring, he made the gesture of tearing something with both hands. "Shall I?"

"Oh, yes, do!" Gerda exclaimed, finding her voice at last, altogether surrendered to his spell. She watched his strong fingers rip through paper and envelope twice, and then push the four pieces into his pocket; for neatness sake, she presumed. A weight was lifted from her; how easily she'd got rid of it — simply by transferring the responsibility . . . now she need worry no more.

That night she even felt more resigned to her lonely bed, because Louis was her friend. Why shouldn't she trust him? He'd trusted her. He'd confided in her, and always been kind and considerate. Relaxing in the spell of acceptance that was upon her, she thought no further. It was as if Louis, courteous, grave, charming, watched over her dreams; with what object she didn't ask: but his face was bright with the dawning elation of someone about to triumph. She assumed that he would triumph over whoever had written the letter. So Val was safe.

*   *   *

The next day Gerda's attitude was unchanged. She was still in her vague absent condition, hardly present. She did not think about Louis directly, or about the letter, or about what she had done. But, in a general way, she felt that the situation had been improved. Louis had been warned, and would be on the alert, prepared to avert any danger that threatened. She was relieved of her too-heavy responsibility; and this made her feel lighter than ever, still more unreal — almost disembodied, she floated through the morning and early afternoon.

Then a visitor came; a plump little neatly dressed man, unknown to her, but evidently well known to the servants, who brought him tea without waiting for orders, to her faint annoyance. Sitting down with the air of one who intends to stay, he informed her that he was the medical officer attached to the Mombello estate, and that Louis had asked him to call on her, being anxious about her indisposition of the previous night.

This brought her back to herself with an unpleasant shock. What an extraordinary thing for Louis to have done: it seemed almost impertinent — interfering. Coldly and rather indignantly she assured the little man that nothing was wrong with her: she'd simply felt overcome by the heat for a moment, not being accustomed to it.

But wasn't it true, he inquired, nibbling with rapid delicacy at a sugared cake, that she'd just left a sanatorium against the doctor's advice?

This made Gerda really angry. She'd disliked the little doctor on sight: an impudent little fellow, he seemed, glancing at her with a kind of sidelong malice as he nibbled away, sitting there as if in his own home. And it was really too bad of Louis; he really had gone too far. Though no doubt he meant well. She must make it clear to him that she preferred to keep her private affairs to herself; not to have them broadcast all over the district. Doing her best to assume an air of distance and dignity, she told the doctor that she was quite capable of sending for him herself, if she thought it necessary; and wished him good-afternoon. But he, not understanding her, or unwilling to leave the tray, merely smiled and lifted his cup of tea. Whereupon she walked out and left him to drink it alone.

A certain uneasiness, due to Louis' behaviour, had settled upon her. But as soon as the visitor left she forgot it, going out into the garden to wait for Val, whose arrival she expected at any moment. He must have walked from his office today, instead of driving as usual, for presently he called to her from the house, which he'd evidently entered from the other side. His angry voice warned her that something was wrong: and she'd barely opened the door before he almost shouted at her: "So now you're going to turn the place into a hospital ... "

"What on earth do you mean?" Not understanding him in the least, her wide astonished eyes followed the direction of his gaze, to focus on the pile of temperature charts beside the thermometer on the table. She did not immediately associate these objects with her uninvited guest; it took her several seconds to realize that the doctor must have left them there. For an instant then, they appeared to her confused, immature mind as part of a vast nightmare conspiracy against her, in which, not only people, but all the inanimate things around her, from the house downward, had joined. Seizing the forms, she started tearing them into small pieces, and scattering them on the floor. "It's not fair!" she cried wildly. "Louis sent the man — it's nothing to do with me — I didn't even know he'd left these — " Suddenly catching sight of her hands, in an oddly vivid flashback she seemed to see Louis' hands, similarly engaged; and, as if for the first time, the full significance of last night's events, for which she could not deny responsibility, dawned on her with a shock of mingled horror and guilt. What she had done the evening before seemed just as incomprehensible and disloyal as not answering Val's letter. She deserved all his angry reproaches: she was worse, far worse, than he knew. Dropping the last fragments of paper, standing there with the torn scraps strewn around her, she covered her face with her hands, her thin shoulders began to shake in a storm of weeping.

Exasperated, the young man turned his back on her, leaving her there, and went into another room, where he mixed himself a stiff drink. He felt both angry and injured. He wasn't meant for this sort of thing; he detested tears and scenes. All he wanted was to live a happy, easy-going life, and for other people to do the same; but ever since Gerda came there had been nothing but trouble — anyone would think the girl was deliberately trying to make things difficult for him. Even when she did do something right, like last night at the big house, she had to go and spoil it all afterwards by giving the impression that she was a sickly weakling —the one thing people here, with their robust health and spirits, despised and hated.

His feelings were particularly strong because he'd come straight from a conversation with Louis on this very topic. His employer had warned him all along to keep the t.b. business under his hat; people were such idiots with their morbid dread of disease, they might be afraid of infection. Now Mrs. Mombello, apparently, was being difficult about it; saying she didn't like having Gerda about the place, which wouldn't have mattered, except that Louis himself was obviously worried, and had finally said she ought to be sent back to the sanatorium. Made angry by this dictatorial attitude, Val had told him straight out that he'd no intention of packing her off like that for anybody. Afterwards, in a more restrained way, he'd tried to persuade Louis that it would be to their advantage to keep the girl here as a kind of shield against malicious gossip. But his employer, unconvinced and unfriendly, had remained resolutely opposed to the idea, upon which Val, particularly since he'd seen the impression Gerda made on his friends, had become rather set.

Louis could at times be aloof and haughty, displaying an

intransigeance and a cold reserve by which Val felt obliterated, and against which he reacted instinctively by outbursts of temper. After their talk, he'd started to be uneasy, fearing he might have gone too far in his resentment of the other man's overbearing attitude. So it was maddening, after perhaps endangering his own position on Gerda's account, arguing in her defence, to come back and find those confounded charts spread out where anybody could see them, as if to prove the falseness of his repeated statement that she was now perfectly well. No wonder he was furious.

However, by the time he'd finished his drink, he began to feel slightly sorry for the girl, and angry with Louis again. Who the hell did he think he was, to tell him he ought to get rid of her? It was too much — he wasn't going to take that sort of thing from anyone.

Going into the other room, sitting down on the couch where Gerda was huddled dejectedly, quite forgetting that he himself had caused her distress, he drew her to him, saying: "Don't be so miserable. It's a damn shame that you should be made to suffer — it's not your fault."

But she only started sobbing again as if broken-hearted, crying: "It *is* my fault — you must hate me!"

"No, no. Don't be silly," he murmured soothingly, thinking that she was hysterical, holding her comfortingly until she relaxed at length, and let her head drop on his shoulder. For several more minutes he continued to stroke her hair absently, while he tried to think what to do.

He hated the thought of having to knuckle under to Louis. His mild intermittent fondness for Gerda now made him overlook for the moment the inconvenience of her presence: he persuaded himself that he wanted to keep her with him; whereas what he really wanted was his own way. The difficulty was to decide just how far he dared go in order to get it, since he was never quite sure where he stood with Louis; whether he was or was not indispensable. He liked to think he was the only person who could alleviate the central loneliness, emptiness, of the rich man's life, by helping him to fulfill his secret desires. But he wasn't certain: there was always about Louis something inaccessible, withheld and secret, even at his most intimate moments, which Val's simpler character couldn't grasp. He didn't want to take any irrevocable step. It would be best, he decided, to do nothing at all for a few days; just to watch how things went.

In the meantime Gerda's adoring love was quite welcome, building him up again after Louis had made him feel small. Val could be indulgent now towards her childish lack of sophistication, feeling that it showed him by contrast as an efficient, experienced man of the world. It was quite pleasant to relax in her uncritical admiration; he was agreeably amused by that charming childlike spontaneous gaiety of hers, that could make her, quite literally, dance for joy.

She, of course, was enraptured by his attention, even though she knew that it would not last — that it changed nothing. Intuition had already told her that, fundamentally, everything was lost. Since the splendour of passionate love had escaped her for good — never again would she lie through the night beside his magnificent young body, held close to his heart — she humbly and gladly accepted the temporary happiness he now offered her. With feverish eagerness, she clutched at every enchanted, dreamlike hour, gay and smiling, fluttering in the ephemeral warmth of his kindly approval, like a late summer flower, which may at any moment fall to the touch of frost.

In the afternoons of this illusory summer, while Val was absent, she went to the pool Louis had showed her, preferring to be outside, even during the hottest time of the day. She had never managed to feel at home in the cottage, or to forget her original sense of rejection; in her imagination, the place not only refused to accept the impress of her personality, but it seemed definitely hostile. But the pool was friendly. Lying in the little boat, put there years before for another woman's pleasure, she would drowse through the languid hours, lost in some vague fantasy, soothed by the soft-sighing willows, as they stirred in an air-current too light to move heavier leaves. If occasionally a dark face peered out of the branches, she unsuspicious, supposed it belonged to one of the gardeners, and took no notice. It was not to escape possible spies that she rowed out clumsily to the middle of the pool, where, lying down, she would be invisible from the shore: but simply because she took a child's pleasure in this cool secluded private world of water and sky and drooping, soft, graceful green. The spring water was unexpectedly clear and deep, reflecting a sparkling, diamond-bright, magic day. The willows grew all round, and a path of flat stones soon brought her to the hibiscus hedge where her own ground began, so that she could quickly escape, if necessary.

But no one ever came to disturb her. As Louis had said, the place was quite private: she alone frequented it, and began to look upon it as her special haunt. Off her guard, drowsy in the afternoon heat, she was dozing there one day when the unusual sound of steps and voices roused her in alarm.

There was nothing of a listener in Gerda's nature: it must have been some muddled impulse, left over from dream, that prompted her to remain silent, instead of calling to the two familiar figures; kept her lying down, out of sight, until it seemed too late, too embarrassing, to make known her presence. Between the warped timbers of the little boat she could watch the pair without lifting her head. She was thinking how engagingly casual and young her husband looked by comparison with his employer, who without a hair out of place, presented his usual appearance of cool, pale, sculptured hardness, absolutely correct and immaculate, when she heard Val say in a tone of chagrin:

"What I can't understand is why she showed *you* the letter, without saying a word to me."

He had told her nothing of the tension still existing between Louis and himself; but she guessed immediately that the two were not on the best of terms, though there was no suggestion of irritability in Louis' peculiar voice, which came to her over the water with an accentuation of its curious flat resonance.

"She might have showed it to anybody — now perhaps you can see the danger."

Could they be discussing her? To Gerda's sleep-slowed mind the possibility seemed so disturbing that she made a nervous movement, rocking the boat slightly. Terrified of attracting attention and being forced belatedly to reveal her presence, she missed what was said next. When she looked out again, the two men were standing together at the water's edge, both their heads bent over some pieces of paper in Louis' hand; which, more by instinct than recognition, she at once identified, beyond all chance of mistake, as the remains of the anonymous letter she'd given him to destroy.

A terrific pandemonium started inside her head, as of a great many voices shouting against one another, accompanied by corresponding feelings of incredulity, anger, disappointment, shame, bewilderment, pain, disbelief. "I trusted him — I thought he was my friend," was the first coherent thought to emerge from this chaos: and then: "I don't believe it." She stared at the irregular squares of paper, which Louis was now holding out in rather an odd way, almost as if to make sure she could see them: but, although she was certain of what they were, she still couldn't believe he had betrayed her trust. No, it simply wasn't possible, she thought; and, at the same time, watching him hand over the scraps to Val, she was thinking: "So that's why he kept them . . . " The crazy interior turmoil was becoming unbearable, she could no longer distinguish any reasonable thought.

Abruptly then, just as her head seemed about to burst, the conflict ended. Since these things were impossible, they couldn't be real. She had a sense of passing into a new dimension, from which she could see and hear all that went on as from the other side of a transparent wall. There was no more need to worry about anything, because none of it was really happening. Profoundly relieved, she lay back comfortably in the boat, relaxing into a sort of torpor beyond her glass wall, watching the scene where reality had been suspended. Words reached her divorced from meaning.

"You still haven't told her about the trip?"

"I'll tell her at the right time," Val replied, carelessly stuffing the pieces of paper into his pocket, as if they were of no further interest. All the same, he'd been disconcerted, just as Louis meant him to be, by the revelation of Gerda's unpredictable behaviour over the anonymous letter. Thinking he knew his wife through and through, it had been an unpleasant surprise to find her capable of actions he would never have expected. Suddenly realising the surly disagreeable tone in which he'd just spoken, he felt a surge of angry resentment against her, as though she were to blame for his loss of control —she always made everything go wrong.

He'd been determined, when Louis proposed walking through the garden with him, to end the coolness between them, which had been worrying him for some days. But as soon as Gerda's name came up, he'd started getting aggressive again, not out of loyalty to her, but because he couldn't stand being ordered about. The most he could feel for the girl was a tepid affection, depending mainly on habit and memory; and this had now been submerged in a sense of grievance — a muddled feeling that she had made trouble between him and his employer. At this moment she was quite unimportant to him. She meant nothing by comparison with the tall man, who was watching him all the time with pale unpenetrable eyes. Why the hell did she have to come here, he thought, in a sudden access of strained emotion, snatching at a dangling branch and breaking it off. He looked rather like an uneasy schoolboy, as he stood twisting and bending the flexible wood, not knowing what to say or how to get the situation back to a point where it could develop as he'd intended.

"Look here, Val, I don't think you're being fair." The queer insistent voice came again. "I don't think it's fair either to Gerda or to myself, to keep her in the dark until the very last moment."

Gerda again . . . Were they never to get away from her? In spite of himself, Val's temper flared up uncontrollably. "You needn't worry about her; I fail to see how she concerns you," he said, in a voice as heated as the other's was cool. He felt on the verge of losing control of himself altogether, under the fixed expressionless gaze of his companion, who, standing on slightly higher ground, seemed to be looking down on him in all senses. Unconsciously stripping the leaves from the branch he was holding, he saw the other's remote supercilious look as deliberately assumed to remind him of his own inferior status as a paid employee.

"Since you don't appear to consider your wife, I suppose it's no use expecting you to consider your word," came in that weird, measured voice, the tone of which never changed, surprising him so much that he almost forgot his anger in sheer amazement, echoing blankly, "My word?" as if it were a term he'd never heard.

"Isn't it your word of honour you're supposed to give when you make a gentleman's agreement with someone?" A faint satiric smile on his lips, Louis looked almost lazily, almost playfully, at the flushed, bewildered young man; with whom he seemed to be playing rather as a fighter plays with a bull, until he gets tired of the game, and kills it. "The main point in our agreement was your willingness to go anywhere with me, at any time. If you back out at the last moment I'll have to put off the whole trip — you'll be doing exactly what you gave your word not to do."

"I'm not going to back out — "

"Suppose you have to? Suppose Gerda won't let you go?" The unshakeably quiet, half-playful voice had an almost hypnotic resonance, going on and on, travelling far into the recesses of the hot afternoon, where it seemed to reverberate persistently for an eternity, before Val said, without much conviction:

"There's no reason to suppose that."

"On the contrary, there's every reason to suppose she won't let you go away for an indefinite period." Even the listener, behind her barrier of the unreal, was struck by the changed tone, suddenly cold and incisive. The speaker had had enough of the game; it was time to finish. "No, Val, you can't work for me, and be Gerda's husband. I've nothing against her — she's charming. But, as a charming girl, she has certain rights that conflict with your obligations to me. She'll always be making demands that interfere with your work. You were useful to me as an independent, unattached individual; as a married man you're no longer free. The whole situation has changed now. I can't count on you any more."

Hurt, his anger swallowed up in confused agitation, Val said impulsively: "If that's how you feel, I'd better resign . . . " Before he'd even finished speaking, he wished the words unsaid. He knew that he'd made a mistake — fallen into a trap. But why should Louis set traps for him? His simple brain utterly confused, he was utterly at the mercy of the man who'd

172

been playing with him; at whom he gazed, throwing away the tattered remains of the branch, in hot, hurt, boyish bewilderment, not understanding anything that had happened. Surely Louis couldn't be going to take his resignation seriously?

Gerda, meanwhile, was thinking how strange things appeared through her transparent wall. If she'd ever had any doubts of the scene's unreality, they would have been abolished by the sight of her husband's dismay. Never in real life, in the real world, could her gay, dashing, confident Val have looked so unhappy, dumbfounded; so diminished in every way as he now appeared, by the side of his tall employer. The odd thing was that, in the unreality of it all, Louis seemed to her the more real of the two; her interest centred on Louis. And he seemed to be more concerned with her, in some odd way, than with his companion. She could feel his awareness reaching out to her over the water, and binding her to him, although he couldn't know she was there. This feeling of being included, against all rational laws, in his consciousness, increased the sense of unreality with which she waited, a long, long time, as it seemed, for him to speak again.

"Perhaps that would be the best solution, in the circumstances."

As the soft insidious voice crossed the water to her, she remembered the dolphins playing around the ship, more playful than anything she had ever seen, for all their weight and size, light and airy as rainbows, and as unreal — boat and all, the voice rocked her in its spell; spellbound, she lay there listening. It was only the sound she heard, not the meaning. Her mind set the words aside somewhere; their meaning could be examined later; now she could only listen, entranced. "Perhaps Innes would come — he seemed rather keen. But I don't want to rush you into a decision. Take your time and think it over calmly and coolly." When the other voice blurted, outraged, "*You* certainly take it pretty coolly," she hardly heard it; hardly noticed how Val was staring accusingly into Louis' face — she was waiting for the spell to return.

"My dear Val, you mustn't misunderstand me. Just because I value your friendship — " It was the same soft, playful sound, gone mock-serious, rather cruelly mocking, and yet so fascinating to the girl . . . who could hear no more now, because Louis took Val by the elbow and steered him round, guiding him away from the pool.

In a sort of stupefaction she watched the two walk to the point where the hedge divided, and stand there for a few more moments before they parted. When he spoke for the last time, Louis had already turned back; his cool, plangent tones again seemed to penetrate Gerda's head; but still they were only sounds, which, like words in a foreign language, she put aside, to be translated later on into meaning.

"I hope this ridiculous gossip about infection won't prejudice people . . . "

Forgetting her husband as soon as he disappeared through the hedge, she watched the approach of the other figure, strangely tall, more than life-size, it seemed to her, like a statue walking. With a kind of sculptured grandeur, aloofness, it came stalking towards her, moving rapidly but rather stiffly, in an indescribable aura of loneliness, mysterious and not unlike glamour.

The sun was sinking, the willows cast their enormous shade, everything within six feet of the ground was in deep green-black shadow. But higher, slanting sun rays caught the impassive face, so that it seemed to burn like a pale light, brighter than daylight, diffusing its own weird radiance of elation.

She was so sure of Louis' awareness of her that, as he came to the water, she waited for him to speak. Incredulity, rather than disappointment was what she felt, when, without so much as a glance at the little boat, he walked quickly past, and vanished beyond a curtain of dense dark leaves.

Sitting up then, pushing back her hair with a characteristic vague gesture, Gerda looked vaguely round at a world suddenly flushed with sunset; golden light flooded the pool and flared on the tree trunks; like countless emerald pendants the leaves hung down, set in unearthly gold. She felt rather dazed; all this brightness seemed an extension of her own unreality, as though she were looking at a scene on the stage. She still seemed not to understand fully what she had seen and heard, though the meaning of the words which the pair had spoken was beginning to disclose itself, a record played in her head, which she couldn't stop. She tried not to listen to it, not wanting to know that her charming, light-hearted husband had been caught at a disadvantage, made to look hurt and foolish. Clinging to the spell put upon her, she tried to go on seeing Louis as the friend he had seemed, kind, gentle and trustworthy. But that spell had broken. And now an entirely different figure began to emerge, ruthless, calculating; bringing a new and frightening principle of uncertainty into the world. Appearances were no longer reliable; nothing was what it seemed. She didn't even seem to know where she was. Suddenly, she had the feeling that she had opened the wrong door, and entered a world where everything was slightly, alarmingly different. She must get back, at once, to the familiarity of her own world.

Hastily bringing the boat to the bank, Gerda climbed up

and hurried along the path, obsessionally careful, as children are, even in this emergency, to tread only upon the stones, as though some catastrophe would overtake her if her foot touched the ground between. The sun disappeared. Instantly, there was a chill in the air. With uncanny speed, the golden light faded, the world began to turn hostile and dark and cold. Between one stone and the next, all colour was expunged. The trees loomed blackly ominous, the water had a gruesome gunmetal gleam.

The girl stopped suddenly, as if listening. She had only known she must return to what was familiar, feeling as if she'd somehow got into the wrong room, where it was dangerous to remain, though the precise nature of the danger wasn't clear. Suddenly now, danger was close behind her: a nameless something that fearfully threatened — slowly she turned her head.

To her horror, the water, the willows, the sky, seemed to have different faces; while she wasn't looking, they'd slyly transferred themselves to the dark, frightening underside of the world, to which the vast, unknown country beyond the trees also belonged. She could feel the alien country, hostile and savage and huge; the endless lifeless hills crowding one behind the other like the waves of some monstrous sea, fearsome masses of earth, horribly heaving up out of nowhere; rearing up in a ghastly black tidal wave, ready to fall upon her. She was lost, utterly, hopelessly lost, out of her world.

Starting forward in terror, her foot missed the edge of the next stone; she stumbled and almost fell. Then, like a child beginning to wake from nightmare, she started running, blindly, with outstretched arms, to find herself, and the safety of her lost world.

*　　　*　　　*

Val had come into the house feeling thoroughly shaken, angry, bewildered, alarmed. He'd never had the least intention of resigning. Somehow he'd been tricked, as by witchcraft, into doing the very last thing in the world he wanted to do. That Louis could be responsible never occurred to him. It seemed to be Gerda's fault; he blamed her for everything. Though he didn't know it, almost all Louis had said had been calculated to set him against the girl; who now, like a bad tooth neglected too long, seemed to poison his whole being—he wouldn't feel right again in himself until it was out. It was incredible, the damage she'd managed to do in a short time, destroying, in the few days she'd been here, the new life it had taken him more than a year to build up; and making a fool of him into the bargain.

175

Scowling, he pulled the torn letter out of his pocket. But, in itself, it was of no interest to him; his thoughts did not remain concentrated on it long enough for him to fit the pieces together. Preoccupied, with an ugly baffled look on his usually serene brow, he sat there unconsciously folding and re-folding the scraps of paper, finally screwing them into a ball which he threw into the fireplace. His goodlooking face was sulky, his body stiff with bad temper. He was angry with himself as well as with Gerda, feeling, exactly as Louis had meant him to feel, a bit of an ass, because he hadn't known what his wife was up to behind his back. But what worried and infuriated him even more than being made to look foolish, was the possibility that her illness might prevent him from getting another job in this country. Louis' last words, artfully implanted at the moment of parting, rankled with particular bitterness.

Stiff and sulky, he sat in his chair, his legs stretched out in front of him and his glass in his hand. Retiring into some truthful part of himself that he seldom frequented, he admitted the stupidity of risking his future for the sake of getting his own way; admitted that, apart from Louis, he *had* no future, being without special talents or training. For over a year he'd been spoiled and indulged, he had developed a taste for luxury that would hit him hard if he had to go back to his former standard of living. He couldn't bear to think of returning to his home country, to some dreary, badly-paid job in a dismal provincial town, after the life he'd got used to.

Suddenly something caught his attention outside — Gerda came running across the garden. Without moving, he watched the little figure approach with flying hair through the dusk. She held her arms stiffly before her, and kept stumbling, as though exhausted, frail thing that she was. As she reached the verandah, he could already hear the sound of her panting breaths, she seemed to be almost at her last gasp, throwing a terrified look behind her as she entered the room — a look so desperate that Val instinctively glanced out to see if she was being followed. But, nothing being visible in the shadowy garden, he told himself furiously that her frightened look was assumed — she was putting on some sort of act to distract him from his legitimate anger.

She advanced, arms outstretched, towards him, imploring protection, the possibility of rebuff not having occurred to her yet. She must get back to safety; that was all she knew. She must find the door. Something seemed missing from her wide open eyes, which as yet hardly saw the real Val sitting there. She was conscious in herself, but not objectively conscious of her surroundings. He thought she looked queer, unnatural, somehow.; something wrong with her face, which seemed strange and wild. But, too angry to consider this odd expression, he attacked her at once. "What was the idea of showing Louis that letter about me?" he asked, although he had no interest in her motives, speaking the words like an accusation.

. Astonished by the cold denunciatory tone, Gerda stopped dead, letting her arms fall. The question she didn't attempt to answer, having heard it as it had been spoken, merely to put her in the wrong. But now she did start to see the man sitting there sullenly, gulping his whisky, and staring at her with an ugly implacable look, concentrated in anger against her, as unlike Val's gay good-natured aspect as possible. Again she was struck by the terrifying unreliability of all appearances. How could she have made such a mistake? She'd thought she was coming to Val; and now here was this angry stranger, whose hard mask-face confronted her in unyielding resentment. For a moment she puzzled over some frightening half-recollection before it sank in a sea of more recent terrors. She could trust no one, nothing: she was lost —it all came to that.

She had not noticed that, as soon as she stood still, she'd begun shivering like a sick person. Now, abruptly, without any sensation of falling she found herself on the ground. What had happened? Why did she suddenly feel so weak and strange? What was she doing down here, all her strength gone; sleek, brown, wet, gleaming sand stretching around her in all directions, unmarked by a single footprint? She was lost . . . lost . . .

Suddenly then, she saw Val's feet, his legs and ankles, quite close to her. They *were* near her; they *were* his; she recognized them with certainty. The shoes she remembered specially, because long ago, in their life together, he'd once expressed a dislike for suede shoes. *Was* it Val, then — the Val she had known? She dared not look higher, at his face; but, shuffling awkwardly forward on hands and knees, threw her arms round his legs and pressed her body against them, whispering: "Val . . . ?" too frightened to raise her eyes.

Far from arousing any affectionate response, the pressure of her thin breast, her clutching hands, filled the man with such acute distaste that he longed to throw her off. Muscles twitched in his legs, as if with their own brutal desire to lunge out at her. He had to exert all his will to keep quiet, only controlling himself through his dislike of inflicting pain. His teeth clenched, his lips pressed tightly together, he sat there in rigid endurance, beyond speech. While in Gerda's throat, as if of their own accord, words started to bubble up like a painful spring, half blocked, gushing out brokenly, in convulsive spasms. "I know I'm too horrible — wicked — I'm not fit to love anyone . . . I deserve to lose you. But, please, Val, let me stay . . . I can't live without you . . . I promise I won't be a nuisance to you . . . You needn't see me — talk to me . . . I swear I won't interfere with anything you want to do. Only, please, let me see you sometimes . . . For God's sake, don't send me away altogether . . . " She had not meant to say anything like this: indeed, it hardly seemed she who was responsible for the distracted, gasping voice, over which she had no control.

Val held himself rigidly all through it, without listening, not taking it in, all his faculties concentrated on self-restraint; straining against his impulse to jump up, throw her aside, and run . . . anywhere . . . to get away. He was thankful when tears silenced her finally. He felt their wetness on his skin under the thin cloth, and the feverish heat of her lips, as she pressed frantic kisses on his knees, his thighs, wherever her mouth could reach, absolutely beside herself and unconscious of everything. It was a horrible position for him, harrowing. It horrified him to have her kneeling before him, abandoned, her pale hair streaming wildly over her shoulders, her poor little thin body shaking as if in fever. But he felt no compassion; on the contrary, any small remaining spark of pity or fondness was now extinguished by this torture she was inflicting on him.

Suddenly, to his immeasureable relief, he heard Louis' car on the gravel outside, followed by that unmistakeable voice calling: "Hello there! Are you ready?"

Val had quite forgotten, in the throes of his personal crisis, that this was the night of some traditional ceremony his employer wished to attend. Now it passed through his mind that, since Louis had come for him, things couldn't be quite as bad as he'd feared: all was not yet lost; perhaps he might still be able to save his job. His muscles tensed, he prepared to jump up. But Gerda was still clinging to him as if demented, clutching his legs in a crazy grip, so that he couldn't move without using force.

Of course he must go; his whole future depended on it. If she wouldn't let go, he would have to push her out of the way. But for a moment he hesitated, delayed by a memory so vivid it was like a vision of the girl, who had, perhaps, once been real, but was now no more in existence than the forgotten honeymoon, from which her inopportune ghost returned, to offer herself with innocent guileless humility, saying: "I know I'm not nearly beautiful enough for you, but I'll adore you for ever and ever . . . "

Getting no answer to his call, Louis, in the meantime, had come on to the verandah, and now looked into the room, to find out what was happening. "It's time we started," he said to Val. And then his eyes contracted suddenly and grew intent, like a cat's when it unexpectedly sees a small bird fluttering near, wounded, unable to fly, at the sight of Gerda, crouching there on the floor. So this was to be the finish — good. In the shadows, with the furniture coming between, he might just possibly not have seen her; and, letting her husband think this was the case, he spoke as if they were alone. "I want someone to take a few notes. But if you don't want to come I can 'phone Innes — I don't believe he's doing anything tonight."

Although Louis gave no signs of having observed her, Gerda could feel his awareness, as she had in the boat. And, though her back was towards him, she knew exactly how he was looming there, enormously tall and frightening behind her, like some overbearing statue of god or demon, with that look on his face, not quite smiling, giving off a mysterious bright elation. As if the sunset still gleamed upon it, she could feel his face shine fearfully in the gloom . . . where terror once more piled its dark tidal wave, about to come crashing down . . .

In pure desperation, she looked up at Val, her lips silently shaping his name, her small white face, wet with tears, raised to him in one last despairing appeal — her whole being was in it, the entirety of her love. Surely, surely, he wouldn't abandon her now . . .

The young man had been gazing resolutely away from her, over her head. But now, against his will, his eyes were drawn to meet hers; enormous, from pits filled with deep grey shadow, they stared at him with a look of anguished exposure, stripped, in this extremity, of some veil imposed by decency at other times.

He was horrified and shocked, disgusted almost. There was to him something almost obscene in this shameless display of emotions that should have been dead. He turned his face quickly aside. But not before he had caught her look of naked terror and supplication which seemed to exude fear. This was something he really couldn't endure to see — it was not meant to be seen. It seemed inhuman to him. And it revived a deep-buried memory he'd tried for years to suppress; bringing back to him the look he'd seen years before, in the eyes of a hare, just before the dogs tore it to pieces, when he was a boy living in the country. Suddenly he felt sick, just as he had then; when, to the farmer's scornful amusement, he'd vomited behind a tree. Now he had to make his escape.

Nausea supplied the impetus for which he had seemed to be waiting. He had to get away from that terribly wounded look; to shut it right out of his consciousness. Oblivious of everything but his overwhelming need, he jumped up, hardly knowing what he was doing, pushed Gerda roughly aside, and started across the room.

She gave a single queer little cry, like a mad person, as she fell, slipping on the polished floor, sprawling with arms flung out. Without another sound then, propping herself on her elbows, she stared after him. Her face had gone suddenly a dreadful grey, as though shadows, overflowing from her eye-sockets, covered it thinly with a shadow like death. Val had deserted her in her utmost need. She had lost him, so all was lost. She had known it, of course, for a long time: but, since she couldn't know it and live, the knowledge had remained unreal, unrealized. Now she was forced to accept the reality of her loss, to realize what it meant, watching Val walk away, as though she were fixedly watching hope itself recede from her.

Louis had recognized in that strange sound she uttered the death cry of hope. And now, watching her, suddenly prominent in her thin face, he could see the small female bones, as if the shape of the impatient skull tried to appear prematurely, eager to rid itself of the living flesh, into which the greyness of death had already entered. He did not see her as a girl, a human being. He was concerned with her only in her abstract capacity of the victim required for the rite's fulfilment, watching her with a rapt far-off lonely intentness. His eyes, impersonal as pale stones, dwelt upon her with the cold inhumanity, the perfect indifference, of his obsession; and then, as he became satisfied by what he saw, they began to glitter in anticipation of triumph. Already he could feel in himself the mystic exultance of the supreme moment, and of all those, ghosts and living, who would participate through him in the climax of dark ancient forbidden magic. With a strange impersonal passion he saw the sacrifice ready, prepared: and knew there was nothing more to be done. Now he was free to go. Confidently, he could await the consummation.

Coming back to himself, he also came back to the young man, of whom he'd been oblivious temporarily. There was no more to be done with him, either; he, too, had been dealt with adequately. Val had of late become over-confident; it had been necessary to put him in his place — to make him aware of his obligations. Now that this had been done, he would doubtless be more co-operative, less aggressive. Since he would have had to be deflated in any case, it was, perhaps, fortunate that Gerda had served as a convenient excuse for the operation. With an indulgent smile, Louis now stepped past him, out on to the dark verandah.

The smile seemed to convey something of his own exaltation to the recipient, for Val felt exhilarated suddenly, as if slightly drunk: and it seemed to erase the image of Gerda finally from his mind. Instantly and entirely, she was forgotten, as though she had never been. All that remained at the back of his thoughts, was a dim impression of something sad and incurable, about which he could do nothing, and which, therefore, it was best to forget. Relief at having escaped from this hopeless unnamed sadness, the antithesis of his own *joie de vivre*, brought a naive smile to his face. Hurrying after Louis down the verandah steps, he felt no urge to inquire into the cause of the sudden cessation of tension between them. For his uncomplex nature it was enough to know that he was at one again with his friend. Simply letting all his cares fall away — all the anxiety, the bad temper — he looked immediately several years younger; a charming, good-humoured boy; handsome, smiling and likeable.

Gerda saw the two smiling faces receding from her in the dusk, and, seized by an overpowering anguish of loneliness, struggled to her feet, struggled after them. But, by the time her stumbling awkward steps reached the verandah, the two men were already sitting in Louis' car, their heads close together in animated talk. Instinctively she darted back, struck by the blow of their utter indifference.

As if to emphasize the abyss between them, the car lights abruptly came on, relegating her to a world of dimness, while they moved in the light. Helpless, she watched the long shining machine glide away from her along a bright tunnel between spectral tree trunks, the blackly-silhouetted heads of the two occupants always closely and mutually absorbed, till, with a sudden swerve, the car darted out of sight, stealthily, like a snake.

Because neither of those two heads had turned to give her a single glance, the girl, now left quite alone, felt an additional isolation — for one wild moment it was unbearable: she looked round frantically, as if her reason were going. Then, somehow, she was beyond it all, and beyond herself. It was all right, almost — almost peace.

In the last few moments night had flowed over the scene, very empty-seeming and quiet, as though, when the car disappeared, not only light, but life, had gone from the world. This was where her own life came to an end, though she did not know it. She had no further reason to go on living.

Having already experienced all the emotion of which she was capable, she now felt no more fear or despair or any particular feeling; only the vague unhappiness of a child that hardly knows it is sad. Her thoughts, too, were childish, confused and vague. She shrank from the idea of contact with human beings. The possibility of a servant coming to find her, to ask her a question, perhaps, about dinner, filled her with dread, and seemed something she must avoid at all costs. Automatically, she started walking away from the house, scarcely knowing that she was doing so. She could move now without any effort, her muscles seemed to work without her supervision: light as a leaf in the wind, she went drifting along.

The chill of sunset had gone, and the air felt warm, heavy with dusty foreign scents she would never learn to identify. The odours of alien men, beasts, flowers, food, vegetation; of cooling sun-parched earth, wood and stone; combined in a breath of hostile primitive feral strangeness. So that she was transiently aware of something sinister and oppressive: as if, for a second before she forgot it forever, the huge landmass beyond the trees forced its primeval ferocity upon her consciousness. But only for a second. And then she had gone on somewhere still further, into a different strangeness, her face empty as a somnambulist's.

It was not very dark, although there was no moon. In the faint diffused luminousness of great flashing stars, flowering bushes stood like girls in old-fashioned dresses, immobilized in a game of grandmother's steps. She thought they didn't want her to play with them, for they put out no detaining branch, but seemed to watch, gravely, silently, as she went by, straying along in the starlight as if in a dream. She had not realized that she was making for the pool; but when she saw the mass of willow foliage map its familiar mountain-range on the sky, she knew she could have come nowhere else. She stood on the bank, just above the black water, brought here by the impulse of an unhappy child to hide her unhappiness in a secret place.

Under black feathery trailing branches, the water, sprinkled with diamond stars, was the ceiling of her private world, the hanging constellations its chandeliers. That was where she wanted to be. With sudden intensity, she longed to escape from all the sadness, the guilt and the not-being-loved, of the world to which she had come unwanted, where nobody wished her to stay.

She had a vague notion that she was to blame for her own unhappiness. But she no longer understood how this was so. She could no longer remember what she'd done wrong —

the things left undone, unsaid . . . It all seemed far away . . . long ago . . . not so very important. She knew she had always been stupid: there had always been so much she did not understand . . . and no one had ever explained. But now it seemed not to matter much any more.

Bending their massive great heads, the willows began to whisper softly among themselves; and as she listened to them, the past slid away from her altogether. Now there was only the black waiting water, gleaming with stars, between the one world and the other.

She had been looking up at the trees. Now she lowered her eyes; and saw, at her feet, like a silver carpet put down in her honour, a radiant path leading straight to the place where she wanted to be — there it lay, her own world, safe and secret, beneath the dark water, its splendid lights, blazing like Christmas stars. She had a sense of enchanted wonder, and of arrival. Now she was nearly home. Very soon she would be in the midst of the bright insubstantial reality of her dream. The great stars poured out their wonder-light, welcoming, not far away. So brilliant, made of pure diamond-sparkle, they shone in their beauty. She wanted to come to them . . . to come to them quickly . . . she kept her wide open eyes fixed on the lustrous stars.

She felt light — lighter than air. And she seemed to be moving towards them with wonderful ease and speed . . . through silver-black glitterings, and cool dark depths, and still deeper darknesses, surrounding her . . . growing deeper . . . She gazed at the brilliant stars till her eyes filled with darkness; till everything was dark in her head: and the stars, as they set their jewelled wreath on her floating hair, seemed to be trying to give her what she had never been given by human beings.

7

PARADISE

THE rich woman's parents could not have chosen for her a more appropriate name than Regina; since height becomes royalty, and she was tall and queenly, always bearing herself with dignity and aplomb. More especially as she grew older, the word regal aptly described the carriage of the wonderfully cared-for body that had always been her one love, in spite of various husbands.

The last of these, the current husband, had been thirty-five when she married him:. and though no one then would have guessed she was nearly double his age, she prudently decided to run no risks but to take him out of reach of temptation. At the same time, he had to be kept interested and amused; so she proceeded to make him a little paradise-world to play with; a kind of super cage of the purest gold.

She was not unpractical. She bought a stretch of magnificent scenery that was first-class fruit-growing land in a climate as nearly perfect as anything is on earth. A thriving young town provided the amenities of civilization without being near enough to be dangerously attractive. Mountains stood in the background; in front was the bright blue sea; and to the space between she devoted her wealth — it went a long way, any amount of cheap labour being available. The woman wasn't really interested in anything but herself; and in the husband, as a sort of extension. But she had a knack of getting the best out of those who worked for her; and, the money being practically inexhaustible, the result was something remarkable in the earthly paradise line.

The man was nominally in charge of it all with the title of The Master. And the administration of the estate, which was ultimately to be self-supporting, was sufficiently complex to give him a sense of responsibility and of doing something worth while. All the actual labour was done by the meek under-privileged people of the dark indigenous race, with whom no communication was possible: but they were directed by men of his own colour, imported at great expense; and with them he spent much of his time. A friendly, rather simple fellow, he would have been lonely in his new grandeur, but for the company of these white overseers and their families, who always seemed delighted to see him when he visited them in their homes.

He was fond of children — the head gardener's little girl Susan quickly became his favourite — and used to beg every year for a children's party at Christmas time. But this one favour the rich woman always refused to grant. Her dislike of children amounted to a phobia, almost; she simply couldn't stand a child anywhere near her. Vaguely, the man connected this with rumours he'd heard of a child of her own; a daughter, dead long ago. But she never mentioned the subject, and he wouldn't have dreamed of asking a question. At no time had there ever been anything remotely resembling intimacy between them.

His whole attitude towards her was oddly deferential. He could never get over the fact that she'd married him, which seemed an undeserved compliment he could never repay. He was a big, strong, well-built, pleasant-faced man, who looked less than his age; obviously a decent sort, honest and open, the very opposite of the gigolo type who might have married her for the money. But, that, for a woman of almost seventy, to have captured and held him was something of an achievement — a triumph, even — never entered his head.

Even after some years of marriage, he remained distinctly awed by the dominant female who had transformed his existence, turning him into The Master, upon whom everybody and everything was supposed to depend. He'd never amounted to anything much in life before, and couldn't help being impressed by the new identity she had created for him. And, having no special talent or bent of his own, he very willingly fell into the ready-made part of the practical idealist, making a paradise both in nature and in *human* nature; everyone was to be happy and good, they would be like one big united family, all friends together.

For a number of years he played quite happily with his paradise-world, adopting, since children were banned, a fatherly attitude to the childlike, dark-skinned workers. He built a model village for them; and when, at different times, he asked for the addition of a dispensary, and then a school, the rich woman agreed unhesitatingly; she considered it cheap at the price.

The husband seldom saw his wife until, dressed punctiliously, they confronted each other throughout the long ceremonial dinner, conversing like polite strangers. His modesty and his real admiration made it seem natural to him to feel, not exactly embarrassed, but tense, on his best behaviour, all the time he was with her. It was always a bit of a strain, and it made him drink more than he would have done alone.

So the weeks and the months went by, and there was always a new toy, a teacher or a speedboat, to occupy and amuse him; he was busy and mainly content. But in that climate growing things matured quickly; the time came surprisingly soon when the garden, the groves and vineyards, were in their prime; from now on their maintenance would be a routine matter. The house was complete too, perfect in every detail, not one more object to be added to it. It was a perfect jewel of a place, inside and out. What more could any man wish than to be master of such a paradise? He didn't know himself why, now that it was perfect, he should begin to feel vaguely restless, and at a loose end.

Partly, it was his age; for he was now definitely middle-aged, and, though he still looked youthful, he knew he had passed the peak of his manhood; the future no longer seemed to stretch before him without a limit. And partly there seemed nothing much more for him to do: which made him see that he wasn't really cut out for the part of the master, after all. A real master would have gone on devoting himself to improving the lot of the native people; there was still plenty of work to be done in *that* field. But he lacked the necessary enthusiasm. He was getting tired of dark faces. They were all alike. And they were numerous as the sands of the sea; his efforts seemed such a very small drop in the ocean; it was all beginning to seem rather disheartening, pointless. He liked to bask in the goodwill of his little world, he did his best, and went on playing the master's part. But now he knew it was only a pretence, and such zeal as he'd had originally seemed to have evaporated.

This was the state of affairs when the rich woman was faced with the first humiliating sign of her beloved body's deterioration. She had to have some teeth extracted; which meant going into a nursing home in the town, where she stayed for a while, deeply shocked, less by the operation than by this intimation of mortality which she could not ignore.

The man, whose first taste of freedom this was since the marriage, was, in his own totally different way, almost as much affected. Of course he visited his wife dutifully each day with fruit and flowers and messages from the staff. The nurses all thought him a model husband. But, once the visit was over, his time was his own; and, having come into the town, he naturally stayed there, doing all the things a paradise had been created expressly to stop him doing — going to theatres, dances, race-meetings; getting to know new people; enjoying himself more and more every day.

The woman hadn't made the mistake all this time of cutting him off completely from social contacts. She had admitted a few hand-picked outsiders to their private world, with whom, through the years, they had regularly exchanged visits, keeping up the illusion of a normal social existence. Submissive and unquestioning as always, the man had made no attempt to enlarge this circle, assuming, when from time to time he was struck by its limitations, that only staid, elderly, retired people lived within visiting distance.

Now, all of a sudden, he discovered this town, full of people of the very sort he liked best — youngish, unpretentious, cheerful and energetic — with whom he might have been friends all along. Freedom going to his head slightly, for the first time in his life he ventured to criticize his wife consciously, deciding that she'd played a mean trick upon him. And he retaliated by inviting some of his new acquaintances to dinner while she was still away — an invitation they jumped at of course, for the place, with its exclusiveness and rumoured luxury, was already becoming a legend.

The man was excited and happy as he had not been since his marriage. His friendly nature could never have been at ease in solitude. But it had taken the shock of his wife's deception and his present exhilaration to make him realize that he'd felt rather isolated and miserable all these years, and had got singularly little pleasure out of living in paradise. The beauties and splendours of his home remained inaccessible and meaningless to him without companions to share its riches. Only now, at last, was he going to enjoy it in the only possible way, with people of his own kind, his own personal friends.

They arrived, these first guests he'd ever invited, with exclamations of delight and wonder. But as soon as they went in to dinner things began to go wrong.

The huge dining-room was dominated by a portrait of the rich woman, painted during a former marriage, in the academic style of the period, photographically realistic, the eyes staring straight at the beholder, embarrassingly lifelike. Considering his friends' comfort in all ways, wanting everything perfect for them, he had ordered the light beneath the picture to be switched off. Now, entering the room, he saw at once that his order had not been obeyed, and repeated it sharply, drawing attention to the portrait more effectively than any illumination. There was an awkward moment while every eye turned instinctively to it, and then moved quickly away.

187

And now a very curious thing happened: it was as if their collective attention, turned for that brief moment to the absent woman while their eyes turned to the picture, had somehow or other invoked her spirit, which all at once began to pervade the atmosphere, filling it with antagonism and constraint. The servants seemed to participate in this, in league with their mistress. The man was astonished, after all his friendliness, to feel them on her side, against him. He looked at the butler, the footmen, with whom he'd believed he was on the best of terms; and was amazed by the malice and disapproval escaping beneath their professional impassivity. The guests, feeling themselves the target of hostile emanations they could neither understand nor ignore, became increasingly uncomfortable and nervous as the meal went on.

Their host did his utmost to relieve the tension and to overcome the enmity and repressiveness in the air, emptying glass after glass in the attempt to spread good humour around the table. But all in vain. Despite his efforts to keep up a cheerful conversation, the silences grew longer and more oppressive; his gaiety sounded always more feverish and artificial. And if, for a second, he did start to throw off the mysterious blight and to smile spontaneously, something fell like a dead hand on his spirits, damping them down, as if a soundless voice announced that in this house there should be no laughter, no pleasure, nobody should feel at ease even — it was forbidden. The visitors left early, anxious to escape from something incomprehensible that had killed their accustomed geniality stone dead.

The man had a thick head the next morning, and that was all he got out of his party. But, meeting the same people again in a neutral environment, everything was all right, friendly and gay, as before. That evening's fiasco seemed like a bad dream; they explained it away somehow: and he, determined not to let his wife's return interrupt these new friendships, made a point of asking them to come again.

Leaving the chauffeur to deal with the luggage, he himself drove the rich woman home, and, approaching the house, was astonished to see the whole staff lined up outside to welcome her back. Nobody had consulted or even told him about it; no hint of any such demonstration had reached his ears. The servants had planned the thing among themselves, deliberately leaving him out.

He had begun to think he must have imagined their hostility on the night of his party. But now, looking at the rows of blank faces, he knew they really did want to hurt and humiliate him. But why . . . ? he had always tried to be both friend and employer, never acting inconsiderately — unlike his wife, who treated them as barely human. They seemed to prefer that, he thought glumly, hearing the butler cut short by her curt word of thanks.

The man was not insensitive though he wasn't clever. What most wounded him was to see the overseers who had been his companions so long lined up with the butler and co. — in the conspiracy against him. Remembering how their faces had seemed to light up when he entered their homes, it mortified him to think that their cordiality had been only a fake; a trap, into which he had fallen. Well, he wouldn't be such a fool as to stick his neck out again. Now he went to the other extreme of behaviour, cool, short and strictly impersonal, with them. Once, when little Susan ran out of the gardener's house after him, he almost relented: but he told himself the child only wanted the sweets in his pocket — cupboard love, that was all it was — and strode on, ignoring her. Convinced they were all sneering behind his back, against his true nature he forced himself to become suspicious, secretive.

He said not a word to his wife about the people he had invited until the very day they were to come, when he presented her with the *fait accompli*. Promptly, she commanded him to put them off, and, when he refused, gave him a baleful look, really witchlike, and stalked out of the room.

Her stay in the nursing home had aged her; or rather, the shock of her body's betrayal—of being forced to acknowledge that it was mortal, which she'd never quite believed — had broken something in her. Outwardly, however, she only appeared harder and more domineering. Bolt upright, with her years upon her, she had become more formidable than she had ever been.

Coiled like a poisonous snake deep within her was her resentment of old age; all the more deadly because even she was powerless against the years. So her vengance should fall on the man who had chosen this, her bitterest hour, to strike his treacherous blow — he, at any rate, could be made to suffer. She would show him up in his ignominious insignificance before these idiots he had encouraged to trespass on her domain. It was hers alone now. Forgetting that he was necessary to her power-fantasy, if only as a subject is necessary to a queen, she deposed him ruthlessly from the position of master which she'd allowed him to occupy while he knuckled under to her.

The butler, the chauffeur, and the rest of the white household staff, had, of course, recognized her as their real boss all along. Their demonstration of welcome had been no less a demonstration of contempt for the husband. To a man, they disliked the rich woman because she was harsh and inhumane; but she possessed some element of true aristocracy which they respected; they had for her a certain kind of regard which this quality alone could evoke. And its opposite, rather than its mere absence, made them despise the man for wanting their friendship, which lowered him in their eyes to an anomalous social position.

He, poor simpleton, in the dark about this, and how much beside, could only hope that his wife would keep to her own rooms when his visitors came. Needless to say, she did not; but, waiting till they were all assembled, appeared in state, in all her splendour, blazing with jewels and dressed magnificently, erect as a grenadier and almost as tall, her face a sculptured mask of cosmetics, her white hair waved and perfect like some white metal.

She had lately lost weight, and, at a distance, her tall figure resembled one of those impossibly etiolated and elongated illustrations to expensive fashion magazines; becoming still more incredible as she approached, sparkling with a whole fortune of gems, the painted face weirdly haggard, deathly, at the top of the poker-straight spine. But for all the eccentricity of her appearance it remained dignified, never deteriorating into the joke it so easily could have been.

The visitors, naturally, were astounded. Easy-going, informal people, with no tradition or particular social standing, they had never seen or imagined anything like this extraordinary vision of grandeur in decay. Looking, in their embarrassment, to their host for a lead, but receiving from him no support, no word, nothing, they became unnerved, and could only exchange among themselves wavering looks of dismay.

The man was incapable of speech. He seemed petrified; as if he'd really been turned to stone by his first glimpse of that Medusa-head, wearing a death-mask instead of a living face. He didn't even see that the woman looked ghastly — almost at her last gasp. Like the strangers, he saw her at this moment as quite inhuman, outside the scope of pity, incompatible with the thought of weakness. Like an apparition, a sort of ghost-queen, she sat stiffly upright beneath her portrait as if enthroned, completing their consternation by turning her stonewhite countenance to one of them after another, offering frigid words of formal politness to each in turn.

The stammering visitors couldn't assert themselves, overawed, just as the husband had always been, by the attribute of an almost extinct nobility, which enabled the solitary, sick old woman to get the better of them, and control the whole situation.

She had won her victory: but at the price of a fearful effort that was to be her last. This unprecedented invasion of her privacy, the insubordination of her subject-husband, had shocked her almost to death; making it seem that, besides the half-belief in her imperishable bodily self, she had lost the precious moral superiority, without which she was at the mercy of the vulgar everyday world.

But, though mortally wounded, she continued the fight, with her servants as valuable allies. Circling the table with impeccably blank well-trained expressionless, they nevertheless distilled into the atmosphere a veiled exultance, which reached its climax when, directly after the meal, the demoralized guests fled in a body, and they escorted them, with uncomplimentary willingness, to their cars.

The strangers were in such a hurry to get away that they hardly paused to say goodnight to the still silent host, standing alone like a passive on-looker beside the porch. Their hasty departure was almost a rout, cars starting up simultaneously and racing along the drive, nearly colliding as the drivers competed with one another to be first through the tall wrought-iron gates; where dark underlings, holding lighted lanterns aloft, rolled wondering eyes at the disorderly exodus.

As the last car took to flight, the servants turned back to the house; and their faces, blanched by bright moonlight, seemed, to the man in the porch's shadow, to glisten with sinister triumph, insolent beyond words. A few more seconds passed, they had all vanished indoors, before his paralysis lifted. Suddenly then he was furious with himself for doing nothing to save the evening, when he ought to have done something drastic — led a revolt. If he'd jumped into his own car and driven off with his friends it would have been better than standing here doing nothing at all.

Even for that it was already too late. The sounds of departure faded; and at once the peculiar atmosphere of the place, disrupted by the turmoil, came flooding back, submerging everything like deep dark water. He was more aware of it at this unlikely moment than ever before; it was all so lovely, the soft air fragrant with a thousand sweet-scented flowers, the moonlight glittering on the sea in the distance. And yet, behind all the loveliness, and the scented pallor of roses unfurling bleached petals beneath the moon, there seemed to be something evil, malign.

Though so far only in a vague unthought-out fashion, he'd often felt something working against his simple wish for everybody to be happy and good. Now it suddenly came clear as a jeering laugh in the stillness, like the voice of the place itself mocking his half-baked idealism.

He was very much ashamed of the way he'd been subjugated by his wife the whole evening, rendered dumb and helpless before his new friends. Now, remembering how her influence had ruined their former visit, he suddenly saw her as the cause of all his failures; identifying her with the opposing force, he blamed her for all that had gone wrong in his management of the estate, as well as for his own lonely unhappiness — everything was her fault. She must have called him The Master as a cynical gibe, since she'd always willed his frustration in the world he was supposed to rule, inspiring it to oppose him, infusing resistance into its very air. Suddenly he hated her, hated the place, and longed to break away from them both.

A surge of unaccustomed rage took possession of him, rising up from the unknown depths of his being. Day after day since the marriage, year after year, his inner dignity had been affronted by his wife's insulting indifference. And, though so deeply suppressed that he didn't even know it existed, resentment had been growing in him all this time: under tonight's emotional pressure it came bursting through to the surface — nothing now could stop the explosion.

He went in, fury abolishing all restraint, and violently accused the woman of having made a fool of him all along: but tonight she had gone too far, turning him into a laughing-stock to his friends; it was too much, he would stand no more —he was leaving. Banging the door behind him, he left the room without giving her time to speak.

She had just begun to recover a little. Encouraged by the strangers' flight and the triumph of her own people, she had almost come to believe she still held the precious secret of power, after all. Then her husband came bursting in, in his rage; and the first sounds of his accusing voice extinguished her faint hopes and turned them into despair. All must be lost, indeed; never would he have dared, otherwise . . . It was agonizing to hear his loud brawling voice dragging her down finally into the mire of the commonplace world; desecrating and laying waste the sanctuary where she'd enthroned herself, safe, she had thought, from the vulgar assaults of life. Now she knew there could be security for her anywhere, since, in the last resort, even the money had failed her.

Had she not always been shielded by her income, the rich woman might have been considered a little mad. All her life, she had been in love with herself, self-absorbed utterly, and indifferent to everything that did not concern her; uninterested in such things as worldly success, love, or fame. She had been content with the glorification of her own self, exalting her own identity into a sort of mysterious secret, folded in her like invisible wings, on which she rose above reality to the nebulous region where she reigned as queen in her imagination. And now, at her age, no change was possible. She could not come back to the real world, she had lived too long with the secret that was her religion, taking the place of human relations, of intellectual interests —of everything. Without this magic make-believe — in which the husband played an unconscious but vital part — her life would be insupportable; she wouldn't be able to go on living at all.

Already, at the first threat to her mystic queenliness, old age, which had long been hovering in the background, had approached and closed with her in an icy clinch from which she would never escape. And now she faced the ultimate degradation: the possibility that, in spite of all her wealth, her husband would go. This she must prevent at all costs; not because of any attachment — she hated him for what he had done and was doing to her self-esteem — but because she must die without at least a shadow of the pretence that she was some sort of superior being, to whom he was dedicated. She saw the situation in those precise and dramatic terms, as, shattered in mind and body, she waited next day, alone in her splendid rooms. When evening came, she could bear no more suspense, and sent for him to find out what he meant to do.

This he hadn't really decided. Last night's outburst having relieved the tension, he no longer felt any urgent wish to escape. Though the voice of middle-age kept reminding him that he couldn't afford to waste his time here, the spell of the place was all the while urging him just as insistently to remain. It wasn't only because of the money, either. In the course of years, the simple warm-hearted fellow had really grown fond of his toys; in spite of everything, he had come to love the small world that had been his whole world for so long.

And, now that he contemplated departure, the place of course turned on all its charm, so that his vision of its malevolence seemed absurd: as if on purpose to disprove it, today it put on an air of delicate innocent playfulness that was the reverse of malign. There was a light wind blowing, everything was in movement, hundreds of gay little wings seemed to be opening and shutting wherever he looked; the sea, the flowers, the leaves, were all dancing together, harmlessly frivolous as the butterflies dancing in the sun.

How could there be anything evil about a place that possessed this innocuous charm, so innocent and so playful, like dancing butterflies, or little soft fluffy kittens playing? The air itself seemed full of peace and goodwill. When he let out the savage guard-dogs, instead of snapping and snarling as usual, they gambolled round him, rolled one another over, ran races, and finally stretched out amicably together in the shade, not even chasing the pigeons that settled near. He half expected a wild-cat to come from the trees and lie down with them, as in a real paradise.

In the evening he got his wife's message, and went, very reluctantly, to her boudoir, sincerely regretting the way he'd attacked her, and expecting an act of reprisal. The delicate atmosphere of the day had left him feeling opened-up, almost tender; the very last thing he wanted was any sort of a row. He had to wait at the door a moment, hardening himself to withstand her. But, entering, seeing her lying, gaunt and hollow-eyed, on the *chaise longue*, he was puzzled, because there didn't seem to be anything to withstand.

It was the implacable will looking out of her eyes that had frightened him all these years and driven him nearly to drink, controlling him all the time, surrounding him with her dominion. Steeling himself now to meet it, with a touch of horror he met her eyes, and, incredibly, it had gone: it was no longer there, that awful fixity of her will upon him, which had made him her thing, The Master, a mere projection of *her* mastery. Now he saw only a curious emptiness in her eyes, looking into the space which before had always been filled by her compulsive will. A sudden sense of freedom uplifted him; of lightness, release. At last he had got himself back, out of her power: she had ceased to possess him.

He could pity her now, seeing her as she really was, feeling no more resentment. She was just a pathetic old woman; incredible that he should ever have feared her. Now she looked truly pitiable to him: and smaller, shrunken, somehow; as if, minus will, there wasn't much of her left.

She asked him if he were really going away. And he said he would stay, if she wished it. To himself he said he'd waited too long; that he hadn't the heart to abandon her as she was now — which was true, in its fashion. He felt that the decision had been taken out of his hands, which was a great relief.

So it was settled that he would stay. But on his own terms; he had won the right to live as he pleased in future.

From now on he would be free in his comings and goings; he would keep his own friends, though, out of respect and consideration for her, he would not bring them to the house. And he refused to resume the title of Master which she had snatched from him; it had always been a farce, anyhow. Let everybody call him by his own name.

Having stated his terms, he was amazed at her acquiescence. She agreed to everything, almost indifferently, hardly seeming to listen. She didn't care any more what he did, provided he left her the pathetic rag of pretence in which to dress up her life as a queen's. Her one stipulation was that he should present himself to her each morning and evening, to show his continued allegiance. Between visits, he could go to the moon for all she cared. She shut her eyes, not wanting even to see him; he was too big and too much alive.

The breakdown of her body and will had left her utterly worn out, exhausted, drained of everything. She felt literally brittle, as if one more shock, even the smallest, would smash her to smithereens. All must be quiet and still around her. Almost over-night, she'd become an invalid; her life resolved itself into the small routines of a sick person. She hardly ever left her suite, except when she went out for drives, or to stroll in the grounds.

Out of sincere compassion, the man offered to accompany her on these outings. But she didn't want him. She always seemed to resent it if he appeared at any other than the appointed times. She complained that his step didn't fit in with hers if he walked beside her. And she preferred the chauffeur to drive her, because he was careful and slow. So gradually, feeling entirely superfluous, the husband withdrew from her, coming only at the regular visiting hours, which he kept religiously. He was always as kind then as he knew how to be, always kissing her hand with reverence, honouring her as a queen still, though an old and infirm one. He was kind because it was his nature, and thought nothing of it. And what her thoughts were no one knew.

He could now, had he wished, have lived a life of luxury and indulgence. The woman never asked what he was doing, she showed no interest in how he spent the time, but seemed quite indifferent to everything. However, his simple tastes didn't alter; and he was eternally conscientious. He enjoyed himself with his friends in a modest open-air way; but he still gave as much time as ever to the running of the estate, really the master now, although not in name.

The mysterious malevolence seemed to have been exorcised; at all events, there was no more opposition. Everything was going smoothly as if on wheels, everyone seemed satisfied with his station. To a superstitious person, the calm might have seemed ominous, almost; but the man had no fanciful notions — why should he? his conscience was clear; he acted invariably with the best of motives.

He took care never to do anything his wife might have objected to in the past, avoiding the small deviations to which her present indifference sometimes tempted him. He was tempted, for instance, when the hot weather came, to give the children growing up on the place the run of the swimming pool; which, filled and re-filled, purified, kept clear of leaves and insects, served only to mirror the surrounding flowers, except when he took his daily plunge. It seemed such a waste — why shouldn't the kids enjoy it? His wife need not even know. But, remembering her strange horror of children — like some women's horror of cats or spiders — he resisted temptation, and, instead, took the youngsters for day-long picnics on the neighbouring sandy beaches.

He noticed that Susan, his old favourite, outgrowing her babyish charm, was developing into a quiet shy little girl who didn't make friends easily with the rest — a typical only child. When they all piled into the station-waggon to be driven home, she hung back as if half-scared of the noisy excited crew, and begged to be allowed to come in his car with him. He agreed, always wanting everyone happy; and was rather touched by her quick and ardent response to the casual kindness. After this, since she always seemed on the look out for him when he passed the head gardener's house, he fell into the habit of taking her with him as he drove about the estate; amused by the way she snuggled against him, he would call her his little sweetheart, and laughingly ruffle her hair.

It was a part of his general impersonal kindness and meant nothing to him; no more than when he fondled one of the dogs. He would have been surprised — even startled, perhaps —had he known of the fantasy being woven about him by this child, left much alone by parents absorbed in their own full young lives. She had decided, in her childish but oddly resolute fashion, that the man from the big house should give her the love which the father and mother seemed to withhold; and when, for several days running, he failed to appear, she screwed up her courage to go and look for him.

This was a desperate step, for, like all the children on the estate, she'd been taught that the immediate vicinity of the house was forbidden ground, and the one unforgiveable sin to trespass there. But now she was impelled by the most powerful of all motives: it was love she wanted; she must, she must, have It. So, in the concrete way of a child, but with almost adult resolution, she set out to find the man she believed would give it to her.

Flat on her stomach, she wriggled with snakelike stealth between the bushes of the dense boundary hedge. No one saw her, and she saw no one; the whole great garden beyond seemed deserted — this gave her confidence presently to sit down on a comfortable cushioned seat in the shade. She only meant to rest for a moment; but, starting to weave into a wreath some flowers she had idly picked, she became absorbed and forgot to move. She was still sitting there, gently swinging, her lap full of brilliant petals, when two people emerged silently from a grass path close beside her.

Looking up at them suddenly, her eyes dilated with fright. Then, to her great relief, she recognized the chauffeur she knew quite well. His companion was an old lady leaning on a black stick; which also seemed reassuring. She had no idea of the rich woman's appearance, having caught only rare fleeting glimpses of her speeding past in her car; but it never occurred to her that this legendary personage could be old, and so she didn't associate her with the new arrival.

Arranging herself more decorously, she assumed her most engaging expression, smiling at the old lady; and in the hope of placating her, on the spur of the moment, offered the clumsy wreath . . . which was instantly struck out of her hand by a vicious blow from the ebony cane.

"The audacity . . . My own flowers . . . "

Susan scarcely heard the outraged voice, more surprised than she'd ever been in her life by this violent act, so at variance with her preconceived ideas of old ladies' behaviour. And now a still more amazing thing happened. The Grimm's fairy-tale-world of thinly-veiled terror, which she thought she'd left behind forever in her babyish past, suddenly claimed her again, a fearsome present reality, as, in front of her eyes, the old lady folded up like a fan. Scrambling off the swing-seat in a panic, she raced for home, never once looking back to see what took place afterwards; not giving a single thought to the man she had come to find. There was no room for anything in her head but this sinister incident, a fearful secret she must keep hidden from everyone, which had revived the belief in witchcraft she had not entirely outgrown.

Almost as soon as Susan got home, the man heard his wife was unwell. He at once sent for the doctor; who later called in another; and still later a specialist came from the town.

After a consultation, the three announced that the rich woman had suffered some sort of slight stroke. There seemed no grave cause for alarm; but she should have a nurse.

The husband, not allowed in the sickroom and tired of hanging about the house, was anxious to make himself useful, and set off immediately in his fast car. He drove both ways with hardly a break, for the nurse was waiting ready for him at the hospital: but by the time he got back with her, his wife was already dead.

The shock stunned him, it was so sudden and unexpected. Somehow, he had never envisaged the possibility of her death. He made arrangements, interviewed people, did whatever was necessary, all in a kind of trance, barely conscious. Only when the funeral service was over did he start to come back to himself, realizing, on his return from the church, that his head was aching. Inhaling a heavy sweetness, looking vaguely about, he saw that the servants, as a last tribute to their mistress, had filled the house with tuberoses, camellias, lilies — all the strongly-perfumed flowers that had been her favourites. The scent was like a weight on his forehead, and, acting blindly, on instinct, he went outside, wandering through the garden bemused, until something caught his eye.

Every day, in the shade of a great spreading tree, a cushioned swing-seat was erected under its canopy, though seldom indeed did anyone make use of it. Someone was sitting there now, gently swinging backwards and forwards; and this motion, where nothing ought to have moved, the man's automatic attention had noted. Dimly, in his obscured brain, formed the idea that some unauthorized person was taking advantage of the general distraction and grief: and, his eternal conscience functioning despite shock, he was impelled to investigate.

Approaching, he saw, with an incredulous dreamlike sensation, that the intruder was a child. But how was it possible? Indignation mounting in him, he asked himself what child would dare disregard the established order on this very day? For a child to come trespassing now, with his wife barely cold in the grave, seemed a deliberate insult to the dead woman.

On the verge of an angry shout, he was silenced by something familiar about the swinging figure, recognizing the tumbled brown head he had often caressed with his hand. Susan was murmuring to herself, or to an imaginary companion, too absorbed to have seen or heard him. In his peculiar shocked condition, he felt a sudden queer access of curiosity at the sight of her flushed oblivious face with its fixed expression: what could be making her so unaware of everything around her?

He went closer, expecting her to look up. But still she remained unconscious of him, though he could almost have touched her now. His whole state was abnormal: and suddenly, seeing the little girl so absolutely oblivious of him, wide-eyed, rapt, his unnatural curiosity was swamped by an equally unnatural uneasiness. Now he would gladly have gone away without making his presence known, repelled by her unchildlike and uncanny-seeming absorption, had he not known his feeling was quite irrational, and fought against it.

"I'm sitting here on your seat, old witch — do you see me? Come back and knock me off with your black stick— if you can . . . "

He listened to the repetitious challenge as if turned to stone. Nothing had seemed real to him since the news of the death; and now the monotonous childish chant reached him with the sound of an incantation — a dreaming sound. But soon a note of triumph entered the low sing-song.

"You're dead, old witch, and you can't come back . . . you're under the ground and you can't get out . . . you'll never get out again . . . "

The quiet triumphant chant, going on and on, started to chill his blood: eerily now, through its childishness, he seemed to catch, like the sound of another voice, unimagineably old and remote, a strange gloating undertone of primitive malice. It was not only a child's voice he was hearing; it was also the voice of primeval man, proclaiming out of the mists of pre-history his unchangeable savage nature.

The listener's heart contracted in horror, amazement. He had always thought of children as being innocent, pretty, engaging creatures, like dancing butterflies or little soft playful kittens — that a child should speak with that pitiless voice of ancient evil malevolence! And, of all children, his Susan, his little sweetheart — little viper, was more like it! Stabbing through his shocked daze, the chant began to throb in his aching head with a sound of madness — maddened by it, he shouted crazily:

"Shut up! Stop that wicked nonsense . . . ! "

He was quite out of himself at this instant of aberration, not knowing what he was saying, or to whom; not seeing the real situation. Something of horror or hate, like a fog in the air around him, prevented him momentarily from seeing or thinking clearly.

The little girl had seen him the moment before, looking up

at him quickly with a happy confiding smile. Now, for a strange and senseless second, she went on smiling with that confident bright expectancy; until a look of wild disbelief preceded the sudden burst of tears that washed away all expression. Quick as a lizard, she darted out of his sight, disappearing immediately among the tall flowering plants; though for some more seconds her running steps thudded, the foliage rustled and waved: and then there was only the empty seat, wildly swinging, to show that she had ever been there at all.

At this moving object the man stared, as if mesmerized, while it gradually slowed to a standstill: then stonily turned his back upon it, and walked away. Once or twice, on his way to the house, without knowing he did so, he pressed his hand to his head, which ached more than ever, oppressively, heavily.

The episode with the child had left him curiously sick at heart. For some reason he couldn't forget it. It kept on coming back to him, intermittently, with inexplicable seizures of uneasiness, almost like guilt; until the reading of the will finally drove it out of his thoughts.

The rich woman had willed the house with all its contents, the whole estate, almost her entire fortune, to the chauffeur. To her husband she left only a meagre life interest, a pittance; and some objects without any special value, as keepsakes.

Also by Anna Kavan and available from Peter Owen

Asylum Piece

ISBN 978 0 7206 1123 6

£9.95

'If only one knew of what and by whom one were accused, when, where and by what laws one were to be judged, it would be possible to prepare one's defence systematically and set about things in a sensible fashion.'
— Anna Kavan, *Asylum Piece*

First published sixty years ago, *Asylum Piece* today ranks as one of the most extraordinary and terrifying evocations of human madness ever written. This collection of stories, mostly interlinked and largely autobiographical, chart the descent of the narrator from the onset of neurosis to final incarceration in a Swiss clinic. The sense of paranoia, of persecution by a foe or force that is never given a name, evokes *The Trial* by Franz Kafka, the writer with whom Kavan is most often compared, although Kavan's deeply personal, restrained and almost foreign-accented style has no true model. The same characters who recur throughout — the protagonist's unhelpful 'adviser', the friend/lover who abandons her at the clinic and an assortment of deluded companions — are sketched without a trace of the rage, self-pity or sentiment that have marked many other accounts of mental instability.

'Pervaded by a sense of intolerable oppression, lit by sudden shafts of delight in the natural world, their concise artistry proclaims how consummately she knew and rode her devils.' — *Guardian*
'Anna Kavan charges the space between her words and the reader's mind with a continuous crackle of electricity.' — *New Statesman*
'A classic equal to the work of Kafka.' — Anaïs Nin

Peter Owen books can be purchased from: Central Books, 99 Wallis Road, London E9 5LN, UK
Tel: + 44 (0)20 8986 4854 Fax: + 44 (0)20 8533 5821 e-mail: orders@centralbooks.com